Murder in a Teacup

Nancy Curteman

ISBN-13: 978-0-9834631-2-2
ISBN-10: 0983463123

Second Edition: April 2017

Dedication

Larry, Jerry and Juli

Chapter 1

Thirty minutes into the tedious two-hour drive from Billings Logan International Airport to Sage Deer, Lysi punched the speed dial number of her partner's cell phone, listened to the irritating recorded message and left a call back number. Skeptical about Cristin Holden returning her call, she clenched her teeth and tossed her phone onto the passenger seat of her rental car. Lysi guessed Cristin was probably in a bar with a cold martini and a hot date.

Cristin told Lysi she got her pragmatic philosophy of life from her "Merry Widow" grandmother who whooped it up until she died at 95 wearing a satisfied grin. "Yup, granny always said, 'Men make life one big joy ride. Lucky for us girls, they're like streetcars; a new one comes along every few minutes. You hop on for a fun jaunt. Hop off when the ride gets too ho hum then just hop right onto the next one.'"

Sometimes Cristin would put her arm around Lysi, give her a wink and declare in a voice dripping with pity, "Honey, you just work too hard. Make time for a little fun. Get some good men in your life, Girl."

Cristin had a pretty big collection of "streetcars." Lysi would be happy with just one. She figured she just hadn't found the right "streetcar" yet.

No longer able to endure the monotony of field after field of jaundiced grass and gray boulders smoldering in the heat of the late morning sun, Lysi stared straight ahead through her bug-splattered windshield at the succession of rolling heat waves on the empty road that seemed to stretch forever in front of her.

"So this is Montana." She raised one eyebrow, blasted air through frustrated lips and grabbed her cell to try Cristin Holden again.

"Hi, you've reached Cristin. You know what to do."

"Cristin. Call me. I need to know how your part of the seminar went. How many knuckle draggers started pounding their chests when you announced the topic? Call me!"

Lysi pulled off the road and crackled onto a gravel shoulder along side a dry creek bed that bordered a field of harvested hay rolled up like giant sausages. An old barn in the distance looked like it might fall over any minute. She needed to work out the kinks in her neck, back and legs. Walking to the back of the car, she noticed a small herd of cows crowded under the sparse shade of a desiccated oak tree, and wondered how anything but lizards and snakes could possibly survive in this desolate land.

Sweat squeezed from her pores, driving her back into the air-conditioned car. After blotting her sopping face and neck with several tissues, she picked up the cell one more time.

Still no Cristin.

She frowned at the phone. Usually Cristin got back to her after the second or third call. Setting the phone on the seat and starting the car, she told herself she was overreacting. It was just that she didn't like Montana and she definitely did not like this assignment.

*

The cell phone on the motel bedside stand had already recorded twelve messages. Its shrill ring tone shattered the calm again. Cristin Holden lay on the bed within arm's reach of the phone but did not turn her head. Her eyes remained wide open, unblinking; through the rings, Lysi's messages, and the profound silence that followed.

*

Ten dry miles later, Lysi passed through the heavy-duty iron gate that separated the well-tended gardens of Montana Nerium Regional Office from the brown world outside the corporate fence. She followed an aspen-lined lane into the employee parking lot behind the new four-story glass and steel building.

An explosion of heat blasted her in the face when she opened the door of the air-conditioned car, a rude reminder of August in Eastern Montana. *I'll never again whine about San Francisco fog.* Sweat started to percolate through her skin.

Taking Cristin's name in vain for badgering her into this assignment, Lysi grabbed her briefcase, took a deep breath, and headed for the Staff Only entrance. On the metal door a poster advertising her seminar dangled by one taped corner. The original poster had read:

Required Staff Training
Sexual Harassment Presentations With Expert Lysi Weston
In the Boardroom Thursday and Friday 4:00 to 7:00 p.m.

Some redneck genius, using all the brainpower he could muster, had taken a thick black felt pen to it:

Sexual Heaven Promised by Sexpert Lysi Weston
In the Bedroom Thursday and Friday 4:00 to 7:00 p.m.

A sardonic grin spread across Lysi's lips. *I guess this is a preview of the* "challenge" *the boss told me I'd* love?

She ripped the seminar poster off the door and shoved it into her briefcase. She dragged in a tenacious breath capturing a pungent whiff of the nearby cow pasture that lay ripening in the sun. Holding her breath, she pushed open the glass door and escaped into the Nerium building.

On the way to the elevator, Lysi mentally revisited the original reason for taking this job—to help victims of sexism in the workplace. She still burned when she recalled the Larksdale School District Director, a chrome-domed lecher who imagined he had the *droit du seigneur* to grope her at will. A complaint to the Superintendent got her demoted to the classroom. Humiliated, she resigned and took a position with Stellar Corporate Development as a management-training seminar presenter. This was her job and she would see it through.

Lysi pressed the elevator button then took out a tissue and dabbed at her damp face. She peered into the mirrored elevator door and tried to smooth the frizz from her short unruly hair. Never mind the makeup that had already sweated into uneven blotches.

The elevator sailed upward to the soft strains of a string quartet until the doors opened on the fourth floor. Lysi's brown eyes wandered over the rich woodwork shining in the glow of decorative lighting. A cobalt blue carpet runner led her past several oversized doors to the Staff Development office. Pretty elegant for a cow pasture.

She blinked at the sudden brightness of the office. The sun beaming through a glass-enclosed roof garden filled with large pots of pink and white dwarf oleanders created a welcome relief from the funereal feeling of the dim corridor.

A no-nonsense secretary squinted at Lysi through rimless spectacles—salt and pepper hair pulled back in a bun, sensible crepe-soled shoes, figure lost somewhere in a baggy, long-sleeved dress.

"This way, Ms. Weston. Ms. Norris has been *waiting* for you for sometime now."

The secretary's voice matched her chastising frown. Two deep grooves running from nose to chin told Lysi the frown was perennial. Her rimless spectacles measured Lysi, assessing her Bernardo sandals, white Tahari pantsuit and fuchsia blouse.

Lysi looked at the secretary. *I guess* you'd *have no problem with sexual harassment.* Instantly regretting her nasty thought, she forced a pleasant expression.

"Sorry I'm late. The drive from Billings took longer than expected."

The secretary raised her eyebrows and executed a tight-lipped teacher stare that made Lysi feel she should go stand in a corner. Then she opened an inner office door that framed a pencil-thin brunette in her thirties who rose from an absurdly large leather chair and strode toward Lysi in high heels that added three inches to her petite stature.

The brunette extended her hand with a warm smile. "Hi. I'm Carolyn Norris, Director of Staff Development. Welcome to Nerium, Ms. Weston. I hope you had a pleasant flight from San Francisco."

"Thank you," Lysi said. "The flight from San Francisco was fine." She didn't add that the drive from the airport was tedious; that she got her fill of sagebrush, macadam and barbed wire fences; and that the graffittied poster in her briefcase confirmed her view that the seminar would probably be a colossal waste of time, money and effort.

Lysi glanced back at the roof garden. "That's *some* garden."

"Thanks. That was my incentive bonus to come here. I had no desire to work in this God-forsaken country. I'm a West Coast girl, too—L.A. So I brought a little piece of home with me."

Carolyn motioned Lysi to a seat on an ivory brocade couch.

A woman who gets what she wants. Lysi noted the designer name embroidered on Carolyn's turquoise silk shirt and the large diamond sparkling on her finger. She liked Carolyn's elegant style and efficient manner. Maybe Ms. Norris was aware of the pervasive sexism at Nerium described in the seminar background report. Maybe she'd be a good support for change. Maybe there was hope after all.

Lysi pulled a blue binder from her briefcase. "In reading the Nerium Montana Background Re—"

"Just one second." Carolyn leaned across her desk and pressed the intercom button. "Ms. Weston's here."

A baritone voice resonated through the intercom. "Great, be right over."

When the door opened a few seconds later, the same voice said, "Miss Weston. What a pleasure to meet you. Hank Jones. Human Resources."

"Soon to be Nerium Montana Corporate Manager." Carolyn flipped her straight, shoulder-length hair back with a toss of her head. "No one deserves it more than Hank."

"Congratulations," Lysi said. Hank's smile radiated artificial charm.

With a sideways glance followed by a wink, Hank said, "You sure don't look like I'd expect a little lady to look who'd spent two years studying sex in some dingy old library."

Lysi bristled. She knew what he meant. All he could see was a tall, fair-skinned blonde with enough curves to merit a second glance. He knew nothing of the years of study for her PhD. She

7

could just imagine what he'd think of her thesis topic, of all her research.

"The title of the project is 'How Sexual Harassment in the Work Place Bankrupts Corporations and Obliterates Careers,'" she said, and glanced at Carolyn. *How about a little sisterhood here?*

Instead, Carolyn lowered her lashes and emitted a soft purr. Her cheeks warmed to the same delicate pink as the rose quartz pin she wore on her lapel.

Turning back to Hank, Lysi could see what had transformed Carolyn from a levelheaded professional to a twitter-brained teenager. Hank Jones looked like a lean, lanky cowboy in his forties. His clean-shaven face revealed a sharp, slightly jutting jaw softened by a deep dimple in each cheek. He had a smile that would melt an iceberg, and deep umber eyes that could ignite any woman's passion.

"Whoa!" Hank smacked his forehead with his palm. "Now you're breaking out the big words. Give me a minute to chaw on that hunk of title. Sounds awful scary to me."

Lysi didn't bite the bait. Instead, she held up the Nerium Montana binder and watched Hank's smirk disappear.

"Mr. Jones, I think you made a wise decision to address the issue of sexual harassment at Nerium. I certainly believe–"

"Lisa, honey—you don't mind if I call you Lisa do you?"

"I don't mind, but my parents would. Both classical lit professors, they named me after Lysistrada, the heroine of a Greek play by Aristophanes. Both the *y* and the *i* sound like *i* in the word *it*."

Hank didn't try to conceal his disdain. "Well, Lysistrada *honey*, I want to be real up front with you." He sidled next to her and draped a big arm over her shoulders, enveloping her in the scent of his expensive aftershave cologne.

"I did *not* put in a request for your seminar. It came from corporate headquarters in California. Someone out there in Hippie Ville seems to think Montana Nerium middle management people need training on how to treat our women. Sexual Harassment. Hah! As we used to say out on the ranch, there just ain't no such critter in these parts."

Lysi raised her eyebrows in question and removed his arm. "So you've seen no evidence of sexual harassment in this plant?"

Hank nodded his head at least three times.

"Interesting." She didn't add: Since the background document on the need for training of Nerium Montana management personnel stated that sexual harassment was pervasive in the Montana branch and named you and one Bill Pitt as transgressors—suggestive comments, lewd pictures, invasive touching.

I'm here, Lysi shouted in her mind, because Nerium Corporate California wants to avoid an expensive lawsuit that would probably name you and Pitt. Of course, you would never consider your behavior offensive, just *friendly*.

As Lysi opened her mouth to rebut Hank's denial of sexual harassment at Nerium, Carolyn recovered her equilibrium.

"Cristin Holden left a message for you, Ms. Weston."

She handed Lysi a white envelope with Big Sky Motel printed in the return address space.

"Ms. Holden made quite an impression with her motivational seminar yesterday afternoon—and at the reception later."

Lysi laughed inwardly, *I'll just bet she did—with every male in the place. I wonder how many 'streetcars' she collected?*

Lysi tucked the envelope from her co-presenter into her purse and moved towards the door. She nodded at Carolyn.

Before leaving, she couldn't resist sticking one last burr under Hank's already sore saddle.

"Mr. Jones, since management of sexual harassment cases is part of the purview of the human resources department, it'll be your responsibility to insure that a workable prevention plan is developed." Her nicest smile accompanied the burr. "See you at the seminar tomorrow."

Lysi hadn't quite clicked the door shut when she caught snatches of a sharp exchange.

"...don't trust Weston...doesn't act like a woman."

"You mean she doesn't respond to you like most..."

"...cold, business like, arrogant about her expertise."

"You're just used to women falling all over..."

Lysi's anger rocketed from a simmer to a boil. She yanked the handle and closed the door with a loud click. She would let him stew about how much she might've heard and what she planned to do about it.

The no-nonsense secretary stopped typing, pursed her lips and cast a disapproving eye when Lysi speed walked past her desk on the way out of the office.

*

Back in the car, Lysi opened the motel envelope and read Cristin's scribbled note.

"Lysi, can't meet for dinner Wednesday. We'll do lunch Thursday before I fly out. I'll call you. Hugs, Cristy."

Lysi knew what that meant. Cristin had already snagged herself a date for the evening, probably for the night. She'll never change. You got to love her anyway.

Lapsing into self-pity, Lysi wished she could go to Cristin right now and grouse about Jones, the heat, this assignment and Montana. She started to crumple the note when a phone number scribbled on the envelope back caught her eye. Could be little Cristy's squeeze for the night. Lysi decided she'd quiz her about it at lunch tomorrow and shoved it into her briefcase. Who knows, she might need to reach Cristin. Then she pressed hard on her partner's speed dial number and hung up before the recorded message ended.

*

As Lysi passed through the town of Sage Deer on the way to her motel, she was struck by the absence of a broad array of city life—no hustling pedestrians dodging cars, no shoppers racing for cabs or buses, no trolleys swallowing and disgorging throngs of people. Instead, the town chugged along like a slow cattle train in the burning afternoon heat. The few townspeople lazing on wooden benches in the shade of squat buildings seemed two dimensional—either white or Native American. She concluded that the lush ethnic mix of San Francisco would wither in this inhospitable place.

A monster sign with the words Big Sky Motel emblazoned in garish blue lights above a cowboy bouncing precariously on a twisting bronco signaled her arrival at the town's grandest motel. The motor inn harked back to the sixties—built in a U shape around a fenced kidney pool with parking spaces in front of each room. Lysi's boss told her it had recently been remodeled. A fresh coat of exterior paint the pinkish color of a kid's cough syrup and several young sapling trees scattered around the courtyard along with new poolside furniture did seem like a feeble attempt at remodeling. She hoped for newly decorated interiors, too.

The flashing neon lights of the Sagebrush Trucker Café next door to the motel reminded Lysi she'd missed lunch. She decided to check in then order a takeout turkey sandwich to eat in the room while she reviewed her notes on Montana Nerium's corporate culture.

After unpacking a few essentials–toothbrush, makeup kit, nightclothes–Lysi changed into a baggy gray tee and shorts, shoved her feet into flip flops, and opened the blue binder titled, "Target audience: Montana Nerium Middle Management Personnel."

On the first page, California Nerium had listed three goals in bold print:
1. Managers will gain a clear understanding of what constitutes sexual harassment.
 2. Managers will train all employees on appropriate behavior in the workplace.
3. Managers will create and maintain a non-sexist environment at all levels.

Lysi put the goals sheet down on the desk, gazed at the ceiling, and slowly massaged her taut shoulders, pressing hard with her fingertips. *I'd have an easier time training cats to ignore a passing mouse.*

She stared at her cell phone, willing it to ring, and wished again she could bounce this assignment off Cristin who always managed to lighten the load with her acid gibes and hilarious antics. Lysi smiled recalling the last night of a seminar in New Orleans two years ago. They had gone out to dinner, got turned around on the way back to the hotel and ended up in the French Quarter. Cristin insisted no one was ever lost for long in New Orleans. As usual, she was right. They ducked into a little jazz club off Bourbon Street and had a couple Hurricanes. When the club closed, Thibaudeau, the dark-eyed Cajun bartender, walked them back to the hotel. Cristin certainly added a bit of spice to Lysi's somewhat conventional life.

Lysi could use a Hurricane or two right now.

She typed a few ideas on her laptop worksheet. Not satisfied, she deleted them. Still chewing the last bite of her sandwich, she reached over to the bedside phone and dialed the night desk clerk. Maybe Cristin would answer the hotel phone.

"This is Lysi Weston in room 20. Please put me through to Cristin Holden, room 29."

There was a pause while the clerk shuffled papers.

"Miss Holden asked not to be disturbed until eleven tomorrow morning. If it's an emergency, I guess I could shove a message under her door." A heavy sigh punctuated the last sentence.

"No. No thanks. I guess it can wait 'til tomorrow." Lysi hung up the phone and shook her head, chuckling. "That's my Cristy girl. A late night with her man of the moment stretching into a lazy morning."

Lysi forced herself to finish her notes. At eleven, she shut down the computer. Satisfied she was as well prepared as could be expected, she showered and went to bed. For a long time she stared into the darkness, unable to escape a cacophony of jarring sounds— engines backfired, air horns squawked, car doors slammed, brakes squealed. She rammed her head under the pillow. *A jackhammer would enhance the ambience of this miserable motel.*

Somehow, exhaustion overpowered the din, and she drifted into a restless sleep troubled by a vague presentiment that had needled her most of the day.

Chapter 2

After a late breakfast, Lysi changed into a two-piece swimsuit and headed for the kidney-shaped motel pool. Swimming laps would have to replace her daily two-mile jog given the oven temperatures in Sage Deer. The blast of cool water sent energy racing through her body. An elderly lady soaking at the shallow end of the pool winked at her. "Nothing like a cool dip. Going to be a hot one today."

Just as Lysi nodded agreement, two overfed teenage boys belly flopped a few feet away, inundating her in their wake. She laughed and raced through her laps, climbed out of the water, and stretched out on one of the chaise lounges to dry. Exercise always reduced Lysi's stress and seemed to clarify her thoughts. She closed her eyes and envisioned the seminar presentation. Soon she would bounce ideas off Cristin.

*

Back in her room, Lysi waited for Cristin's call. By one o'clock, the phone had not rung. Cristin must have quite a catch. Well recreation is over. It's time for lunch then work for me, and a flight home for you. Lucky.

She dialed Cristin's room number. The phone rang five times.

No answer.

Lysi let it ring a few more times. "Come on, Cristin. Playtime's over. Pick up the phone."

No answer.

Lysi checked her watch and frowned. She stepped outside and followed the sun-baked walkway to Cristin's room, tapped on the door and listened for a response. When there was none, she knocked harder. A small wave of concern rippled through her. *Something's not right. Cristin prides herself on keeping commitments.*

This time Lysi hammered on the door with her fists. "Wake up, Cristin. You'll miss your plane."

No answer.

Lysi's chest felt tight. She hurried down the steps to the motel office. No one stood behind the desk. She looked around the room. The only sound came from a television in the corner broadcasting some soap drama. Trying to control the uneasy feeling in her stomach, she banged the little silver bell on the counter several times.

A blurry-eyed teenager wearing a wrinkled cowboy shirt, a baseball cap with Judo Jock embroidered across the crown, and an irritating scowl shuffled from a backroom to the counter.

"Yeah, Lady?" He pinched at a painful looking zit on his chin.

Lysi eyed him suspiciously. "Are you the desk clerk?"

"Nah, my ma is. She had to step out for a few minutes." He tipped his head towards a sitting area. "Wait on one of them couches over there. I'll get her."

Lysi looked at the ashtray overflowing with cigarette butts sitting on a coffee table in front of the leather couches and decided to wait at the counter.

After an interminable ten minutes, the desk clerk appeared. Apologizing for her absence, she settled her corpulent body on a small stool behind the desk, opened a bobby pin with her teeth and pinned back a stray strand of stringy brown hair. Her heavy exhale communicated exhaustion.

"What can I do for you?"

"I'm Lysi Weston, Room 20. I just came from my partner, Cristin Holden's room—29. She didn't answer my knocks or my phone calls. Has she checked out?"

The desk clerk dragged her finger down a ledger page. Lysi resisted the urge to grab the ledger and search it herself.

With a long breath, the clerk said, "No. In fact, check out's at eleven. She owes us for another night." The woman's voice sounded as if it had struggled up from deep inside her bulk.

Lysi choked back the anxiety that clawed at her throat. "Look, she's going to miss her flight. I need you to check her room."

The clerk reached under the neck of her faded cotton dress and pulled up her bra strap. "I'm sorry Miss. It's our policy never to intrude on the privacy of our–"

"Now!" Lysi's eyes burned; "or I call the police."

The desk clerk opened her mouth, but closed it without speaking. She slid off the stool, fingered a key that dangled from a dirty string around her neck, unlocked a drawer and pulled out a master magnetic key card. She trudged from behind the counter and padded out the door to the stairs that led to the second story. Clutching the railing, she pulled herself up each step, already breathing heavily by the time she had ascended half way. Lysi followed at a safe distance behind.

The woman knocked on the door to room 29. "Desk clerk, Miss Holden."

No answer.

After a few more knocks, the hefty woman inserted the master key card and slowly opened the door. She edged her head inside. "Miss Holden, it's the desk clerk."

Lysi, now frantic, pushed past her and looked through the door.

The draperies were drawn against the harsh afternoon sun leaving the room bathed in a gray darkness.

Cristin was still in bed.

Feeling relieved, but embarrassed at her childish outburst in the office, Lysi called out, "Wake up, Cristin. You'll miss your plane."

When Cristin didn't move, Lysi decided to give her friend a jovial shake and chide her for oversleeping.

Then suddenly she knew. Before she took one step, she knew.

Cristin was dead.

Lysi stared at the unnatural Modigliani-like angle of Cristin's head, auburn hair cascading over the pillow, lacey black nightgown partially hidden by a shimmering satin robe. She felt queasy looking into Cristin's lifeless blue eyes—wide open, gazing at nothing. How horrible to see her fingers, spread apart as if frantically grasping at something. Where was the diamond and ruby ring she always wore? The question hung in the air for an instant then fragmented and disappeared in the dark sea of sorrow.

A tear trickled down Lysi's cheek as she gazed at Cristin's face, her body. Laugh lines around her mouth that had always signaled a boisterous sense of humor were now silent. The sweet scent of Cristin's favorite French perfume, like flowers in a funeral chapel, lingered in the air; but her partner—her friend—was gone.

During their five years at Stellar Corporate Development, Lysi Weston and Cristin Holden had become one of the company's top management training teams.

The Holden/Weston Duo was the brainchild of Charles Stone, Stellar's CEO. When Lysi first met Cristin, she protested the partnership. Cristin Holden neither looked nor acted like she could convince corporate management personnel they needed to develop anti sexual harassment plans.

Stone hired Holden anyway, asserting she was a motivational speaker only. A cheerleader. Her role was to soften employee resistance before Lysi brought in the big guns.

Lysi worked her first assignment with her short curvaceous colleague at a corporate employees' team-building program in Texas. Lysi's Sexual Harassment seminar followed Cristin's motivational warm up.

When Cristin walked on stage in her clingy red dress and six-inch spike heels, every male face in the audience radiated motivation. They seemed captivated by her icebreaker games or as Lysi suspected, her luscious curves and luxurious hair.

Lysi, in turn, delivered the hard sell, a no-frills description of the consequences of sexual harassment—frayed office relations, employee turnover, lawsuits, job loss, jail—and how to avoid this unpleasantness.

To Lysi's surprise, Cristin's warm up did mellow the audience. Their partnership presentation met with such success that Stellar Corporate Development had booked them as a double feature ever since.

Now it was over.

Labored breathing and a faintly acidic odor intruded on Lysi's grief. She jerked her head around and looked right into the sweat-soaked face of the desk clerk standing inches from the bed, gaping at Cristin.

"Go call 911," Lysi said, wanting to shield Cristin from the curious stare.

The clerk slapped her hand over her mouth and backed out the door, her eyes so wide the whites showed all around the pupils.

Lysi's eyes darted around the cluttered room. An empty bottle of champagne and two tall flutes shared the nightstand with a small box of chocolates. Cristin's binder, laptop and pens lay on the motel desk, her dress draped over a chair, red heels underneath.

In the silence, Lysi heard her heart pounding as she returned her gaze to Cristin's lifeless body. She felt a need to touch her friend one last time. In slow motion, she extended her fingertips to Cristin's white hand. Instantly, she drew back in shock at its coldness, terrified that healthy, vibrant Cristin was dead.

Chapter 3

At the sound of someone clearing his throat, Lysi jumped and a frightened little wail escaped her chest.

"I'm sorry. I didn't mean to startle you, Miss Weston."

Lysi blinked and turned toward the voice. A tall man in a brown tweed jacket filled the doorway. As he moved towards her, Lysi caught a fresh outdoor whiff of alfalfa. His heavily silvered black hair fell in a thick fringe over half his forehead. Lysi judged him to be about her own age, fifty something.

The man held up a badge. "I'm Detective James Tennyson, Sage Deer Police Department. I have to ask you to step outside. We need to cordon off this room. It's standard procedure in cases like this."

Lysi had no idea how long she'd stood riveted next to Cristin's bed. She stared blankly at the detective, hesitated, and licked dry lips.

"I'm sorry. I don't think I understand. What do you mean, 'in cases like this'?"

Detective Tennyson tucked his badge away and looked at Lysi through sensitive blue eyes. "Mrs. Pry, the desk clerk, called the department and reported a possible homicide."

"Homicide," Lysi said, her voice barely above a whisper. "I can't believe this is happening."

Her eyes strayed to the door where two police officers stood with rolls of yellow plastic tape in hand, waiting impassively for her to vacate their crime scene. Suddenly aware of the detective's eyes on her, she switched her vacant stare to him.

"I understand completely," Detective Tennyson said. "This must be a terrible shock to you."

Lysi nodded and moved slowly towards the door.

"I know Miss Holden and you had worked seminars together for quite a few years," he continued.

For an instant, Lysi wondered how this stranger knew so much about her—name, job, and history with Cristin.

"It would be helpful if I could ask you a few questions," the tall cowboy detective said. "We can talk in the motel office or at the Department if you prefer. It's ten minutes from here." He hesitated a moment, his attention intently focused on her face like a doctor evaluating a patient, then added, "I can drive you."

Lysi took a slow breath, and heard a distant voice that was her own reply. "I'll tell you what I know." She pressed her fingers to her temples to quell the throbbing in her head. Feeling relieved that the questioning could take place away from the motel, she said, "My car's parked in the lot. I can follow you."

*

Lysi barely noticed the green Ash trees that lined Sage Deer's main street or the modest shops and businesses crowded into the small downtown district. She looked straight ahead, trailing Detective Tennyson's car—stopping when his brake lights glowed, accelerating when they dimmed, turning when his signals flashed. Her thoughts raced around in her head like aimless mice in a circular maze. She tried to find some thread of logic in this increasingly macabre nightmare. Cristin was dead, but murder…murder was incomprehensible. Cristin had never set foot in Montana until three days ago. It's impossible that one of these strangers in this alien place would want to kill her.

Still in shock, Lysi followed Detective Tennyson's car into a gravel parking lot, parked beside him in the shade of an Elm tree and waited like a lost child for him to lead her to his office.

The two-story mission style building with its brownish-orange stucco exterior reminded Lysi of home. The soft curves of the three arched parapets that extended above the roofline evoked comforting images of California Spanish architecture. Suddenly, Lysi desperately wanted to catch the next flight to San Francisco. But what about the seminar? She was already contracted. She'd just have to stick it out.

Lysi stopped and stared when Detective Tennyson led her under a wide arch through a recessed door opening on a central lobby. A heavy wrought iron candelabrum hung from the domed ceiling casting a warm glow on historic murals painted on large sections of all four walls.

She caught her breath at the mural of a young Native American woman with long ebony braids seated in front of a buffalo hide tipi. The maid embraces a tiny baby and gazes at a bare-chested brave. Clutching a feather-bedecked spear in his right hand, the young man fights to control the spirited horse he has mounted. The plains surrounding the scene are covered with a profusion of gay little brown-eyed susans that contrast with the deep sadness in the big dark eyes of the new mother.

Allowing her imagination to wander through the details of the painting provided a temporary respite from the pain of Lysi's reality. The mural reminded her of the historical frescos in Coit Tower on San Francisco's Telegraph Hill; a place she and Cristin discovered together.

Detective Tennyson seemed to read her thoughts. "A Cheyenne woman painted this mural as a tribute to her tribe. The model for the maiden is a student at Lame Deer High School on the Northern Cheyenne reservation not far from here."

"It's beautiful."

The town hall building housed three agencies–County Courthouse in the South wing, Police Department in the North wing and City Offices on the second floor. The wide marble stairway with its ornate banisters resembled many of the stairways Lysi had seen in treasured old French buildings while a student at the University of Nice. This kind of building in Eastern Montana seemed surreal, similar to the thick mist clouding her understanding of recent events.

Detective Tennyson guided her into a small office in the North wing. The simple room fit Lysi's preconceived notions about Montana much better than the striking Mission style lobby. Neat stacks of file folders lined one half of a utilitarian metal desk along with a beaded Indian pot full of pencils and a framed photograph of someone she couldn't see. A computer station stood behind the swivel desk chair, a file cabinet to the right of it. Two wooden chairs in front of the desk completed the furnishings. Lysi noted one extravagance, a large oil painting that took up most of the wall space opposite the desk—a magnificent landscape of silvery green sagebrush.

The detective motioned her to a seat in one of the wooden chairs and offered her a choice of coffee or iced tea.

A little surprised at the offer of iced tea in a cop's office, Lysi said, "Uh, tea. Thank you."

He left and returned a moment later and handed her a cold glass. She accepted it gratefully and really looked at him for the first time. Sun exposure had tinted his fair complexion to a slightly ruddy tone accentuating a deep cleft in his chin that gave him a rather boyish look despite the dark stubble of a tough beard. The smile creases at the outside corners of his almond-shaped eyes blended into the laugh lines around his full lips giving him a perennial smile even during serious moments.

James Tennyson removed his well-broken-in jacket and sat down in the chair next to her. Lysi appreciated this more informal approach to interrogation. Catching the outdoorsy alfalfa scent again, it crossed her mind that he was a comfortable man like a pair of warm slippers.

He eyed Lysi with the same concern he had shown at the motel. "Do you need a few moments?"

"No, no. I'm fine." Her hands shook when she tried to sip the tea. "Really, I'm fine."

"You have a full schedule, so I'll be as brief as possible." The detective took a yellow pad and pen from his desktop and began writing as he questioned her. "Did you know Miss Holden well?"

Lysi hesitated. Oh yes, she knew Cristin well.

As a friend—caring and steadfast. Nonjudgmental, always supportive. But, as a professional colleague Cristin's dedication left a lot to be desired. Her actions often conflicted with the anti sexual harassment doctrine she preached.

Lysi's mind raced back to an incident that seemed to characterize Cristin's erratic philosophy. At a seminar reception outside of Houston, Cristin had used her sharp tongue to verbally castrate a boor who tried to force her to have a drink with him. Not ten minutes later a tall, good-looking Texan put his arm around her and suggested they get together a little later. Cristin flashed a smile, and they ended up in her motel room. Somehow the boor found out and nearly broke the door down before the police hauled him off to the drunk tank.

Lysi knew this kind of thing had happened more than once. Could it have happened this time?

"Yes, I guess I've known her about five years." Lysi tried to keep her voice calm.

Cristin reminded Lysi of her vivacious younger sister, Jessica. Since her early teens, Jessica had had the same devil may care attitude as Cristin. Lysi adored Jessica and accepted her hedonistic lifestyle as just part of her outgoing personality.

It seemed like only yesterday a loud pounding on the door in the middle of the night followed by her mother's heartrending cry, changed Lysi's life forever. Jessica had died in a DUI car crash along with the driver and two other passengers. That was over thirty years ago, but the pain still surfaced each time she thought of her little sister.

Detective Tennyson inclined his head toward her and stared with raised brows. "Miss Weston?"

Lysi blinked several times. Had he asked a question? "Sorry, what was that?"

"Can you think of any reason someone might want to harm Miss Holden?"

Lysi bit her bottom lip and provided a limited response to the detective's question. "Cristin had a wonderful personality. Everyone liked her. I can't think of any reason someone in Sage Deer would want to harm her." Her stomach wrenched. *Could Cristin have hooked up with the wrong Sage Deer cowboy?*

Detective Tennyson leaned closer to Lysi and rephrased the question. "Do you know of anyone, anywhere who might want to harm Miss Holden?"

Lysi shook her head. "No. No one. As I said, everyone liked Cristin."

With a slight tinge of resignation, Detective Tennyson moved to a different line of questioning. "When did you last see Miss Holden?"

"Two days before she left San Francisco. We touched base on our presentations."

"Did she behave in any way out of the ordinary? Seem anxious? Mention any names?"

Lysi knitted her brows. "No, not that I recall."

After several more questions, the detective asked, "What led you to ask the desk clerk to unlock her room?"

"Cristin and I were supposed to meet for lunch. I called her room and when she didn't pick up the phone, I decided to knock on her door. She didn't answer. I was worried so I got the desk clerk to open the door and when she did I..." Her eyes misted and she quickly took a sip of tea.

James Tennyson tapped his yellow pad with the pencil eraser three or four times then leaned back in his chair. "Thank you, Miss Weston. That's all the questions I have for now."

He handed her his card. "Call me on my cell phone if you think of anything else or...if you need anything."

Lysi nodded. "Cristin's death is such a nightmare." She squeezed her eyes shut. "I need to know what happened."

"I understand. We'll do everything possible to find out for you."

He stood and extended his hand. His voice sounded solicitous. "May I see you to your motel?"

Lysi tucked the card in her purse and took his hand. It felt warm against her icy fingers—supportive and comforting. She looked up at the detective. "Oh no. Thank you."

Her voice sounded distant, preoccupied, even to her own ears. A glance at the big round wall clock told her the interrogation had lasted almost an hour. She needed to rest—to recover—before the afternoon presentation.

Just before opening the office door to leave, she turned back to Detective Tennyson.

"There's one more thing. Cristin had a diamond and ruby ring. It's missing."

He wrote down the description and Lysi sleepwalked out the door.

*

As Lysi drove towards the Big Sky Motel, she caught sight of Detective James Tennyson in her rearview mirror. At first she thought nothing of it—probably out on a duty call—but when his image remained in the mirror, worries began to plague her. Did he suspect she had not fully responded to his interrogation questions? Had she said something suspicious? Didn't he believe her?

The detective followed her to the motel and as soon as she opened the room door, he gave her a friendly nod and left.

Her gaze trailed him out of the parking lot. *Is he concerned about my welfare? Or does he think I'm a murderer?*

*

Lysi dreaded the call she had to make to her boss, Charles Stone. Twice she'd punched in his private number and hung up. Now she forced herself to stay on the line while each ring of the phone thundered in her ear. Tears streamed down her face and she didn't bother to wipe them away. She didn't know what to say. She didn't know how to tell him about Cristin. She didn't know how he'd react. All she knew for sure was she couldn't go through with the seminar. Not now. Not without Cristin. Not with Cristin lying dead somewhere cold and alone.

"Charles Stone speaking."

Lysi's sniffled into the phone like a child, her shoulders heaving. Somehow the normal sound of Stone's voice brought more tears. Nothing was normal anymore.

"Who's calling please." His voice had an edge of impatience.

Lysi drew a ragged breath. "It's me, Charles. Lysi."

"Lysi, what's going on? You sound terrible? Are you okay?"

The words poured out of her. "It's Cristin. Oh, Charles. Someone murdered her. I can't go through with the seminar. You have to cancel it. I just can't do it."

The silence on the other end of the phone seemed endless. Finally Lysi said, "Did you hear me, Charles? Cristin's gone."

"Yes," he said on the exhale. "Do they know how…"

"No. But they're investigating it as a homicide. Charles, I'm coming home."

"Listen to me Lysi. You're not coming home. You will do the seminar. We have a contract—an obligation. We have to separate the seminar from Cristin's death. I…we are devastated by her death. We care about her and mourn for her. But Lysi we cannot risk losing thousands of dollars over a breach of contract suit. Do you understand what I'm saying?"

Seconds passed before she answered. Then she said quietly, without inflection, "Yes."

Charles Stone may have said something else but Lysi didn't hear it because she disconnected and went into the bathroom retching dry heaves.

Chapter 4

The sun inched across the sky scorching the town into idleness. James Tennyson cruised slowly past storefronts along Dull Knife Street, nodding at townspeople seated on benches under sun-bleached awnings fanning themselves with newspapers and magazines. Even though it was already past 3:00, out-to-lunch signs still hung on shop doors. The air conditioned café bulged with customers lingering over cold drinks.

Tennyson turned the car air conditioner up two notches and thought about Lysi Weston. For starters, she was not what he expected. When the police chief told him a female professor would be conducting a training seminar on sexual harassment at Nerium and the mayor expected town leaders to attend, he had envisioned a shrill, in-your-face woman—acerbic, aggressive, mannish. Now he reproached himself for buying into sexist stereotyping. *I guess I need that seminar as much as anyone else in this town.*

An appreciative smile spread across his lips as a picture of Lysi floated through his mind's eye—a tall woman, conservative dress and makeup, a cameo beauty; strong character tempered by a deep vulnerability, a cross between Ingrid Bergman and Audrey Hepburn. The fine lines around her eyes and mouth told him she had reached that age where it's difficult to determine a woman's years, perhaps somewhere in her late forties or fifties. The one time she smiled while in his office, she had filled the room with a warm glow.

James slowed when Jet, the hardware store's half-deaf hound dragged its old arthritic body across the street in front of him. He shook his head and grinned. That old dog would be a goner if everyone in this town didn't look out for him.

People watching out for each other was one of the things James liked about Sage Deer. The town had the family feeling of his grandmother's Cheyenne village. People knew your name and cared about you. He'd spent enough time in big cities full of strangers to know that life would never work for him.

After Jet made it safely across, James inched on down Dull Knife Street, his mind back on Lysi Weston. Something about the interrogation kept gnawing at him. He knew one thing for certain; she hadn't been totally forthright in her responses to his questions. Her long pauses didn't match her short answers. He had a gut feeling she might be hiding something. Two big questions pounded his brain—What? And why?

After pulling off the main street into the gravel parking lot of the city offices building, James lingered in the car a few minutes pondering the questions. Maybe the shock of losing her colleague was too much. Maybe she was on overload with the seminar only a couple of hours away. Or, maybe she knows someone who threatened Cristin Holden.

He would follow up on the ring, the only solid bit of information she provided. Could robbery have been a motive?

He knew one thing for sure—his interrogation of Lysi Weston wasn't over yet.

Chapter 5

Three hours later Lysi waited on the Nerium conference room stage, her face devoid of expression; thoughts of Cristin pushed aside. She sized up her audience while staff development director, Carolyn Norris, read her introduction bio to the audience.

Lysi's eyes flickered around the large mahogany-paneled room scanning the group seated on cushioned folding chairs in front of her. Another captive audience required by upper management to attend a seminar. Some in the group openly glowered at her; arms crossed, well-fed double chins tucked into porky chests, eyebrows knitted together. Others wore bored or preoccupied expressions, probably overworked and resentful of time away from their desks wasted on another useless training session. A few sat with pencils ready to take notes on her comments. Out of twenty people, she counted only four women.

Hank Jones, seated about four rows from the stage, had his eyes trained on her as if daring her to chip away at his little fiefdom. No one else looked familiar. She scrutinized the other faces. Which ones vandalized her poster? Well, she had a few little surprises of her own for those adolescent pranksters.

Lysi considered which of her basic approaches she'd choose and decided her "scare the hell out of 'em" strategy would do nicely. She'd cite a couple of devastating sexual harassment lawsuits like the Global American Corporation, a travel conglomerate that had to pay out $47,000,000 to plaintiffs.

Maybe, she mused with a sardonic smile, they'd get a little laugh out of the Ishizawa Recreational Vehicles lawsuit in which the corporation had to cough up 51 million for the class action suit victims plus several millions more to private plaintiffs bringing similar complaints.

She wondered if they'd be able to figure out that managers' heads rolled when these companies had to pay out the big bucks? Sometimes a punch in the gut's the only way to get their attention. Lysi had trouble keeping a gleeful glint out of her eyes. Inwardly, she wondered why the lack of awareness of audiences like this still surprised her.

In the midst of planning an attack, her gaze drifted to a familiar figure seated in the first row, arm draped over the back of the chair, long legs stretched out in front of him. His eyes twinkled as his lips curved into an easy grin. The unexpected pleasure of seeing him brightened her spirit, and she couldn't resist flashing a quick smile.

It struck her as rather odd that a detective would participate in a Nerium seminar; and again she wondered if he considered her a suspect. Maybe he was there to keep an eye on her. Yet, in some way Detective James Tennyson's presence soothed her.

The sound of the audience's grudging applause interrupted the private chemistry between Lysi and James Tennyson. She walked to the podium, thanked Carolyn for the introduction, took a deep breath and began.

"Recently, a corporation about the size of Nerium filed bankruptcy, closed three regional branches, and laid off 800 employees, 37 of whom were middle and upper managers."

A rumble of comments told Lysi she had gotten audience attention.

"The issue, perceived by the CEO to be minor, was a complaint by a female office clerk that her supervisor made frequent suggestive comments to her and attempted to fondle her anytime they were alone. These advances resulted in the employee's nervous breakdown and inability to continue in her job.

"A sharp attorney who decided to survey all employees of the corporation, discovered several other incidents of a similar nature and filed a hefty lawsuit on behalf of the victims. He demanded a

15.6 million dollar financial settlement on top of which he wanted an additional 6 million for managers creating a hostile workplace and another 3 million for their dismissive treatment of the complainants."

Lysi paused for another wave of whispered comments, then added in a strong, matter-of-fact voice, "He won."

She waited a moment to allow time for pulse rates to accelerate and blood pressures to soar.

"This alone would have bankrupted the company, but a shareholder then sued the corporation stating that the management's dismissive treatment of employee sexual harassment complaints wrongly cost the stockholders millions of dollars that had to be repaid."

Lysi paused again and locked eyes with several in the audience.

"Sexual harassment can be quite costly."

I'll give them a moment to gnaw on that. She figured they might not think a suit like this could happen here at Nerium because they probably didn't see their own behavior as harassment. After all, is it against the law to be sociable? It would be her job to describe offending behaviors well enough for them to see themselves.

She put on a pair of reading glasses and flicked on her computer. The seminar agenda materialized on a large screen behind her. Pointing to each bulleted item, she summarized the two-session presentation.

"This afternoon I'll define sexual harassment and explain how it harms both victims and perpetrators, and lessens the productivity of the work place."

"Tomorrow afternoon I'll offer ways to identify and eradicate sexual harassment, and guide you in outlining your own plan for its elimination here at Montana Nerium."

Feet shuffled, eyes rolled toward the ceiling, tongues clicked, and snorts bounced around the room. She halted her presentation and deliberately made eye contact with several of the more restless members of the group. After a few moments, the room quieted and she continued.

"The Equal Employment Opportunity Commission defines sexual harassment as any conduct of a sexual nature that creates an intimidating, hostile or offensive work environment. Sexual harassment includes groping, fondling, lewd and/or suggestive jokes, comments and behavior; and—" She held up the graffittied seminar poster she had removed from the staff entrance door—"obscene graffiti plastered in work areas."

A dark haired woman in a tailored beige summer suit exclaimed from a back row seat, "Oh, my God!"

Lysi dipped her chin and looked over her glasses.

"Oh yes, there *is* sexual harassment here at Montana Nerium."

Immediately, a man with a head like a basketball and a face almost as red as his power tie, guffawed. "Hey, that poster's pretty clever." He bobbled his head around the room.

"Good laugh, eh? Eh?"

Several people snickered. A shrill whinny from a pretty woman in her thirties formed an unattractive counterpoint to Basketball Head's snorts. Her blonde hair piled on her head with springy little tendrils dangling over her eyebrows and tickling the fronts of her ears, reminded Lysi of an unkempt poodle.

Now's the time Lysi decided, and she advanced her attack. "There's been a dramatic increase in the number of sexual harassment suits in the past few years." She cited the lawsuits at Global American Corporation and Ishizawa, and went into great detail regarding the types of transgressions, the devastating financial settlements, and the mass firings of management personnel.

She crossed her arms, leaned over the podium, and stared hard at the audience.

"The bottom-line question is this: If Montana Nerium loses a million dollar sexual harassment suit, will it be *your* head on the bloody block?"

Nervous faces paled as anxious eyes seemed to look inward examining past behavior, except for Basketball Head, who shot Lysi a menacing glare.

Lysi plowed forward with the presentation, referencing several supporting charts and distributing pertinent handouts.

When she checked her watch, two and a half hours had passed. "Our time's almost up. I'd be happy to take any questions you might have."

She looked around the room. No one raised a hand.

"Perhaps you might have questions later. If so, just write them on the question cards in your packet and place them in the blue box at the back of the room.

"Tomorrow afternoon we'll learn procedures that'll enable you to keep your head attached to your body—" No one laughed. "—and make the workplace hospitable to all employees. I thank you for your attention."

Lysi nodded to a few scattered handclaps, gathered her papers from the podium and walked in a relaxed but deliberate way, off the stage straight to the parking lot exit door. Carolyn Norris intercepted her before she could open it.

"Terrific presentation, Lysi." She sounded sincere.

"Just want to remind you we're serving light refreshments and some hors d'oeuvres in my office."

Taking Lysi's arm, she turned her towards the elevator. "We want to give staff an opportunity to talk with you informally."

"Great," Lysi said, trying not to betray her true feelings. *That's just what I want to do, hobnob with Neanderthals.* She immediately repented her rush to judgment. Wasn't it her job to persuade them to change their behavior?

Carolyn pressed the up button and the elevator doors opened framing Hank Jones in front of a body-to-body mob. Carolyn's breathing crept toward hyperventilation, color rose to her cheeks, and her eyes grew moony as though Adonis himself had miraculously appeared.

In a voice as smooth as soft butter Hank said, "Come on in, girls. There's plenty of room if we kind of squeeze together."

Lysi recognized Basketball Head's guffaw from somewhere in the back of the group echoed by Poodle Girl's same shrill whinny from the seminar. *Do those two always do duets?*

Carolyn wedged into the stuffy elevator next to Hank. "Hmmm, nice," he said, playfully pressing closer to her.

Lysi stepped back. She had no intention of playing rub and grope with her seminar attendees. "I'll meet you up there. I need to put my materials in the car."

*

Returning from her car at a snail's pace, Lysi passed a kid wearing an olive drab shirt with large letters on it that spelled out *Clean Team.* His head bobbed to the rhythm of some inaudible tune from earphones wedged in his ears. He trudged along leaning on a barely moving cart loaded with mops, toilet brushes, sponges and various bottles of liquid cleaners. As he passed, she read *Judo Kid* on his cap. The desk kid from the motel; He must have two jobs. His rating inched up a notch on Lysi's approval meter.

As she drew near the Staff Development Office, Lysi heard the mellow voice of Willie Nelson belting out a tune about getting on the road again. That's what she'd like to do. Get on the road out of here. What she wouldn't give to be sitting in a quiet San Francisco bar nursing a cold drink and a long conversation with Cristin; or even just grabbing a quick coffee and bagel with her. *Cristin, I miss you so much.* Day after tomorrow, Lysi would be out of Sage Deer before dawn. She didn't care that she'd have to spend half the day in the Billings Airport sitting around waiting for her afternoon flight time, she just wanted out.

Pursing her lips, Lysi resignedly opened the door just as a new song started with the words "all my ex's live in Texas" followed by a couple of loud whoops from somewhere in the room. *Montanans sure do love their country-western hurtin' tunes.*

Lysi's tastes ran more to Classic Rock—music by Linda Ronstadt, Elton John, Billy Joel and the Beatles. To this day, Paul McCartney still made her heart turn flip-flops.

Her eyes widened at the Staff Development office converted into a party room. It smelled like a well-used barbecue pit. Instead of the large reception desk in front of the glass-enclosed garden, she saw a long table laden with catered food—deviled eggs, Buffalo wings, garlic bread, black bean wraps, and a minuscule vegetable tray with a creamy dip. It looked like an all-you-can-eat restaurant, the kind of place her father used to call a *trough.* People sat around tables, drinks in hand, munching finger foods from heaping paper plates. *This is* light *refreshments?*

"Lysi, come on in," a voice called over the music. She turned toward the voice. In a corner opposite the table, Hank Jones stood behind a portable bar stocked with wines and liquors. Sparkling glasses hung from a rack above his head. He motioned her over.

"The drinks are on us. What'll it be, Lysi? A *screw*driver?"

"Mineral water. Thanks."

"I bet you want plenty of *ice*, right?"

Lysi nodded.

He set the drink on the bar and leaned toward her. "You know you ruffled a few feathers today. I think you need to slow down a mite. We like to kind of ease into things around these parts."

Lysi noticed Hank didn't call her 'honey'. Maybe there was hope. She took a sip of her drink. "Thanks for your input."

Hank looked at her with mocking eyes and just a hint of anger, causing Lysi to wonder if he had a stake in maintaining ignorance at Nerium.

Lysi searched the room. A brief wave of disappointment passed through her when she didn't see Detective Tennyson among the revelers.

The raucous laughter, loud voices, and jovial backslapping told her people had already had more than a couple of drinks. She decided to mingle briefly and then exit as quickly as possible.

Lysi had just turned away from the bar when she recognized Basketball Head's raspy voice. "Time to belly up to the bar, eh?" He held up his empty glass and tottered over to stand too close to her.

He slammed his glass on the bar. "Well, Hank, what have we here?" he said while looking straight at Lysi through bloodshot eyes. His whiskey stench forced her to hold her breath.

"Why Bill. You must remember Ms. Weston?" Hank blinked wide, incredulous eyes and grinned at Lysi.

"Yeah, yeah, I remember her. But did you notice, Hank? This little gal doesn't pull any punches, does she?" He reached up and poked his ten-gallon Stetson hat back with one finger.

Lysi eyed the hat and guessed he got his etiquette lessons in a barn. She grimaced at the big silver belt buckle half hidden by his mountainous belly and the string tie with the long horn clasp. He fits the worst of all cowboy stereotypes.

"Nope, she sure doesn't. She's just doing her job," Jones said. "Lysi Weston meet Bill Pitt, Director of Sales."

Lysi extended her hand to the man who'd been named a major offender in the background material on Nerium. He ignored it and went on talking.

"I got a couple questions for Ms. Weston here." He put a nasal stress on the word *Ms.* and stretched the z sound out like he was an overstuffed bumblebee.

"Well, she's right here Bill. Why don't you just ask her those questions?" Hank splashed whiskey into Bill's empty glass.

Lysi scowled at Hank. She wanted to shout, "Don't keep filling his glass. Can't you see he's already smashed?" Instead, she turned to Pitt.

"Do you have some questions I can help you with?"

"Well, Ms. Weston, exactly why are you wasting your time giving speeches here at Nerium?"

Lysi considered telling him he was the reason. But said, simplifying her response to the level of a six year old, "Your corporate headquarters contracted with Stellar for the sexual harassment seminar and the company assigned me to do the job."

Pitt hitched his belt up over his big gut. "Sexual harassment my eye! Show a little friendliness and some women take it the wrong way and go whining to the cops. Why I—"

"Mr. Pitt, I'm not here to debate decisions made by your CEO. Do you have any questions concerning what I've presented so far?"

Pitt rocked unsteadily on his heels. "Okay. Tell me, darlin', have you ever been sexually harassed? I mean...you just might enjoy it."

Lysi reached into a small portfolio, pulled out an index card and wrote Bill Pitt's name at the top. She handed it to him along with a pen.

"Mr. Pitt, here's a card. I'm asking people to write down their questions so I can respond to all of them tomorrow during the group presentation. That way I don't have to answer the same question several times, and all the participants can benefit."

Looking hard at him, she added, "Put it in writing. Be assured, I will give you full credit for this question."

Bill Pitt, mouth hanging open, stared at the card in his hand as if it were a strange insect about to crawl up his arm. Hank Jones threw his head back in explosive laughter. It jolted Pitt from his hypnotic state and he thrust the card at Lysi, snatched his drink, and stalked off without another word.

"Don't mind Bill. He's looped. His mouth gets bigger than his stomach when he's had too many. Won't remember a thing tomorrow." Hank seemed to enjoy Bill's big scene.

Lysi bent down and picked up the card. She took her mineral water without looking at Hank and walked across the room to join Carolyn Norris who was deep in conversation with a thin, brown-haired woman with hunched shoulders.

"Hi, Lysi," Carolyn said. "Meet Elizabeth Scot, Information Technology."

Lysi recognized the woman in the seminar who had expressed shock over the graffittied poster.

"Elizabeth just installed a new company-wide management information system. She claims it'll be ten times more efficient than the old one. Right now, it's making us all crazy. She's the only one in the company who understands it."

Elizabeth flinched. "It's mainly the e-mail component that's causing people problems. It'll all come together. You'll see."

Carolyn hooked her arm through Elizabeth's. "Lizzie and I've been friends since grade school in L.A. When this job opened, I knew she'd be the perfect candidate, so I recommended her. Math and computer science have always come easy to Elizabeth. Instead of dating and dancing, she spent all her spare time romancing the computer."

Elizabeth smiled at Carolyn then looked at Lysi through thick glasses with rims the same brown as her comfortable oxfords. Lysi studied Elizabeth's fine features and intelligent eyes. She'd look quite pretty with a touch of makeup and an updated hairstyle.

"I really appreciated your presentation." Elizabeth pumped Lysi's hand. "I hope you plan to discuss the procedure for filing complaints and, more important, how to do it without losing your job."

Lysi almost asked Elizabeth if she had a complaint, but deemed it inappropriate at the moment. "There's a step-by-step filing procedure to protect victims. I'll walk everyone through it tomorrow."

A slight man in his early twenties standing alone near the door caught Lysi's eye. He hesitated then grinned, peeled himself off the wall and approached the group. He drew a handkerchief from the pocket of a waist-cinching, European cut jacket that fit snuggly over his gold jersey. After a couple of discreet dabs at his nose, he peered at Lysi through soft brown eyes and introduced himself in the changing voice of an adolescent.

"Hello Ms. Weston. I'm Denny Robbins, Director of Finance. I guess you'd call me the money guy, not that I have any to speak of. I just get to watch it fly by me. I monitor cash in and cash out." He sniffed and dabbed at his nose again. "You'll have to excuse me, I've had allergies ever since I got here. I think it's the dust and chaff."

Lysi knew what he meant. A dry throat had plagued her since landing in Billings. She liked Denny's open, friendly manner; the way he raised his eyebrows while speaking with lots of dynamic expression. He reminded her of a puppy in his eagerness to please. "A pleasure to meet you," she said

"I was so excited when I heard you were from the Bay area. I live in San Francisco." He sighed and closed his eyes. "Oh, how I miss that glorious morning fog and those soft misty days."

"How did you end up here?" Lysi asked. Denny in Sage Deer was like Beluga caviar at the local H Salt Fish and Chips.

"I'll spare you the long sad story. I'm a temporary transfer."

Elizabeth patted Denny's back. "Tomorrow Lysi plans to address the procedure for filing complaints without losing your job."

A smile warmed Denny's face. "Cool. If tomorrow's seminar is anything like today's, it'll be fantastic."

"Why thank you, Denny. I really appreciate positive feedback," Lysi said.

Denny glanced over his shoulder, as if checking to see if someone might be listening. He lowered his voice. "It interests me that men can file complaints. When you can spare a few minutes, I'd like to talk to you about a problem I'm having."

Lysi suspected she already knew his problem. She opened her PDA to the calendar and set a time to talk with him.

A familiar whinny interrupted the quiet conversation. "Ms. Weston, I'm KiKi Kavenaugh, Sales Administrative Assistant. I'm pleased to make your acquaintance."

Carolyn Norris glanced at KiKi and, without greeting her, turned to Lysi. "I have to circulate a bit. I'll be back shortly."

Lysi remembered the blonde haired, curly-headed poodle from the seminar. "It's a pleasure to meet you, Ms. Kavenaugh."

"Please, call me KiKi." The dimples in her cheeks deepened as she gushed on. "I just wanted to tell you what a great place Montana Nerium is to work. I'm so lucky Billy—I mean Mr. Pitt— took a chance on hiring me. Why, if it weren't for him, I'd still be serving cocktails at the Cattle Rustler's Lounge. I'm awful grateful and I try to show it, if you know what I mean." Her big smile revealed two slightly protruding canine teeth that reinforced her poodle image.

KiKi's last sentence set off an alarm in Lysi's mind. *Is she a victim or a predator?*

Bill Pitt staggered up and encircled KiKi with one beefy arm, pulling her so tight against his big stomach he forced an involuntary squeak out of her.

He slapped Denny on the back, nearly toppling him. "You look just stunning today. I love the gold jersey. It's so..." He shrugged his shoulders. "Oh, you know."

Denny lowered his eyes. "Hello, Bill." Then he said to Lysi, "I have to go now."

Pitt roared as Denny walked away.

Lysi wanted to knee the fat cowboy where it'd really hurt.

"Now I hope you aren't trying to poison the mind of my little filly here," Pitt said to Lysi.

KiKi whinnied and Pitt tipped her chin up with his index finger and planted a sloppy kiss on her mouth. He looked at Lysi and slurred, "Tell me something honey, how'd a frigid piece of ice like you ever get together with a hot little chili pepper like Cristin Holden, eh?"

For an instant, KiKi's eyes flamed. Then she pursed her lips into a jealous little pout and said, "*I'm* your hot chili pepper aren't I, Billy?"

The color drained from Pitt's face and he said in a don't-get-mad-at-me voice, "You bet you are, Toots. You know I didn't mean a thing by that."

Images of Cristin's lifeless body passed through Lysi's mind. The possibility that Pitt might have been Cristin's man for the night disgusted her.

She pulled out the same index card on which she had written Bill Pitt's name and calmly handed it to him.

"Write your question on the card, Mr. Pitt."

He snatched it from her, tore it up, threw it on the floor and stumbled away muttering.

Lysi caught the word, "Bitch!"

KiKi grinned.

"He's not normally like this. He just had too many shots. He shouldn't drink."

She hustled after him.

After KiKi left, Carolyn reappeared, hooked her arm through Lysi's and tipped her head close to Lysi's ear.

"Ignore him. He's only here because he's one of the good old boys, sort of our token Montana hire. Corporate seemed to think Nerium would have better PR if we put a few of the local yokels on the payroll."

Lysi raised an eyebrow and nodded as if to say, "I got it." She was beginning to like Ms. Norris more and more. Clearly, Carolyn had a sense of the company's sexist attitude."

Carolyn checked her watch. "I'll have to stay here until the party's over. God knows when that'll be." She did a quick visual survey of the room.

"Everything seems to be going okay for now. How about stepping into my office for a short respite? I'd like to debrief on your presentation and talk about tomorrow's seminar."

Lysi breathed a sigh of relief and followed Carolyn into her office. Carolyn closed and locked the door. They sat on each end of an alpine green couch.

Carolyn set her drink on a glass coffee table and kicked off her size 4 heels. She turned to Lysi.

"About some of the responses to your presentation—I hope you didn't take their brainless drivel personally. Most of these managers are castoffs from other regional offices. They're here because they're either close to retirement and just putting in their time or have become problems to head office. L.A. Corporate thinks it owes them something for their years of service and doesn't want to just fire them."

"Why not a golden handshake? Why place them here? Wouldn't they want their best people to get a new plant off to a good start?"

"I guess they didn't know where else to put them, so they just pastured them here in the outer limits. Placement at Nerium Montana is kind of like putting them out to graze. Frankly, I think head office will eventually bribe them with some kind of payoff to get them to retire early."

Lysi felt tired. She drew a ragged breath and exhaled heavily. "Then why are they bothering with this seminar?"

"Probably because they want to avoid expensive legal action. Most of those jokers out there still think of women as play things and treat them that way."

Lysi pursed her lips and nodded resignation.

Carolyn reached over and touched Lysi's hand. "I really respect you going through with this presentation today. It must have been terribly difficult so soon after losing your partner."

Lysi swallowed a lump in her throat and lowered her head.

Carolyn scooted next to Lysi and patted her arm. "I'm sorry. I shouldn't have said anything."

"No, no. It's okay." Lysi locked at Carolyn. "You know, the police think someone murdered her."

Carolyn's mouth dropped open. "Murder! The people around here may be a little rough around the edges, but I don't think any of them would be capable of murder. What on earth makes them think that—did they find something in the room like prints or…or… whatever it is they find?"

"I don't know. A detective came to the room right after I discovered her body and—"

"Oh no, you were the one who discovered her. You poor thing."

Lysi knitted her brows. "Carolyn, I've been thinking about something you said this morning in your office."

"Yes."

"Well, you commented that Cristin made quite an impression at the reception following her presentation. What exactly did you mean?"

Carolyn averted her eyes. "I really didn't mean anything. I just noticed she attracted several of our male employees. That's not very hard to do."

"Do you think she attracted Bill Pitt?"

"Bill Pitt? Sick!" Carolyn jabbed a finger at her mouth a couple of times. "Yeah, probably. You just have to be female and not dead to get his testosterone flowing." She narrowed her eyes. "Why do you ask?"

"I know Cristin. She wouldn't even glance at a guy like Pitt. This may sound silly, but it occurred to me that Pitt might have approached her, gotten a quick brush off, festered into a rage and…you know."

Carolyn seemed to consider the possibility before she answered. "No. I don't think so. Bill has his hands full with KiKi. She watches him like a hawk. He doesn't dare step out of line."

Lysi remembered KiKi's overreaction when Pitt called Cristin a hot little chili pepper at the reception. She recalled how Pitt tensed up and fell all over himself trying to pacify his nippy little poodle.

"If not Pitt, then who?" She leaned her elbows on her knees and rested her forehead on her fingertips. "It just makes no sense. Cristin had never set foot in Sage Deer before this seminar. She didn't know anyone. Why on earth would someone want to hurt her?"

Carolyn was silent for a moment. She seemed thoughtful.

Then in a deliberate voice she said, "Come to think of it, Bill did brag to a few people that he'd had to fight off Cristin's advances. Nobody thought anything of it; he's such a blowhard. He does have a fragile ego though and a belligerent attitude to match. I heard he's got a real nasty temper, too."

Lysi's eyes sparked. "I can tell you, there's no chance Cristin came on to Pitt. He lied."

Carolyn looked incredulous. "You really think Bill had something to do with Cristin Holden's death?"

"I don't know. Maybe I'm grasping at straws. I just feel I owe it to Cristin to find out who did this." She pressed a finger against one tear duct then the other.

Carolyn put her arm around Lysi's shoulders.

"Look, you don't need any more of this party crap. You're coping with enough. Go home. Get some rest. I'll make your excuses."

Carolyn led Lysi from her office into the reception room while Kenny Chesney sang to the strum of his guitar. She navigated through the whooping, toe-tapping crowd, running interference for Lysi until she was safely out the door and in the hall.

She squeezed Lysi's shoulder. "Don't worry about the reception. I'll take care of everything. I'll call you."

When Lysi got into her car, she sat staring into the darkness for a few minutes. Bill Pitt has a fragile ego and a nasty temper—a recipe for violence.

Chapter 6

When Lysi pulled into the Big Sky Motel parking lot, a red glare blazed from her side view mirror causing her to squint. The gaudy neon lights in the window of the Sagebrush Café blasted *OPEN* in six inch flashing letters. She parked, but instead of going to her room, walked toward the beckoning sign telling herself she needed a late snack. She wasn't hungry, but a feeling of isolation had plagued her ever since she'd discovered Cristin's body. She couldn't force herself to go back to the room just yet.

A bell jangled as Lysi opened the glass door of the café. Football schedules and class pictures plastered the walls along with a Sage Deer High pennant and hand-scrawled menu specials for the day. Two large gold trophies filled a small shelf behind the cash register.

The room was empty except for a waitress. The platinum blonde woman raised a deeply tanned face from behind a Soap Opera Digest. She straightened one of the skinny straps of her orange tank top and smiled.

Lysi had her pick of tables, but walked straight to the counter and slid onto a round vinyl-covered stool. The waitress stared at her through almost transparent blue eyes.

After a moment, she handed Lysi a tissue.

"What's the matter, honey? Is it a guy?" she asked in the gravelly voice of a long-time smoker.

Feeling a tear dampen her cheek, Lysi accepted the tissue and dabbed at her eyes.

"Hey, I know it hurts." The waitress held up a coffee pot in an unspoken question.

Lysi nodded.

The waitress scooted two mugs onto the counter and splashed coffee into them, splattering a few drops on the green Formica top.

"Some men can be real weasels. I had one drop me like a hot branding iron when I wouldn't put out. Just 'cause I'm a waitress doesn't mean I'm easy."

She poured an avalanche of sugar into her black brew and clinked a spoon around in it.

"Yeah, he found himself a conniving little alley cat over at the Cattle Rustler Lounge. She gives him whatever and whenever." The waitress rolled her eyes and pulled at a dangling silver earring.

Lysi poured cream into her coffee. "No, no. It's not a man. I just lost a long time friend."

The waitress scrutinized Lysi for a moment. "Say, you're staying over at the Big Sky aren't you?"

Lysi stared into her coffee cup. "Just for a couple of nights."

The waitress stared into her coffee for a few seconds then looked up. Her mouth formed a perfect *O* as she gulped air. "Hey, she was your friend. That woman they found dead over in room 29. Holden. Right? Cristin Holden."

Lysi nodded and felt a lump rise in her throat.

"Oh God, I'm sure sorry. I got a big motor mouth."

Lysi wondered how the waitress knew about Cristin. She started to ask, but remembering how fast news spreads through small towns, she figured the desk clerk had probably raced over to tell her all the juicy details. "It's okay. Cristin *was* my friend."

"Man, that's got to be tough."

The waitress shook her head and handed Lysi another tissue. For a few moments, the two women sat silently sipping coffee; each seemed to be caught up in her own private thoughts.

Finally the waitress said, "I'm not saying I know how you feel, but I do know what it's like to lose a best friend except my friend didn't die—just our friendship did. Her name's KiKi."

"KiKi Kavenaugh?" Lysi recalled Bill Pitt's giggly blonde poodle. "She works for Nerium. I met her at the seminar today."

The waitress' eyes rounded. "Hey, you're the one that's got everyone so all fired up with your anti guy talk. I'm gonna tell you right now, honey, I'm with you. I–," She slapped her fingers over her mouth and fell silent for a few seconds then said in a soft voice, "Miss Holden was your partner, too."

"We worked together for five years. I'm going to miss her."

"You know, honey, the hardest thing that ever happened to me in my life was losing my mom when I was just out of high school. It still hurts when I think about her. But you know what I do? I just make myself think about all the nice things about her. I mean, I'm not saying you have to do that about your friend. I'm just saying...well, it works for me."

Lysi swiped at her eyes with the napkin. "She was a great friend. Always there when I needed her ...when I'd start a new assignment... whenever I felt down. When my mother passed away she stayed at my house for a week, slept on my couch and made breakfast every morning. She was like a sister."

"Sounds like you two got along real good."

Lysi looked over her coffee cup. "We were so different yet we balanced each other. I'm tall and angular. She was short and curvy. I'm reserved and serious. She was outgoing and funny. I'm a workaholic. She liked to play—she *taught* me how to play."

Lysi set her half empty cup on the counter, stretched tight neck muscles, opened her eyes wide and sighed.

"Honey, you look beat. The waitress patted Lysi's hand. "You better hit the sack, Gal."

"I guess you're right." Lysi knew she was over tired, but she also knew sleep wouldn't come easily tonight.

The waitress extended her hand. "I'm Jade Green. The coffee's on me."

"Nice to meet you, Jade. I'm Lysi Weston." She swallowed the last of the coffee and slipped off the stool. "Thanks for the coffee and the sympathetic ear."

"Anytime, Honey."

"And my seminar isn't anti male."

"Hey, doesn't matter to me." Jade Green picked up the cups and stashed them under the counter. "Oh, just in case you didn't notice, I saw Jimmy Tennyson tail you into the lot earlier today. He's our local gendarme."

"I know." Lysi wondered again if she was a suspect in the murder of her friend.

Jade's eyes turned dreamy. "Now there's a man! Today's young colts can't even get close enough to eat the dust of that stallion. Most any Sage Deer girl'd love to corral him."

"Good night, Jade."

Chapter 7

Lysi jerked up from a sweat-soaked pillow. She scanned the room—taking in the beige walls and draperies, standard motel desk and chairs, and the gray-faced television. The Big Sky Motel.

She dropped her head back to the pillow and tried to block out the hazy images that had floated through her restless sleep; Cristin—eyes sparkling, pink lips smiling, cheeks flushed with happiness. Cristin—fading into a soupy mist as the arms of Bill Pitt encircled her. Cristin—reappearing in a smoky brown cloud—face white, eyes empty and arms flailing as if to keep from sinking.

The nightmare seemed so real. Remorse crushed Lysi's chest. If only she'd telephoned Cristin as soon as she arrived on Wednesday. If only she'd checked on her early Thursday morning. If only she'd insisted the night clerk shove a note under the door. If only… Maybe she could've saved her.

All she could do now was try to help find her partner's killer. Lysi squeezed her eyes shut and tried to concentrate on what she'd learned from Carolyn about Bill Pitt. When Pitt bragged that Cristin came on to him, no one listened to his blathering. Maybe Pitt tried to hook up with Cristin, and she blew him off. Pitt had a temper and probably couldn't handle rejection. Pitt could be capable of murder.

Lysi's heart raced. She bit hard on her lower lip as facts stampeded through her head. Cristin's diamond and ruby ring, her most cherished treasure, gone. She always wore it. Had she told the detective about the missing ring? Yes. Yes she had. The killer must have it. Find the ring. Find the murderer.

The clock alarm on the bedside stand burst into a peppy rendition of "Camelot." Seven a.m.

"Sage Deer is no Camelot." Lysi hit the alarm.

Forcing herself to think about the day's tasks, she slid out of bed and brewed a cup of watery coffee in the less than gourmet coffee maker. She set the cup on the desk and opened the draperies. In the field across the road the colors of the tall grass changed from brown to beige to yellow as it rippled in an invisible breeze. It looked like a beautiful golden sea. Still, it couldn't compare with the lush green she saw on her bike rides through Golden Gate Park. Tomorrow she would be home. That thought gave her the strength she needed to make it through the day.

A monstrous silver semi truck roared by on the highway and eclipsed the view along with her pleasant reverie. She turned back to the desk, rummaged through her brief case, found the packet of question cards from the Nerium comment box and spread them on the desk. There were the usual unsigned questions: *Do you want to outlaw sex because you're not getting any? Are you frigid? What have you got against men? Are you a lesbo?* She shoved these out of the way and categorized the relevant question cards.

Several questions related to procedures for filing a complaint and protections for people who file: *How do I file a complaint? Could I lose my job if I file? Could my supervisor retaliate? Who do I file with if my boss is the one who harasses me?* She jotted down response notes to use at the afternoon presentation.

After a sip of cold coffee, Lysi checked her PDA for appointments and saw Denny Robbins' name next to nine o'clock. Time to get ready.

She'd just slipped into yesterday's fuchsia silk blouse and summer white pantsuit, one of three outfits she'd brought, when the phone rang. She hadn't expected a call on the motel phone line and stared for a long moment before answering on the fifth ring. "Hello?"

She immediately recognized the shrill voice on the line. "Hi, Lysi. This is KiKi Kavenaugh. Remember me from the reception? I work for Billy Pitt."

"Of course. What can I do for you, KiKi?"

The growl of heavy-duty trucks passing in the busy morning commute distracted her. She glanced out the window at the garish parade of primary colors glistening with chrome. It struck her that they probably all had gun racks.

"Oh, it's what I can do for you." The now familiar whinny vibrated from the receiver. "Elizabeth Scot from Information Technology and me are taking you out to an early supper or late lunch before your presentation today. Oh, let's just call it a 'sunch.'" KiKi chortled at her idea of a clever play on words.

Ramming my head into one of those trucks would be more palatable than 'sunch' with KiKi. "That's very nice but"—

"It'll be on the company, of course. We'll meet you at 2:30 at the 'palace'. That's our nickname for the Nerium building." Another whinny. "Just come on up to Staff Development."

"That's very kind of you but completely unnecessary. I wouldn't want to impose."

"No, no we want to. It's kind of a regular thing we always do for new people, just to be neighborly. Besides, Carolyn figured you might need a little cheering up. We took Cristin out, too. Rest her soul. I read about her tragic demise in the paper this morning."

Ignoring the comment about Cristin and eager to get off the phone, Lysi said, "When you put it that way how could I possibly refuse? I'll meet you in Human Resources at two-thirty; and thank you."

Lysi hung up the phone and rummaged around in her purse for lipstick. *It takes forever to find anything in this big gunnysack.* The purse was an impulse buy at a boutique sale in Monterey because she fell in love with the adorable baby otter embroidered on the front of it. *She really needed an orderly purse with lots of compartments.* She determined to shop for one as soon as she got back to San Francisco.

In frustration, she dumped the contents of the purse on the bed. That was when she spotted Cristin's note. She picked it up and examined the phone number on the envelope back. She had first noticed it when she opened the note in the car outside Nerium, but had not thought about it since. Now it seemed very important. Whose number was it? She looked at the motel phone. The Sage

Deer area code was 406 the same as on the envelope. A local number.

Lysi hesitated; then reached for the phone. She had punched in two numerals when she heard a timid knock on the door. After stuffing the envelope back into her purse and cramming the rest of the stuff in on top of it, she opened the door to Denny Robbins' intense face.

"Mr. Robbins, it's a pleasure to see you again." She invited him in and motioned him to a chair beside the desk where she had been working earlier.

"Thanks for letting me come."

His eyes strayed to the unmade bed. Lysi could see his discomfort at having to meet with her in a motel room, but he'd wanted to meet some place private. She suspected he was afraid of possible reprisals.

"Just think of this as my private executive suite," she joked.

Denny managed a nervous laugh and sat down beside the desk. Lysi returned to her own seat. "You wanted to share some concerns with me."

"Yes," he said, rubbing his fingers across his forehead. "I guess I'd better begin at the beginning. I'm with the San Francisco office. Corporate sent me to Montana Nerium for a couple of months to train a new Finance Manager. The problem is I've been here four months already and we still haven't hired one."

Lysi looked confused. "I'm afraid I can't help you with hiring practices, I'm—"

"No, no. That's just some background information." He clicked his tongue and stared into space. "I'm gay."

Lysi took in Denny's purple crewneck and the silk scarf knotted around his throat, his delicate fingers clutching an envelope. How has he survived so long in "Marlboro" country? She touched his hand.

"As you know I'm from the San Francisco Bay area too," she said, hoping to convey her acceptance of his lifestyle.

Denny leaned toward her and blurted out, "I'd give anything to be home in the Castro. My life's been hell ever since I got here."

He reminded Lysi of a little boy whose dad forced him to play football even though none of the boys wanted him on the team, and the coach made him warm the bench for the whole game.

Denny pulled a note from an envelope and smoothed it out on the desk top in front of Lysi. "Look at this."

Lysi read the dark, angry pencil strokes scrawled on a piece of binder paper:

Our boys aren't for sale. Signed, The Good People of Sage Deer.

She looked at Denny. "What does this mean?"

He explained he had inserted a five dollar tip into an envelope for the kid who delivers his newspapers and later found it shoved back under his door with the tip still inside—and the note.

"It sounds like they're accusing you of soliciting young boys."

Denny's whole body drooped. Lysi knew her comment wounded him, but in her experience in dealing with homophobia, clear specific facts were critical.

Now he sat with his legs crossed, elbows on knees, chin resting on one fist. "I guess," he said to his knees.

"Denny, this disgusting note may violate several statutes. I need to ask hard questions to find out."

Denny nodded.

"Have any similar incidents occurred since your transfer to Sage Deer?"

Denny nodded again. "This whole thing started at Nerium."

He told her he'd found a computer-generated picture with his head on the body of a bikini-clad woman tacked on the staff room bulletin board. He found disgusting notes taped to his computer monitor and ugly comments on his voice mail. Once someone had even draped women's lingerie over his desk chair.

In a desperate tone he said, "I don't know what to do. My partner, Thor, is coming out to visit soon and I'm afraid for his safety."

Lysi studied the furious writing on the note. Denny had reason for fear. She knew gay bashing incidents occurred even in liberal San Francisco. She worried something more deadly might happen here in cowboy land. Right now, a homophobic fanatic probably wanted to scare Denny. But if one gay triggered such antipathy, imagine the virtuous wrath that would be wreaked on a gay couple.

"Do you have any idea who might be involved in this?" she asked.

"I know who it is. It's Bill Pitt and his cronies. They've tortured me ever since I got here—making little side comments, mimicking me, giving me nasty looks. I can't prove it, but I know it. He tapped the newspaper boy envelope. "And now it's spreading through the whole town."

Denny stroked his temple with his fingertips.

"I begged for a transfer back to San Francisco, but corporate refused. I have to stick it out until they hire a new Finance Manager because I need the job. My partner and I just bought a Victorian house near the Castro, and the remodeling is taking every penny we earn."

He held his head in his hands. After a ragged breath he said, "You're my last hope."

Sympathy and anger welled up in Lysi's chest. "I can help you, but you'll have to work with me."

"I'll do anything." His voice cracked and his little-boy eyes watered.

"I'll need copies of every degrading note and picture you've received—including e-mails. From now on, don't erase any sexist comments on your voice mail. If you haven't erased your previous voice mails— don't. Document any obnoxious behavior on the part of Pitt. Record the time and place it occurs and describe it in detail."

Denny's face brightened. "You're my last hope. I'll do it."

Lysi didn't like being someone's last hope, but he seemed so childlike in his desperation. She didn't know whether to pat him on the head or shake his hand. She got up and followed him to the door where he turned and grabbed her hand. "Thank you," he whispered. He looked left and right then raced to his car.

Lysi's foot scraped against something near the threshold. A newspaper. She stooped and picked up the Sage Deer News Roundup. Apparently someone had left a copy of the weekly outside on the mat.

She closed the door, walked to the bed and unrolled the paper. The inch-high, bold typed headline on the front page buckled her knees and she dropped down on the bed as the painful reality hit her—**Foul play suspected in woman's motel death**.

Chapter 8

Detective James Tennyson waited while Dr. Angus MacKinnon eased into one of the chairs in front of his desk and crossed his legs revealing a patch of white skin above his black socks. He unbuttoned a snug-fitting suit jacket and pulled a gold pocket watch out of a green and black MacKinnon plaid vest.

"I have a patient at ten, so I'll have to make this fast."

He replaced the watch and smoothed the front of the vest. He had worn the MacKinnon clan tartan as long as James could remember. It kept alive a dream of one day visiting his clansmen in North Mull, Scotland, his birthplace.

James grinned at the doctor who had tended him as a child and ministered to his grandfather and father as well. When James's Cheyenne grandmother, on her deathbed, begged to spend her last hours out of doors, Dr. Mackinnon had her bed placed under a shady cottonwood and held her hand until she passed.

James's English-born mother had chosen Dr. Mac as the family physician over a more experienced Polish doctor because his Scottish ancestry served as a link to the British Isles for her. It proved to be a wise decision.

He's got to be over eighty, James mused, noting the doctor's thin white hair, creases in his pink complexion, and the thick spectacles that magnified his sharp eyes.

"I won't take much of your time, just tell me what you got and you're finished," James said.

Dr. MacKinnon pulled a notebook from his medical kit, licked his thumb and turned several pages before he found some scribbled words only he could read. He skimmed the page, coughed twice and peered over his spectacles at the detective.

"Well Jamie, you know I'm no expert in these matters, but after a preliminary examination, keeping in mind that I'm no forensic specialist, the data, skimpy as it is, says homicide."

He raised his bright blue eyes to James. "You're planning to consult the Billings' forensic specialist, aren't you?"

"Only if you think it necessary. I have complete confidence in your judgment."

Dr. MacKinnon made a definite nod of his head. "I do think it's necessary." He cleared his throat again and turned back to his notes.

"Time of death was between 9:00 and 11:30 or so on Tuesday night. I found bruises on the neck that point to some form of strangulation."

James leaned forward. "What do you mean some *form* of strangulation?

Dr. MacKinnon uncrossed his legs, reached across the desk with a little grunt and dragged a pad and pencil over to his side. He sketched a neck, shaded several small patches on it and added some perpendicular pencil lines. Moving his gnarled finger around on the drawing he explained.

"Now this is what the neck might look like in your sort of every day strangulation: disc-like finger-tip bruises, linear finger-nail scratches from the assailant—or even from the victim struggling to remove the assailants hands from her neck—maybe hemorrhaging under the neck skin and bruising of the strap muscles; damage to the larynx."

He drew another neck and shaded in one small area. "This is the only bruise I found on Miss Holden." He tapped his index finger on the shaded area. "It's right on the carotid artery."

James looked thoughtful; then said half to himself, "Compression of the carotid triangle—a martial arts choking technique."

"That's right. It's quick and easy. Doesn't take much strength, and the victim is unconscious in about twenty seconds. Just got to know where to exert the pressure." The doctor pressed hard on the shaded part of the picture.

Dr. MacKinnon checked his watch again and hoisted himself from the chair with another little grunt.

"Well, got to get going. Let me know if I can be of any more help." Shaking hands with James, he added, "I'd be interested in knowing what the Billings forensic pathologist has to say."

"Sure thing," James said. "And, thanks."

The doctor walked to the door. "Regards to your mother."

James nodded while the face of a murder suspect congealed in his brain.

Chapter 9

Since Cristin's death, Lysi had had very little appetite. She picked at food never really tasting or enjoying it. After Denny left, a growling stomach drove her to the Sagebrush Café where Jade talked her into the Cowboy Bonanza Special–eggs, sausage, bacon, home fries and baking soda biscuits, quite a departure from her usual morning fare of coffee, juice and cereal. It tasted so good she wolfed down most of it.

Stuffed but satisfied, she lumbered across the courtyard and mounted the stairs to her room. The bedside phone rang as she rummaged through her cluttered purse trying to locate the magnetic swipe card. The adorable baby otter embroidered on the front of the bag wasn't worth the mess inside. Maybe she could replace it with a cheapie here in Sage Deer.

Finally her fingers closed on the card. She jammed it into the lock slot, but the door didn't open.

The phone kept ringing.

"Damn you," she said to the persistent phone ring. She kept flipping the card around until it finally clicked. Once inside she tossed the purse on the bureau, dived across the bed in one continuous movement and grabbed the phone. "Hello!"

"Hello, Miss Weston," said a calm male voice. "It's Detective James Tennyson." He paused for a moment.

"You sound a little out of breath. I hope I'm not disturbing you."

"No, no. I just got in from breakfast." She punctuated the sentence with an unladylike hiccup.

James Tennyson's deep, rich laugh vibrated in her ear. "Sounds like you had a good Montana breakfast."

"I had the Sagebrush Cowboy Bonanza."

She caught her reflection in the closet mirror and winced at the crimson waves of color flooding her neck and cheeks. She was definitely starting to notice James Tennyson.

Not sure exactly what she had expected a Montana detective to be like—big belly, big boots, big hat—she knew one thing for sure, Detective Tennyson blasted her preconception to smithereens.

"Uh huh. You may not need to eat for a week." Again the smooth laugh. "Well, I called for a couple of reasons. First, I wanted to tell you that I enjoyed your presentation yesterday. It gave me some things to think about."

"It surprised me to see you there. I expected only Nerium employees."

"I'm afraid it was a command appearance." Tennyson sounded resigned. "Town support for Nerium projects is the mayor's latest brainchild. He wants to stimulate economic growth in Sage Deer now that the state offers business tax incentives and has eased regulatory compliance laws. Nerium's his baby and he's worked hard to get the corporation to settle here. I can't blame him. Nerium's already committed to building a recreation center with a swimming pool and playground along with a couple of sports fields and several bike trails.

"The mayor decided it'd show good will to invite all the town departments to send a representative to your seminar. I got elected to represent SDPD."

"I see." She failed to keep the disappointment out of her voice.

"Don't get me wrong. I *did* have negative expectations. But now I'm glad I went."

Lysi wanted him to explain, but he changed the subject and switched to his on-duty tone.

"I want to update you on the case. First, we've checked the pawnshops in Billings. None recognized the ring."

"That means the thief still has it," Lysi said.

"Maybe. The other thing you probably already know is the preliminary examination of Miss Holden's body points to homicide. Bruises on her neck indicate strangulation was the probable cause of death."

Stunned at hearing the word *strangulation* officially spoken by the detective, Lysi barely managed to speak above a whisper. "Someone strangled her?"

"We've requested a complete autopsy by a medical examiner from Billings. He'll perform it tomorrow."

Lysi tried to speak, but the words stuck in her throat.

"Miss Weston?"

She swallowed the lump blocking her speech. "Yes, yes, I'm here."

"Since the death has now been officially declared a homicide, I'm afraid I have to ask you to stay in town for awhile, until the investigation is complete."

"What! That's not possible. I have a flight out tomorrow afternoon. I need to help Cristin's sister with...funeral arrangements." She forced the words past a new lump in her throat.

"I'm sorry. We're not ready to release Miss Holden's body, yet. You'll have to cancel the flight," he said in a tone that Lysi considered brusque and unyielding.

"I can't stay in this place. Not after what happened. Find me another place—maybe a hotel in Billings. I don't care. Anywhere!" Lysi choked on her words, tried to swallow and convulsed into a cough.

"Miss Weston. Please try to calm down. Billings is over two hours from here. We just need you for a few more days." Detective Tennyson spoke in a worried voice. "How about a room away from the crime scene? Maybe next to the office."

"I don't know," Lysi said. Her thoughts scattered into little beads of quicksilver, impossible to pull together.

"I'll arrange to have you moved right away."

Before she could protest further, he added, "The department's beeping me. I'll call you as soon as I have more information. See you at the seminar this afternoon." He hung up.

Lysi stayed perched on the edge of the bed holding the receiver against her ear and listening to the dial tone. Sad angry tears streamed down her cheeks.

"I can't do this. So help me, I can't," she whispered.

The receiver slipped from her hand and thudded on the floor. Jarred by the sudden sound, she wiped her eyes with the back of her hand, bent down, picked up the receiver and took a deep breath.

"I can and will get through this. I owe it to Cristin."

Chapter 10

Lysi turned sideways and squeezed between chairs, trying to keep up with the mini-skirted hostess who adroitly zigzagged through the boisterous diners to a table situated in the dead center of the Cattle Rustler Restaurant. Cowboy hats and baseball caps filled the room. Even the marble-eyed buffalo head over the bar sported a gray Stetson. The smell of beef and beer proclaimed the restaurant specialties. Lysi sat down and looked around. *The Cattle Rustler Restaurant certainly lives up to its name.*

KiKi Kavenaugh's eyes glittered with excitement as she flitted around the tables in the noisy restaurant. She whinnied and waved at several of the diners. One of them, a barrel-chested guy in a black tee shirt with "I'm your mom's worst nightmare" printed across the front in big red letters, slapped her on the tush and shouted, "Hey, KiKi baby. When are you coming back? This place just ain't the same no more without your classy chassis scooting around."

KiKi shot him a playful punch to the shoulder. "Cal, honey. I bet you say that to all the girls."

When they sat down, Elizabeth Scot pressed two fingers to her throat and surveyed the crowd. "This is not the restaurant I would have selected."

Neither would I. Lysi raised her eyebrows and tried to smile. "Looks like the menu offers lots of choices."

Lysi perused the list of carnivorous delights–flat iron steak, buffalo burgers, rib eyes, T-bones, prime rib. It also boasted thirty beers on tap along with beer-battered fries. Where were the green salads?

"Now Elizabeth, loosen up." KiKi saluted with her glass and chugged down her first drink of the meal—obviously not her first one of the day. She leaned toward Lysi as though Elizabeth wasn't sitting at the table.

"Elizabeth just doesn't know how to party down. Can you believe she's still a virgin?" KiKi's pointy little poodle fangs appeared when she erupted into laughter.

Elizabeth raised her glasses and rubbed the bridge of her nose with her thumb and index finger. The haggard expression in her soft eyes spoke volumes about her many unfortunate experiences with the garrulous KiKi.

After the waitress had taken their orders, KiKi chattered nonstop about her Nerium colleagues.

"Hank Jones is kind of the corporate Casanova. Carolyn Norris gets cow-eyed whenever he's around. Who wouldn't? He's one gorgeous hunk of beef." She giggled and added in a breathy whisper, "Don't you ever breathe a word to Billy that I said that."

Lysi didn't answer, feigning great interest in the platter-size porterhouse steak and mashed potatoes the waitress had just delivered.

Elizabeth frowned. "KiKi, I'm sure Lysi doesn't wish to listen to your prurient office gossip."

KiKi looked daggers at her under heavy-lids and shoved a bite of rare prime rib into her mouth.

Lysi turned to KiKi hoping to avoid a scene and maybe learn a little more about Pitt. "How long have you known Bill Pitt?"

Still chewing, KiKi said, "Since good old Sage Deer High, I was a cheerleader and he was football jock." Her voice sounded wistful. "We only just got together a few months ago. But I think he always kind of had a yen for me. It just took him a while to catch on to it."

Lysi chose her words carefully. She wanted to encourage KiKi to share more about Pitt without sounding too inquisitive. She didn't want KiKi to alert Pitt she'd been asking questions about him. "Anyone can see Mr. Pitt adores you."

KiKi's lips curved into a coy grin. "Yeah."

"At the reception, I did notice he got a little irritated," Lysi continued with caution.

"Aw, he's got a big old ferocious bark, but he'd never hurt a flea. He's nothing but a humungous pussycat." KiKi slapped her hand over her mouth. "Oops, there I go again. Don't you ever breathe a word to him that I called him a pussycat." She turned to Elizabeth. "Or you either."

Both Lysi and Elizabeth shook their heads emphatically.

KiKi cut a piece of prime rib, dabbed some mashed potato on it, and deposited it in her mouth.

Lysi turned to Elizabeth. "Technology seems to be a major thrust here at Nerium Montana. It must be exciting to be spearheading the effort."

"In some ways it's very exciting. In others it's frustrating. For example, people seem to be paranoid about our new communication system. Half my job is"—

"Computers make me crazy." KiKi grimaced at Elizabeth.

Elizabeth took a patient breath.

"I know, KiKi. Seems like they make everyone crazy. That's why half my job's racing around the building solving minor problems and reassuring everyone things will improve. Of course, there're always some glitches to iron out with any new electronic system. People just need to be patient."

KiKi whipped her head to Lysi, as though the topic of technology had ended. "Now where was I about Nerium directors? Oh yeah. Denny Robbins—Finance—now that guy's as queer as a three-dollar bill. We lock up the young boys when he comes to town."

Lysi winced at the remark. KiKi and Bill Pitt are perfectly matched. "I guess Denny's a major annoyance to a big masculine guy like Bill."

"Oh yeah! But Bill knows how to keep queers like Robbins in line."

Lysi wanted to pump KiKi for more details, but Elizabeth interrupted. "That's enough, KiKi. You're making a fool of yourself."

"Yeah? Well, maybe she'd like to hear how Cristin Holden threw herself at everything in pants at the reception."

"Stop it, KiKi. Show a little respect."

Elizabeth turned to Lysi. "I'm so sorry. She doesn't know what she's saying."

Elizabeth eyed the empty shot glass on the table and the beer chaser in KiKi's hand. "Too many boilermakers. I hope you won't judge the rest of us by her behavior."

Lysi started to say she understood, but KiKi interrupted, raising her voice above the nasal twang of the country western singer blaring from the corner jukebox,

"Let's be honest, Elizabeth. You saw how Cristin Holden panted after Hank and Bill–and even Denny, for God's sake. She kept swinging her fat little butt around and flashing her hooters like she was the only game in the room. It made me sick! I couldn't—"

"KiKi, for Heaven's sake!" Elizabeth cringed at the glances from neighboring tables. She seemed to shrink into her chair as more people cranked around to get a better look at the spectacle. She clicked her tongue and waggled her head so hard her glasses nearly jounced off her nose.

"That's it! Lysi and I are leaving–with or without you."

Lysi got up and followed Elizabeth out the door, wishing she had never set foot in the Cattle Rustler Restaurant or Sage Deer or Montana.

Chapter 11

The seminar began promptly at four o'clock. Lysi faced a more subdued audience–none of the scornful looks and bored yawns of the previous day. She wondered if the change related to in-depth consideration of her remarks or the headlines in the morning paper about Cristin's death. Bill Pitt, forehead lined in thought, looked straight ahead. Hank Jones's scornful expression had disappeared. Denny Robbins looked sad but hopeful. She noticed KiKi's empty chair next to Bill Pitt. *Probably snoozing off the liquid portion of her "sunch"*.

Although still upset at Detective Tennyson's rather cavalier insistence that she cancel her flight and remain in Sage Deer indefinitely, Lysi's eyes strayed to the front row seat where he had sat yesterday. Relieved to see him there, she acknowledged his nod with a chin bob.

Carolyn Norris spoke quietly into the microphone. "Will you kindly join me in a moment of silence in remembrance of Cristin Holden." She lowered her head and so did everyone else.

A small lump rose in Lysi's throat as she felt the quiet sympathy of the audience; the considerate show of respect on the part of Carolyn meant a lot to her.

After Carolyn's introductory remarks, Lysi stepped to the microphone. She thanked the audience for the gesture of respect for Cristin, then swallowed hard, took a deep breath and opened the seminar with a brief review of the previous day's comments. She launched the day's topic saying, "Behaviors you may have previously considered innocuous might in fact be illegal." She paused to let the audience chaw on this disagreeable morsel.

They remained quiet.

"By the time you leave here today, you'll have created a preliminary draft of the Nerium Sexual Harassment Policy that will help your company avoid costly suits and perhaps keep you from losing your job."

She distributed a sheet titled Guidelines for Curbing Sexual Harassment, moved to her laptop, flipped on the Power Point presentation and projected the questions she'd received on a large screen behind her.

"I'll address all these questions before you leave the seminar today." A glance at Bill Pitt told her he was relieved she'd left his questions off the list.

She flipped to the next slide and highlighted the first line.

"Your plan must define sexual harassment–any unwelcome sexual behavior—physical, visual or verbal—that creates an uncomfortable or hostile work environment."

Confused expressions greeted this comment. Carolyn spoke for everyone. "Can you be a little more specific?"

"Yes, of course."

Lysi flipped through her Power Point slide show to a list of offenses. She pointed to the first slide and stared straight at Bill Pitt. "Things like remarks about a person's body, gender or sexual preference; display of offensive or derogatory pictures, are among the more reprehensible offenses." She watched him sink down in his seat, head facing straight forward, eyes shifting about the room.

She flipped to the next slide. "Physical contact such as touching, patting or pinching; leering; other obscene or offensive gestures; sexual assault. And maybe most important, the inference that an employee's submission to or rejection of such conduct may be used as a basis for employment decisions affecting the employee."

Feet shifted in the audience. Elizabeth Scot glanced at Bill Pitt who coughed, sank lower in his seat, eyes on his lap. Even Hank Jones cringed.

Lysi flipped back to the opening slide and highlighted number two.

"You need a procedure for filing and investigating complaints. You need to designate individuals who will be responsible and accountable for the timely resolution of complaints."

She looked at Hank. "Often this responsibility lies with Human Resources."

Hank swallowed, would not look at her, but fixed his stare on the screen.

Lysi moved to number three.

"Disciplinary action for substantiated complaints can range from a verbal or written reprimand that may include a recommendation for counseling, suspension, or even dismissal."

Lysi underlined the next two sentences.

"If sexual harassment has been substantiated, the incident must be documented in the offender's personnel file. Not good if you're applying for a new job."

Strained looks on the faces of some of the audience told Lysi reality had hit home.

She moved to the last item and concluded the Power Point presentation by saying, "All employees must be trained and regularly updated on sexual harassment policies."

Lysi suggested management consider posting copies of the policies where employees and customers could easily read them. "Include them in the employee handbook."

"In short, federal and Montana state laws governing appropriate behavior won't go away."

She held up the legal document. "Companies must do whatever it takes to comply with this."

She flipped off the computer. "Any questions?"

After responding to a few questions, she said, "Let's get started."

She divided the management team into four groups and assigned each group a section of the guidelines and directed them to generate a rough draft of a Nerium plan. In less than an hour, the small groups had roughed out their ideas based on the sample plan Lysi provided. They began sharing them with the other participants. During the next hour, the whole group pulled together a final draft of a proposed Nerium Plan.

Lysi ended the seminar by saying, "As managers, it's your responsibility to keep your eyes and ears open. Conduct regular assessments of the work environment to determine whether sexual harassment is a concern among employees. If it is, address the concern."

She checked her watch and gave an affirmative nod to the audience.

"Congratulations, you developed your basic document in record time. In fact, you finished ten minutes early. You're ready to proof it and recommend it to the Corporate Services Committee for review and approval. Good Job."

The audience applauded.

James Tennyson winked at her.

Chapter 12

Lysi let her head fall against the back of Carolyn's couch, grateful Carolyn had ushered her right off the stage into the office before too many people cornered her with questions.

Carolyn poured two Dubonnets into crystal goblets. "This time they *heard* your presentation."

She handed Lysi her glass and clinked it with her own. "Congratulations."

Lysi took a sip. "Thanks. I left the room thinking the managers got the message—even Bill Pitt. They really impressed me with the policy draft."

"When are you heading home?"

Lysi shrugged before answering. "Not for awhile, I'm afraid. Detective Tennyson's decided I have to stay while they investigate Cristin's case."

Carolyn shook her head sympathetically.

Lysi recalled her last image of Cristin lying on the bed—still and pale, her fingers clutching at nothing. The missing ring floated onto Lysi's mental screen. Maybe Carolyn has seen it.

"Carolyn, Cristin had a ring she always wore. She treasured it because someone she loved gave it to her, maybe her mother or sister. She never told me who. It has a one-carat diamond in the center and two blood-red rubies, one on each side of the diamond."

Lysi pictured the ring. "Oh, and the engraving on the inside is a small heart with her initials, a C on one side of the heart and an H on the other."

"Sounds gorgeous," Carolyn said.

"The thing is, I didn't see the ring on her finger when I found her."

"Maybe she took it off for some reason."

"No, no. She never took it off. Like I said, someone she really cared about had given it to her a long time ago."

Lysi looked down at her hands. "No, I think her murderer stole it."

"God, it just keeps getting worse." Carolyn took Lysi's hand. "You poor thing."

Lysi looked through hopeful eyes at Carolyn. "I wanted to ask if you might've seen someone with it."

Carolyn nodded. "No, I haven't. I would've definitely noticed a ring like that."

Lysi drooped against the back of the couch. "Carolyn, I have to find that ring! I believe it will lead me to Cristin's killer. Find the ring. Find the murderer."

Chapter 13

Jade Green's head popped up from behind a romance magazine when Lysi's entrance jangled the bell on the door of the restaurant.

A man in a brown tee shirt with *Central Transport* printed in orange letters across the back and a hat labeled the same, glanced towards the jangling doorbell then continued to swab the last bit of gravy on his plate with a chunk of roll. He pushed his plate back, picked up the check, pulled some greenbacks from his wallet. placed them on the table and nodded to Jade.

"Keep the change, babe."

The last customer saluted Lysi on his way out the door.

Lingering scents of fried steaks and gravy were all that remained of the supper rush. The Sagebrush Café would remain empty until the early morning breakfast crowd arrived except for the occasional traveler who stopped for a takeout coffee to stave off sleepiness on the night road.

"Hey, I heard you were quite a hit today." Jade reached for the coffee pot and a mug.

Again struck by the speed at which information races around small towns, Lysi pictured people skittering about like mice, dropping juicy tidbits everywhere. She guessed that some of the Nerium employees had rehashed the seminar while eating dinner at the Sagebrush.

"It went pretty well," she said without a smile.

Lysi should have felt good about the successful seminar, but depression and fatigue dampened her spirit. She felt weighted down by an avalanche of problems—the death of her colleague and friend that turned out to be a homicide; the harassment of Denny Robbins that could escalate to death threats; and now Detective Tennyson forcing her to remain in Sage Deer maybe as a possible suspect in Cristin's murder. Lysi sighed and let her chin sink.

Jade reached across the counter and smoothed Lysi's forehead with warm fingertips. "Frowning can cause wrinkles, honey. What's up?"

Lysi placed both hands around the coffee cup and tilted her chin towards the ceiling. She dragged in a breath. "I got a call from Detective Tennyson this morning."

The waitress flashed a knowing grin. "You don't say. Not bad for only two days' work."

"It's not what you think."

Lysi explained that Tennyson had insisted she cancel her morning flight home because she might be needed for further questioning in the murder investigation.

"You mean he considers you a suspect?"

Lysi sighed again. "Probably. At any rate, I didn't like his inconsiderate attitude. He doesn't understand or even care that I have commitments. When I phoned Cristin's sister, she was so distraught that I promised her I'd help with funeral arrangements. Now I don't know when I'll get to go home."

Lysi lifted submissive eyes to Jade. "I guess I'm stressed out. I know he's just doing his job."

Jade patted her arm. "You're wrong about James, honey. He does understand. He's been through a lot himself. He lost his dad when he was only ten. His wife died five years ago."

Lysi listened with unexpected interest as Jade explained that Tennyson's mother was English. His parents had met when his father, John Tennyson, traveled to London to research his English heritage.

Lysi arched her eyebrows in question. "It seems strange that a person from a cosmopolitan city half way across the world would settle in a place like Sage Deer." Lysi knew she could never live here. She could barely stand it for a week.

"Maybe a more important question might be—Why would she marry a half-breed with all the trouble that can bring?"

Lysi didn't try to hide her surprise. "A half-breed. You mean Detective Tennyson has Native American blood in his veins?"

"Yup, I know it doesn't seem like it, his being so white and all, but his grandmother was full-blood Cheyenne. He got his straight black hair from her. Light skin and blue eyes came from his mom. He got his good manners from her, too."

Lysi shook her head. "Detective Tennyson is part Cheyenne. I would never have guessed it."

"'Course, it took some time for the Cheyenne to accept him as one of their own because he doesn't look like them. But I tell you, his heart is pure Cheyenne."

"I guess Detective Tennyson's mother returned to England after his father died," Lysi said.

"No way!" Jade looked at her like she had an IQ of twelve. "Sure, James's mom had to make a big adjustment when she married a young deputy-sheriff and moved to Sage Deer. But I tell you, that lady took to Montana like she'd been born and raised here."

Lysi took a sip of coffee. "How so?"

"Well, for one thing, she became a member of the Historical Society and got the whole town interested in Cheyenne handicrafts and festivals. Of course, that made John Tennyson real proud, his being half Cheyenne and all. Then, before you knew it she joined the Sage Deer Garden Club and started a section on native plants."

Lysi could hear the admiration in Jade's voice when she said, "Deborah Tennyson is a real aristocratic lady. No one ever calls her Debbie. It just wouldn't fit right."

A smiling James Tennyson filled Lysi's mind—fair complexion and blue eyes contrasting with black hair streaked with silver; tall, slim body and erect posture; slight British accent; the way he clipped his words. Of course, it was his English mother's influence that prevented him from fitting what Lysi considered the Montana cowboy mold. The comfortable, earthy quality she had noticed during the interrogation in his office must have been a gift from his Cheyenne grandmother. Interesting man.

Jade poured herself another cup of coffee and leaned her chin on her closed fist. "Yeah, after Sheriff John died, Deborah

Tennyson never remarried. She raised James with the help of a Cheyenne nanny that she had adopted shortly after James's birth. I think Namida, that's her name, is sort of a distant cousin. Anyhow, she was about twelve when her parents died of tuberculosis."

Lysi knew from experience that life is never the same after the death of someone you love. "How did Detective Tennyson's wife die?"

"Now it's a real sad story about James's wife. The poor thing died instantly when a drunk driver ran a stop sign and hit the car broadside. After that, seems like James only thought about one thing–putting drunk drivers in the calaboose. To this day he always says: 'Cars and bars are Montana's curse.'"

Jade held the coffee pot over Lysi's half empty cup. "Warm up?"

"No, thanks. I'd better not. I'd be awake all night."

"Suit yourself." She looked hard at Lysi. "Honey, there are only two men in this town worth looking at, one is James, who shows no interest in any woman; and the other is Hank Jones, who wants to sip sweet nectar from every damn flower in the meadow."

Lysi had no use for Hank Jones, and she certainly didn't care about James Tennyson.

Or did she?

*

On the way back to her new room, Lysi stopped by the lobby to request a couple of extra pillows.

The irritating teenage kid perched on the stool behind the desk, hunched over a judo magazine—insolent face half hidden by the bill of his Judo Kid cap; chin bobbing in rhythm to music that blared so loudly through the earphones Lysi could hear the pounding rap beat before she reached the desk. Doesn't he ever take those things off?

He didn't acknowledge her. She waited a few seconds, trying not to hear his labored attempts to breathe through a stuffy nose. When she banged on a little bell about eight inches from the boy, his head shot up and so did his temper. He yanked off the earphones. "Yeah, Lady?"

"Where's the desk clerk?" Lysi said, thinking any request she made of this kid would vanish from his brain before she even finished the sentence.

"She ain't here. I'm doing the desk. What's the prob?"

Lysi concluded he didn't consider the needs of motel clients high on his list of priorities. She took a pen and scrawled her request on a notepad.

"Give this to the clerk when she gets back."

"Okay, but that won't be 'til tomorrow." He slouched over the magazine again and began readjusting his headphones.

Lysi drew an exasperated breath and squinted at the name on his ID badge. "Maybe you could try to fill it–*Choki*. I'll read it to you."

"Hey, Lady. I can read. What is it with all you out-of-town chicks? So uppity. Why do you always have to look down on small-town guys? First you act all nice like you like us, then you act like we're all stupid or something." Choki's zits lit up like miniature tree lights as his face reddened.

Lysi didn't remember giving any indication that she'd even noticed him, much less liked him, but she did feel a little guilty about her demeaning comment.

"Look, I'm sorry. I've had a long day. Can you just get some pillows over to me?"

"Yeah, I guess," he said without looking at her and flipped a couple of pages in his magazine.

*

When Lysi returned to her room, she noticed the phone message light blinking. She plopped down on the bed, kicked off her high heels and pressed the message device button.

In a stressed-out voice, Denny Robbins said he had the packet of information she had requested, but didn't want to leave it at the motel desk and wondered if it would be all right to drop it by after eight this evening.

The clock radio showed 8:45. Lysi dialed Robbins' number and told him he could bring it over right now if he wanted. In truth, she really needed to stretch out on the bed and grab a few winks before writing the closing evaluation report on the seminar, but his stressful tone worried her.

"I really don't want to inconvenience you. It's just that—"

"No, it won't be any inconvenience at all. See you in about a half hour."

In less than thirty minutes, she heard a knock on the door. "Be right there, Denny."

She wedged her swollen feet back into shoes that now seemed three sizes too small and hobbled to the door.

A startled yip escaped from her throat when she opened the door and found herself nose-to-nose with Choki instead of Denny Robbins. He held four new pillows, still in the original store plastic and four clean pillowcases.

"Since you were so nice, I decided to take care of this myself. Where should I put them?"

"On the bed. Thanks."

Lysi noticed Choki had changed into a plaid shirt, cord pants and wore his cap backwards, the adjustment strap low over his forehead. Oil from his hair had darkened the lower part of the strap. It smelled as if he'd taken a bath in a saccharin-sweet men's cologne.

He dropped the pillows on the bed and took his time putting a pillowcase on each one; he arranged them carefully, smoothing invisible wrinkles with his hand.

"Can I do anything else for you? Is the new room okay?"

He peeked into the bathroom. "Toilet flushing?"

"Everything is fine. Thank you again for the pillows." Lysi pulled her wallet from her purse and took out a five-dollar tip.

Choki turned to her with a smile she didn't like. "Not necessary. I did it for you—special."

She walked to the open door. "That's all I need."

After Choki left, she started to tuck her wallet back into her purse when she noticed the corner of the white envelope with the phone number Cristin had written on the back. She took it from her purse and stared at it for a moment. One number was smudged. It looked like a three—no an 8. Her hand moved with uncertainty to the phone. Should she call? After a pause, she pressed her teeth against her lower lip and punched in the number.

"We're sorry. The number you are trying to reach is not in service at this time. Please check the number and dial again."

Lysi disconnected and closed her eyes in both relief and frustration. So the number's a three.

She punched in the number again, substituting three for eight. It rang four times; when she heard the message on the answering device, her mouth dropped open.

*

The knock startled Lysi. As soon as she opened the door Denny, his face pale with fear, walked right past her to the desk, opened a manila envelope and spread out the contents then dropped heavily onto a chair. Breaths coming in short gasps, body stiff, hands shaking, he watched as Lysi, with the precision of a surgeon, examined each scribbled note and lewd picture. One was missing.

"Where's the bikini picture you told me about?"

Denny licked his lips and spoke to the desktop.

"I didn't want anyone to see it, so I destroyed it."

Lysi shook her head and massaged taut neck muscles. Why does she bother?

"Denny, look at me. I have to have everything. You destroyed one of the most damning pieces of evidence. I can't help you if you won't help me."

He looked like a scolded puppy. "I'm sorry. It's just that it was so…degrading. Miss Weston, I don't know what I'm going to do if this doesn't stop. I'm so afraid. I…"

She touched his shoulder.

"I know, Denny. I'd be just as frightened. I'm going to help you through this."

"If only you can."

Lysi felt her energy draining. She just wanted to keep plowing ahead, get finished and lie down.

"Tell me about this one."

She picked up a piece of paper on which someone had pasted a swimsuit-clad male figure from a magazine or catalog. They had cut a circle out of the crotch area leaving a castrating black hole. Underneath, they had written:

Touch one of our boys and you will look like THIS!

"I found it on my desk this morning." His voice quavered. Hurt and disgust mixed in glassy eyes.

Lysi slid the picture next to the note about the paperboy tip and studied the writing on both. The same heavy pencil strokes, the same angry capital letters.

She turned the swimsuit paper over. Blue marks at the top caught her attention. "These look like they might be the lower parts of letterhead. Does this paper look familiar at all?"

Denny took the paper from her hand and moved his index finger over the blue marks. "It looks like it might be off one of the standard notepads distributed to all Nerium employees."

He pulled a pad from his briefcase and pointed at the letters printed across the top. "Look, those blue marks match the bottom part of the word *Nerium* that's imprinted on these sheets. So this is more proof that it's a Nerium employee."

Lysi studied the pad. "It proves it's someone who has access to these pads and to your desk."

*

After Denny left, Lysi sat down at her laptop to work on the final seminar evaluation report; she had managed to type the title and date when a truck's air horn from somewhere shattered the quiet night. She raised her head from the report and listened to see if it would sound again. Hearing nothing, she forced herself to type a couple more lines.

The glaring lights of passing trucks on the highway distracted her again, and she stared out the window for a long time at the irregular flashes of white, red and yellow, then decided to close the draperies. Instead, she got up and opened a window.

The restful chirping of crickets and the hypnotic circling of insects around a bare bulb by the ice machine provided a short respite. She closed her eyes and pictured San Francisco with flocks of gulls soaring and dipping above its emerald bay. She sighed. *After this is over, I'll take a few weeks off and vacation in my city— Golden Gate Park, Fisherman's Wharf, North Beach, a couple of musicals and dinner in a different restaurant every night. If only I could do it with you, Cristin.*

Another truck sped by and spewed gaseous fumes. She slammed the window shut.

After drawing the draperies, to eliminate further distractions, she went back to the computer, reread what she had typed and deleted it. A huge, teary yawn blurred her vision. She decided to do the report in the morning.

As she shut down the computer, her gaze strayed to the white envelope on the bed stand. She still couldn't believe the voice on the message machine. She went to the phone and punched in the number again wanting to be sure she had not misdialed the first time.

The same message resonated through the phone:

"You have reached Hank Jones, Nerium Corporation Director of Human Resources. I'm either away from my desk or on another line. Please leave a message and I'll return your call as soon as possible. Have a nice day."

She slapped the receiver down without leaving a message. What if the number was an eight and not a three and the number really had been disconnected? No, impossible. Too great a coincidence. This was the correct number.

Lysi sat motionless holding the envelope in her hand, grappling with conflicting details. Didn't it make perfect sense for Cristin to call the Director of Human Resources? After all, he works in concert with Staff Development to organize corporate training. On the other hand, the Director of Staff Development is usually the contact for presenters. Why would she need to speak with Hank Jones directly?

With her index finger, she traced around the number. This looks more like a Cristin fling. Hank Jones would fit the mold perfectly. It all comes together. Pitt panted after Cristin, she rebuffed him and planned a little tryst with Jones instead. Pitt found out about it. Would he have been angry enough to strangle her? Lysi had to find out, but how? Maybe she should tell Detective Tennyson about the phone number. But what if it means nothing? Or what if it turns out to be important?

Lysi looked at the clock. *How did it get to be eleven-thirty! It's too late to call anyone. I can't think anymore.* She decided to put Pitt and Jones out of her mind. She would go to bed without setting the alarm. She would sleep until she woke up naturally. All her problems would seem less overwhelming after she had rested.

Chapter 14

The jangle of the phone jolted Lysi out of deep sleep. Eyes still closed, she dragged out a groggy breath and groped for the phone, knocking the receiver off the cradle. She scrambled for it and almost disconnected before getting it to her ear.

"Hello." She couldn't disguise the sleepy sound of her voice. She blinked at the radio. *Eight o'clock. I should be up.*

"Miss Weston?" The male voice on the other end of the line sounded apologetic. "This is James Tennyson. I hope I didn't wake you, but I needed to talk with you before you left for the day. Have you had breakfast yet?"

"No. And no, you didn't wake me," Lysi lied. She felt a little rumble in her stomach signaling breakfast time. "I was just heading out to grab a bite."

"Well then, I'm glad I caught you before you left."

She detected a touch of amusement in his voice, giving her the uncomfortable feeling he knew she wasn't heading out for breakfast and worse that she hadn't even gotten out of bed yet.

Wide-awake now, Lysi replayed his words in her mind. "I needed to talk to you before you left for the day." *That's a laugh. I can't go anywhere. I'm stuck here until you release me, as you well know!* Again it entered her mind that he had decided she was a suspect and wanted to question her further.

"What can I do for you?" she said in a tone that would make icicles shiver.

"I had a little pang of conscience about having to require you to reschedule your flight home. I'd like to make it up to you by taking you to breakfast. I also need to talk with you about the case."

Lysi swallowed and rubbed her eyes. She had nothing to hide and nothing better to do. "Sure, what time will you be here?"

"I'm here now. Look out the window."

Lysi threw the covers back and shivered in the over air conditioned room. A robe to cover her thin lilac nightgown would have been nice. She dragged herself to the window and gingerly pulled the draperies apart.

James Tennyson sat smiling up at her through the open door of his car, a mobile phone at his ear.

She jerked away from the window and raced back to the phone. Sucking air to calm herself, she said, less casually than she would have liked, "I'm not quite ready. Tell me where the restaurant is and I'll meet you there in about half an hour."

"Nope, not a good idea. The restaurant is a little off the beaten path. The directions would be confusing. Anyway, I have some reports I need to do. I'll just park and do them. You can come down when you're ready. There's no rush."

She heard the grin in his voice again.

"Right—Thirty minutes."

She hung up the phone and hopped into the shower. Half an hour later, hair still wet, she climbed into James Tennyson's car.

"Thank you for waiting, Detective Tennyson."

"It's James. Call me James."

"James…What did you want to talk to me about the case?"

"Can we hold off on cop talk until after breakfast?"

"Okay, if you promise not to ask me anything about sexual harassment."

"It's a deal."

His smile gave her an annoying rush. She hoped he hadn't noticed her cheeks flush.

*

Lysi gazed out the window as they drove along the main street leading out of town. Small homes and businesses gave way to open space as they traveled along Highway 39. About twenty miles North of Sage Deer, flat prairie changed to pine-covered, rolling hills. When she commented on the tall pines, James told her about the small timber industry located in Rosebud County.

"But the big industry in southeastern Montana is cattle," he said and told her his grandfather had been a cattleman.

"A cattleman. So he's one of our famous Western cowboys."

"Actually, he became kind of a legend in these parts, sort of a land baron. My dad told me the homestead boom in Montana really began in 1906 when the word got out that Montana was a farmer's paradise. By 1918, more than 100,000 immigrants had flooded into the state. Forty thousand of them filed homesteader's claims making Montana the most homesteaded state in the Union. My grandfather was one of them."

"A 100,000 immigrants! Where'd they all go?" Lysi said. From the internet search she had done on Montana she had learned the state's population was pretty sparse.

"When the dry season came a few years later, there was a mass exodus and within seven years, 70,000 people had left the state. My grandfather decided to hang on to his land. He married a beautiful Cheyenne woman and stuck it out. He changed from farming to cattle ranching, got a loan from the bank and bought thousands of acres of land at rock bottom prices. He started with a small herd of cattle and just kept growing."

"He sounds like quite a guy."

"He was. Both my dad and I looked up to him. But Grandpa always said he owed his success to my Grandma Ninovan. Her Cheyenne wisdom got him through the tough dry years. She taught me the Cheyenne way."

Lysi studied James. She'd never met a man like him before— a man with the blood of two cultures coursing through his body. Who *is* this man? What are his passions?

She wanted to ask him what it was like to be part Cheyenne but didn't want to risk offending him. Instead, she looked out the window at the tall pines. "I must say I never expected a timber industry in southeastern Montana. That's a surprise."

"Montana is full of surprises," James said, as they rounded a curve in the road. "Look down there to the left. That's Castle Rock Lake."

Lysi stared at the unexpected azure lake nestled among dark green ponderosas.

James pointed toward a slope overlooking the water. "There's our breakfast house."

The three-story, natural pine house stood in perfect harmony with the unspoiled beauty that surrounded it.

They turned off the highway onto a gravel drive. Colorful masses of native plants crowded each side of the lane—yellow sunflowers, snowy yarrow, golden coneflowers, and purple prairie clover.

"These are all Montana wildflowers," James said. He pointed to a clump of pink flowers. "That's the Montana state flower, pink bitterroot."

"It's so delicate and beautiful," Lysi said.

She rolled down the window and captured the heady mix of anise-scented goldenrods and the spicy perfume of silvery-gray sagebrush. Castle Rock Lake was a whole different world from Sage Deer.

James parked in front of a rustic pinewood sign. Carved letters spelled out *Wild Flower Inn*. A wreath of carved painted posies like the ones lining the entrance drive, seemed to dance around the name.

He guided Lysi through a rose-covered trellis to the entrance of the inn. The front door opened on a guest parlor. A three-story cathedral ceiling with exposed beams imparted a feeling of spaciousness. They crossed the muted pinks and blues of an oriental carpet and sat down on a turquoise velvet settee with lilac throw pillows. Quaint flowered lampshades and a painting of a bouquet of daisies matched a vase of real daisies sitting in a large stone fireplace at the far end of the room. Sunlight from high windows flickered about the brass andirons in the hearth.

Lysi admired the warm traditional English decor. She smoothed her hand over the satiny, lilac pillows. "Exquisite."

James winked at her. "I sure like the way you look in lilac."

Lysi started to thank him, but realized she was wearing a pale yellow sundress. Puzzled for an instant, her thoughts whipped to the deep lilac nightgown she'd been wearing when she peered through the window at James sitting in his car. He saw it!

James politely averted his eyes as her color rose, and didn't comment further, but the grin lurking around his mouth told her he enjoyed her reaction.

A few moments later, a short round Native American woman padded into the room, her cotton print dress hem brushing the tops of her beaded moccasins.

James jumped to his feet, and she threw her arms around him. "Migisi, my Eagle," she said as his embrace lifted her off the floor.

Setting her down, James looked at her fondly.

"This is Namida, the best nanny in Montana. Namida means Star Dancer in Cheyenne, and she's still one of the finest dancers in her tribe."

Namida giggled and punched James in the arm. He fell back on the settee and whimpered, grabbing his arm in feigned agony.

"Stop it," Namida said and broke into another fit of giggles, her round cheeks jiggling like gelatin.

"Yes, Nanny." He reached up and yanked one of her long black braids. "Only please don't beat me anymore." He rose with exaggerated caution, slipped his arm around Namida and pointed to Lysi.

"This is Lysi, my friend from San Francisco."

Namida's lips spread into a grin and her doe-like eyes sparkled. She shook her own hands, making the Native American sign for friend. "Welcome."

At that moment, a tall silver-haired woman in a pale turquoise pantsuit approached, extending both hands in welcome. James encircled her in his arms as though she were a fragile China doll.

"Mother, you look beautiful, as always." He kissed her on the forehead.

She backed away taking both his hands and looked up at him with affection.

"We've missed you. It's wonderful to see you," she said then turned her vivid blue eyes to Lysi.

"Mother, I'd like you to meet Lysi Weston. She's here from California doing a seminar at Nerium. Lysi, my mother, Deborah Tennyson."

"I'm delighted to meet you, Miss Weston." Deborah Tennyson had a marked British accent. "It's, indeed, a pleasure to welcome a guest from so far away. I hope you're enjoying your stay in Montana."

"What a lovely inn! The lake and the scenery are spectacular," Lysi said, avoiding any mention of her aversion to Montana.

"Come." Deborah hooked arms with both of them. "You must be famished. Let's get you settled down to breakfast."

She led them through large double doors to a long deck. At a table near the deck railing, Lysi noticed a young couple holding hands and gazing into each other's eyes. The other tables were pretty much empty except for an elderly gentleman with a curly white beard reading the Wall Street Journal. Well, there's another Montana surprise—the Wall Street Journal here in the boonies.

Lysi gazed at the lake framed by petunia-filled flower boxes along the deck railing. Hanging pots of pink geraniums danced in the gentle morning breeze. Deborah showed them to a white wicker table, set with English lace place mats and a petite bouquet of daisies.

James pulled out a chair for Lysi while Namida poured tea from an English china teapot into two matching cups and set a basket of homemade blueberry scones on the table.

"I hope you're hungry because you're about to taste my mother's less greasy version of the traditional English fry-up. She substitutes grilled bacon and poached eggs for the fatty fry, keeps the tomatoes and mushrooms and serves it with a big helping of baked beans because she considers beans 'brain food.'"

"Your mother's right, beans are 'brain food,'" Lysi said in an authoritative tone that brought a smile to James's lips.

"When I was still at home she used to add 'bubble and squeak' whenever we had left over cabbage and potatoes from the night before," James continued.

"Bubble and squeak?" Lysi squeaked playfully on the word *squeak*.

"Oh, that's cute." James seemed to enjoy Lysi's vivacity.

"It's basically left over roasted vegetables fried to a golden brown in hot oil. I always liked it."

Lysi took a sip of tea, closed her eyes and inhaled the cool morning air. "It's wonderful here."

"This is where I grew up. When I went off to Cal Berkeley, my mother and Namida turned it into a bed and breakfast. It's small, only six rooms, but it's always full. People come all the way from Billings to stay here for the weekend. It's also a tourist stop for travelers on the way to Yellowstone and Glacier Park."

"You went to school in the San Francisco Bay Area? That's my home."

He nodded. "It's a beautiful part of California. I'd like to go back sometime."

Lysi couldn't understand how he could possibly have returned to make his life in Montana after having spent several years in California, but she didn't ask. She said,
"Tell me what life was like for an English kid growing up in Montana."

"First of all, since I'm part Cheyenne, both my mother and grandmother saw to it that I spent a lot of time running free on tribal lands with my older cousins. They made sure their pale face cousin learned what it meant to be Cheyenne. I not only have Cheyenne blood gushing through my veins, the Cheyenne spirit is in my soul."

Lysi stared into James's eyes for a long moment. She could hardly imagine his life growing up in a culture so different from her own. Yet something about this man drew her like some kind of powerful magnet.

"Lysi?" he said.

His voice startled her. "Oh, I was just thinking about your interesting growing up experiences." she said, struggling to recover her equilibrium.

*

Not until they had finished breakfast did Lysi broach the subject of Cristin's death.

"James, I have some information that might relate to Cristin's case."

James's eyes narrowed. "And what is that?"

"Well, two things. First, I found a phone number on the back of an envelope Cristin had left for me at Nerium." Lysi hesitated. Should she tell James she had called the number?

"What's number two?"

Lysi noticed a tinge of annoyance in his voice. "It's probably not important."

"What is it?" Now the tinge of annoyance had morphed into serious irritation.

"I called the number and got the Nerium Director of Human Resources, Hank Jones."

James took a long breath. "What did you say to him?"

"Nothing. I got his voice mail."

James stared at the table for what seemed like an hour. Finally, he raised his eyes to Lysi. His look was definitely not jovial.

"Lysi, listen carefully because I only want to say this once. This is a murder case and withholding information could make you liable for obstruction of justice and an accessory after the fact."

"I know, but"—

"Now stay with me. I'm the detective assigned to this case—not you."

"I know, but"—

"Last word. Please let me do my job. Do not interfere. Is that clear?"

"Yes." She felt like her father had just chastised her for commenting during one of his you-better-behave lectures to her brother.

With a sharp dip of his chin, he ended the topic. "Okay."

He took a sip of tea and said, "Now here's some good news. I have a suspect. This afternoon I'll be escorting my suspect to an interrogation party at the SDPD headquarters."

"A suspect? Who?"

"You'll know soon enough. I just can't tell you right now."

Lysi immediately assumed it was Bill Pitt, but didn't say so. "You can't imagine how relieved I feel."

"I told you the preliminary examination revealed cause of death was strangulation. We think it was a martial arts choking technique. The sad thing is the technique isn't meant to kill. It's meant to render the victim unconscious. She could have been revived by simply massaging the carotid triangle to open up the collapsed artery."

The color drained from Lysi's face.

*

James heard the old mahogany grandfather clock in the parlor chime eleven and then the tinkling strains of "Westminster" floated into the dining room. Breakfast had lasted more than an hour. He looked across the table at Lysi—brown eyes that seemed to take in everything around them, hair tousled by the lake breeze, shining with blonde highlights that resembled little captured sunbeams; and lips that expressed her every emotion even before she spoke. He didn't want the morning to end. He hoped she felt the same.

Their easy conversation made him feel as though he'd known her for years. She seemed to enjoy herself, but he'd spent so little personal time with women in the past few years that he couldn't be certain. All his female contacts were business associates or casual friends—until now.

When she looked up and caught him staring, he coughed and said, too loudly and too quickly, "How's your time? Anything pressing?"

Lysi made a show of checking her watch.

"Hmmm, let me see. What is on my schedule for today? Oh yeah, nothing. Nothing at all. I have no schedule, at least not anymore. But then you already know that, don't you?"

Her eyes sparked in mock anger. "I'm basically playing a waiting game as you are well aware, Detective James Tennyson, since you're holding me a virtual prisoner."

"Right," he said, catching the humor in her tone. "Look, I had no choice but to detain you. At least I didn't lock you up."

Lysi laughed. "Well not behind bars, anyway."

"If you could possibly find it in your heart to forgive me, maybe you might join me on a little after-breakfast walk. The English say it's good for the constitution."

"Let me think. You *didn't* put me in jail. You *did* bring me to a beautiful inn and treat me to a delicious English Fry." She turned her head slightly and looked sideways at him. "You don't look dangerous at all. Actually, you seem quite civil in an English sort of way."

Pursing her lips and squinting as though grappling with a very tough choice, she took an I've-made-a-hard decision breath and jumped up from her chair. "Sure. Why not?"

With a surge of confidence, James leapt to his feet, grabbed her by the hand and led her to a back door exit.

From the corner of his eye, he saw his mother and Namida exchange smiles. He knew they had eavesdropped on the whole scene.

*

James and Lysi strode down a narrow gravel path that wound through pines and low- growing hydrangeas. The pungent scent of pine pitch swirled around them on the currents of warm air. They stopped at a small gazebo by the lake, about three quarters of a mile from the Inn. Inside the natural pine wood gazebo, high-back benches encircled a small round table.

As the midday sun rose higher and the temperature began to climb, James worried that Lysi might have suffered from their stroll in the heat of a Montana summer day. He almost wished he hadn't suggested it. He eyed her, checking for signs of heat exhaustion.

The air inside the shady gazebo, cooled by the breeze off the lake, seemed to refresh her. She dropped down on a narrow bench, tilted her head against the high back and fanned herself with an open hand. She kicked off her sandals and inhaled the sweet scent of the honeysuckle vine that entwined through the latticework of the gazebo walls. "The sweetest scent on earth," she said.

James eased down beside her, loosened his tie and relaxed.

A moment later, he nudged Lysi's arm and pointed at two deer standing quietly among the pines, heads raised towards the leafy branches of a low-growing dogwood tree, seemingly unconcerned with the noisy twittering of the birds above them. Lysi watched until the deer turned and loped noiselessly into the forest.

"I don't remember the last time I sat in this gazebo," James said and turned his eyes to the lake. "See that island?"

He pointed to a small island about a quarter mile from shore covered with low growing shrubs and large boulders. A wooden dock, sun-bleached to a silver gray, stretched precariously from the island into the water.

"When I was a kid, I used to row out there, build a campfire and fry fish I'd caught. Actually, I planned my future while sitting there feasting on bass or pike; college on the West coast, police academy, law enforcement job in Montana, marriage, children. My life took some unexpected turns, but for the most part my plans materialized."

"I've found we can realize most of our goals through planning and hard work. It's unexpected events beyond our control that knock us for a loop," Lysi said.

He thought about the unexpected death of his wife and his lack of interest in any kind of relationship since that horrible day. Not even a glimmer of interest—until now.

James looked at Lysi who continued to study the island. He resisted a desire to touch her cheek and run the back of his fingers along her jaw line, down her neck and over her bare shoulder. When she turned and caught him staring again, he laughed uncomfortably.

"I must be boring you."

Ignoring his last comment, she said, "I've always been a planner. Trouble is, I don't adjust well when something interferes with my plans. I usually get mad and start working myself into idiocy trying to overcome the obstacle."

James considered for a few minutes. She's probably like me, not interested in emotional entanglements. He felt a sting of disappointment.

"I tend to throw myself into my work, too." he said. "The problem is I neglect other things–important things." Flooded with ambivalence, he hesitated. Maybe he shouldn't say anymore. Why would he? He barely knew this woman.

Lysi looked into his eyes, her voice warm with understanding. "I'm the same. I take big risks in my job, but I walk on eggs when it comes to my personal life."

Encouraged by her candidness, he added, "I haven't really cared about anything besides work–until…recently."

Blue eyes met brown eyes and the tension was palpable. Impulsively, he took her hand and pressed it to his lips. His heart pounded as much from his unaccustomed boldness as from the feel of her skin. He noticed she didn't smile, but she didn't pull away either. *Maybe I should apologize.*

He didn't. Instead, he stood and put on his hat. "I could stay here all day, but I have to get back to the department."

Lysi seemed to be at a loss for words.

Still unsure of himself, but wanting to test the waters, he asked, "How would you like to see Namida dance at a real Cheyenne Festival?"

When she didn't reply immediately, his confidence plunged. He stepped down from the gazebo, saying, "Duty calls. I guess we better get going."

"I'd love to…" She rose and extended her hand to him for balance while she slipped into her sandals. "…see Namida dance at a real Cheyenne Festival."

He stared at her for a beat, his heart thudding. Keep it light. Don't get silly over this woman. She'll be gone in a few days.

All he could say was, "Okay."

Chapter 15

Lighthearted, her mind replaying the delightful morning with James Tennyson, Lysi entered her motel room nearly stepping on a note someone had slipped under the door. She picked it up and examined it. Who would write a note to her here in Sage Deer? She unfolded it and read the words printed in smudgy pencil on a piece of lined paper ripped from a three-ring binder.

Lysi, I like you. I think you and me should get together. I'll come to your room after I get off work. Choki

Adolescent boys—cocky and clumsy. She tossed the note into the wastebasket and didn't give it another thought. She would simply tell him through the door she had things to do and wouldn't have time to play with him this evening or any other time.

The blinking light on the phone registered three messages. Lysi stood by the bed and listened to the first. A whispery voice said, "If you need me, I can come any time. Just buzz the desk." She recognized Choki's adolescent tenor.

"You annoying little insect, you're barely out of diapers." She hit the erase button.

When she pressed the button for the second message her knee joints melted and she dropped to the bed.

Bill Pitt's voice boomed through the receiver. "Miss Weston. Bill Pitt. I'd"—

Lysi hung up the phone. Pitt! Why would he call her?

She stared at the phone for a long moment then pressed the message button again to hear what he had to say.

"Miss Weston. Bill Pitt. I'd like to meet you at the Sagebrush Café at seven tonight. I just feel I need to say a few things. You don't have to return my call. I'll just be there at seven and you can come if you want. I won't blame you if you blow me off."

Lysi hung up the phone. *This is crazy. Wasn't he the murder suspect James talked about? Didn't James have him in custody? She needed answers to these questions. She had to call James.*

When he answered the phone, she blurted out the question. "Isn't Pitt in jail?"

After a short pause, James spoke in a slow easy tone. "Hello Lysi. I'm fine. Thanks for asking."

"I'm sorry. How are you?"

"Good, good. My right elbow's been bothering me a little. An old football injury. And my left leg always thinks it's going to rain. And"—

"Really, James. This is important. Please answer the question."

His response surprised her. "He's not the suspect. Why is it so urgent that you know?"

Lysi thought about whether she should mention Pitt's call and decided she wouldn't. *After all, if Pitt isn't a suspect, then she wouldn't be interfering in the murder investigation.*

"I…I thought he was the suspect." *That's the truth, I did think that.*

"Well, he's not. I still can't say who it is yet. Try to be patient a little longer. Sorry, got to go. Call on the other line."

Lysi replayed Pitt's message. She had no use for Pitt after his boorish behavior at the reception. She poised her finger to hit the erase button then reconsidered. *Wasn't she being paid to enlighten cavemen like Pitt? Besides, she needed some answers from him, and the Sagebrush seemed like a safe public place to ask him a few questions. It'll be the pits to meet with Pitt, but maybe I should.* She chuckled at her silly play on words.

In the third message, Jade Green had left her phone number with a request for a return call as soon as possible.

Lysi had just picked up the phone to call Jade, when a metallic sound jerked her attention to the door. A chill began at her neck and slinked down her spine as she watched the deadbolt knob turn and heard the door click. Four grimy fingers grasped the edge of the door and slid it open without a sound. She instinctively looked around the room for something to hurl at the intruder.

A second later, her anxiety dissolved into surprise then annoyance when Choki stuck his head through the half-opened space, mouth fixed in a moronic grin, *Judo Kid* hat perched on his head at a cocky angle.

"Hey, Lysi. I got off early. I'm ready for our *visit*." He tried to pitch his squeaky changing voice low and sensuous.

Lysi stared at him, lips parted in disbelief as she watched him ooze into the room and close the door. The thought crossed her mind that he might've left a slime trail behind him like the snails in her San Francisco garden. He leaned his elbow on a high bureau next to the door and eyeballed her.

Annoyance changed to indignation. "Choki, what the hell are you doing? Get out of my room!"

"You didn't have the chain on so I figured you were expecting me. I didn't want to disappoint you." He raised one eyebrow.

Lysi stifled an urge to laugh he looked so ridiculous. He reminded her of the eighth grade boys at Alvarez Middle School her first year of teaching—all playing can-you-top-this with fantasy stories about their prodigious virility.

Phone still in hand, she shook it at him. "Get out, Choki, before I call your mother and have your allowance taken away."

"That ain't funny." His dull eyes ignited and his loose lips tightened across tobacco-yellowed teeth. He took a step forward.

Lysi's eyes whipped to her leather purse on the bureau less than a foot from Choki's elbow. If she could just reach the keychain pepper spray inside it.

Maybe her father was right when he had insisted on giving her the spray along with a lecture on self-defense after she took the job with Stellar Corporate Development and needed to travel. She carried it only to please her elderly father. She hadn't seen a need for it—until now.

Choki clenched his fists and took another step toward her. "Why do you act so nice; then spit in my face? You're just like her."

You're just like her. Who's he talking about? Cristin! He means Cristin. Lysi's eyes snapped and bored into him. She sprang up from the bed and shot to within inches of him. Standing a head taller, she glared down at Choki, her voice an ominous growl. "Her? Who do you mean–her?"

"Nothing." He drew back, blinking as if a gnat had flown into his eye.

She pointed a stiff arm at the door. "Out, Choki! Get out!"

"Okay, okay. I'm going." Now at a safe distance from her, he smirked out of half his mouth. "You know where to reach me if you get lonesome."

Lysi had to restrain herself from throwing the phone at him.

On the way out the door he added over his shoulder, "'Course, you'd probably rather get it on with fags like that Robbins guy instead of a real man." He clicked his tongue, licked the tip of his ring finger and smoothed it over his eyebrow.

His high-pitched laughter grated on Lysi's ears. She slammed the door behind him and fastened the chain. Tonight she would wedge a chair under the knob.

Lysi leaned against the door, heart pounding, mind racing. Choki must have watched Denny come to her room. How long had he been spying on her?

A picture of Choki's head sticking through the crack in the door wearing the *Judo Kid* cap flooded her brain followed by James's words about the cause of Cristin's death, "strangulation by a martial arts choking technique."

Choki's words resurfaced in a frightening flash, *"You're just like her."*

Lysi stopped breathing as an image of Cristin's body, cold and still, returned. She swallowed hard. Choki did it.

The phone slipped from her hand and dropped to the floor. She scrambled to pick it up. Controlling her shaking hands, she dialed Jade's number.

"Sagebrush Café. Uptown food at down home prices."

Lysi tried to steady her voice. "Jade? Lysi. I'm returning your call."

"Lysi, what's wrong? You sound awful."

"I just had an unnerving experience." Lysi lowered herself to the bed and took a calming breath. "You know that teenage kid who sometimes works the motel desk? Choki?"

Lysi could hear Gretchen Wilson belting out "Redneck Woman" in the background accompanied by enthusiastic yips and hoots. Jade spoke just below a shout. She probably figured since she couldn't hear Lysi very well, Lysi couldn't hear her either; and solved the problem by raising her own voice.

"His name's not Choki. It's Noah...Noah Pry. Choki's some way-cool Judo handle he made up. Why?"

"Does he seem a little weird to you?"

"If you think Freddy Krueger and Norman Bates are weird, then yeah. That kid's got a few missing spark plugs. He used to come into the restaurant after everyone had gone and sit on a stool watching everything I did. I guess he thinks he's some kind of Romeo, the way he comes on to women–mostly older ones–like he's got a mother complex or something. He doesn't come around me anymore. I told him I got a few friends who'd get a real kick out of turning him into a soprano." Jade laughed so loudly Lysi pulled the receiver away from her ear.

"Jade, he used a master keycard to get into my room. He acted as if I had encouraged him. I tell you, it made me feel creepy."

Jade lowered her voice. It sounded muffled, as though she had cupped her hand around the receiver.

"Just between you, me and the bedpost, Noah's got a real head problem. His mom forked over big bucks taking him to a psychiatrist over to Billings, but all that shrink did was spend a whole lot of time talking to him. Personally, I think he ended up worse."

"Interesting," Lysi said. Again, her mind flashed on the Judo cap and James's preliminary report about the cause of death being a martial arts choking technique.

"If he tries anything like that again, don't mess around. Call the cops. In fact, you better get on the horn to SDPD soon as I hang up."

"You're probably right." Lysi decided James would be her next call. He'd definitely want to know about this. Then she asked Jade the reason for her message.

"Oh yeah. I thought it might interest you to know I saw Bill Pitt's company car parked outside Cristin's room on the night she died."

"Are you sure? That could make Pitt a murder suspect." Lysi had trouble fitting this new information into her evolving idea of what had happened to Cristin. James said Pitt wasn't the suspect, but this could change everything.

"Sure I'm sure. The car had *Nerium* on the side of it in humungous blue letters."

"Have you reported this to the police?"

"No way. I have to live in this town. I can't get involved."

"You're already involved."

"You don't know this town. I could lose my job."

"Jade, please. Call James. I know he'd be discreet if you asked him."

There was a long pause. Lysi thought Jade might be considering a report to James. Then, in a voice that allowed no further discussion, Jade made her final comment on the topic.

"I won't call James. I won't take that chance. I told *you* about Pitt. *You* call James."

Lysi understood Jade's unwillingness to alienate Sage Deer people. Small town folks stick together. If it turned out Pitt wasn't involved, she might very well lose her job. Lysi liked Jade and would never want to cause her any trouble.

"All right, Jade."

Lysi started to ask more about the car when a gruff male voice blasted through the phone. "Hey, Jade! You going to hang on that squawker all night or get a paying customer some coffee?"

"Don't you get your jocks in a knot, Pete. I'm conducting some business here. If you're in such an all-fired hurry, you know where the pot is. Get it yourself."

Jade lowered her voice again, "Look, just forget what I said. Bill hasn't got the guts to kill anyone."

Lysi ignored Jade's comment. "How long was the car parked there?"

"I don't know exactly what time he got here. I looked out the side window about 7:30 and saw his car. I got busy and didn't get a chance to look again until around eleven. No car."

Possibilities raced around in Lysi's mind. Could Pitt have killed Cristin? Seven-thirty to eleven is plenty of time for a visit to turn nasty and end in murder. He's strong enough to strangle a small person like Cristin. But Jade doesn't think he's capable of murder.

"Lysi?" Jade's voice broke into Lysi's conjecture.

"I'm here. I'll call you tomorrow."

Lysi almost hung up, but decided to tell Jade about the message from Pitt.

"One more thing; Bill Pitt called and asked me to meet him at the Sagebrush tonight. I think I'm going to keep that date. Maybe he'll have some information for me."

"Whoa! That's interesting. I wonder what that's all about."

"I have no idea, but I'm going to find out."

"Well, watch out, his zipper's got vertigo and it's on a fast track." Jade snorted. "I'll—"

The gruff voice again. "Hey, Jade. Would you quit yakking long enough to get me a slice of that cherry pie?"

"Yeah, yeah. It's coming. More pie's just what you need to keep that giant grocery tumor of yours fat and happy.

"Got to go, honey. A customer's ragging at me. I'll be dying to hear how it goes with old Billy Boy. Oh, don't tell him I told you about his car."

*

You're just like her. Choki's comment kept swirling around in Lysi's head. She felt certain he was referring to Cristin. An unaccustomed chill rose in her chest at the thought of a kid with psychological problems running around with a master keycard that enabled him to enter any room at any time. She no longer felt safe in this new motel room. The slightest thing seemed to send adrenaline racing through her body—a dog barking in the distance, footsteps on the stairs, the roar of a diesel engine. When a shadow passed by the draperied window she jumped then felt silly. *Stop, your blowing this all out of proportion. He's just a dumb kid trying to act like a big hot stud.*

She flicked on the television in an effort to divert her thoughts. It didn't work. She cut the television and opened the novel she'd started on the plane. The printed words wouldn't stay in her brain. She closed the book and dialed James's mobile phone number. She'd tell him about Choki. As for Bill Pitt—it wouldn't hurt to wait until after the meeting at the Sage Brush before reporting Jade's story. After all, James already has a viable suspect.

With a forced casualness in her voice, she told James about Choki using a master key card to barge into her motel room. She described his belligerent attitude when she ordered him out. "Something he said made me think he might have pulled the same thing on Cristin."

James did not comment right away so Lysi continued. "He said I acted nice to him and then spit in his face—*just like her.*"

"Just like her? What are you trying to say?"

"I think he tried to hit on Cristin and she brushed him off or as he put it, 'spit in his face.' I know Cristin. She could reduce him to a gelatinous mass with a couple of swipes of her caustic tongue. I think she humiliated him and he decided to get even. I think..." Lysi took a breath and stopped short of voicing her final thought—Choki killed Cristin.

James finished her sentence. "You believe Noah Pry might have murdered Cristin Holden?"

"I just don't know. He seems so young. But if you could have seen his angry face when I kicked him out of my room."

When James spoke again, Lysi could hear concern in his voice. "Lysi, I don't want to worry you unnecessarily, but I want you to be cautious. I've never known Noah to be violent, but he is unpredictable...always has been. I'm going to post a police officer outside your door."

"I really don't think that's necessary. I"—

"It's not your decision to make. Call me if he comes anywhere near you again."

Lysi detected more than a professional concern in James's voice. Ambivalent thoughts moved through her mind. On the surface, she felt flattered by his feelings for her. On a deeper level, she wasn't sure she was ready for anything more than a light friendship.

She clicked off her mobile and stared at the motel phone. How many times had Choki listened in on her calls? Had he listened in on Denny's calls? James's calls? Jade's?   From now on she would only make and receive calls on her cell.

Outside her window thin, wisp-like strands of curvy cirrus clouds streaked through high-level turbulence in an otherwise clear blue sky, mirroring the tumultuous pounding in her brain—*...just like her... just like her... just like her*. Choki did it. He had a strong motive for murdering Cristin; but Bill Pitt's car was outside her room; he bragged that Cristin chased after him—a lie. Those two have the same motive, revenge for a bruised and bloodied ego. Bill Pitt's car outside Cristin's room makes him a strong suspect. Choki's master key makes him a strong suspect. Which one of them did it?

Chapter 16

In the bright late afternoon sun, James Tennyson sat in his car outside Nerium and waited for Choki to arrive for his weekend cleaning job. He kept the motor running and the air conditioner on high. Lysi's phone call had troubled him more than he had let on. He hadn't told her he too suspected Choki, because he didn't want to involve her. Now he felt even more strongly that Choki had murdered Cristin Holden and that Lysi may have narrowly escaped being his second victim.

At the growl of an engine, James turned his head toward the passenger window and watched Bertha Pry chug up to the main gate in a dilapidated Chevy that belched to a smoky stop. Choki slid out the passenger side yelling at his mother, "Don't rag, Ma. I said I'd clean it up when I get back and I will." He slammed the door, turning Bertha's angry reply into a silent movie.

James turned off the engine and rolled down a window. "Hey, Noah. Come here for a minute."

James always called Noah Pry by his real name. It galled him that Noah had decided to call himself Choki after the famous early twentieth century Judo master, Choki Masa. The name was the only thing Noah Pry and Choki Masa had in common.

Choki strutted over and leaned against the car. "Yeah, Dude. What'd I do now?"

James had the urge to slap the surly look off Noah's face. He knew about Noah's long list of juvenile offenses—stealing toys at ten, vandalizing cars and bikes at thirteen, hot-wiring trucks and taking them on joy rides by the time he was sixteen.

He knew Noah had lived a rough life. His father abandoned the family while Noah was still a toddler. His uneducated mother worked at any job she could get to keep food on the table. All through school, girls treated Noah with contempt; and boys seemed to delight in taunting and bullying him. His mother got him Judo lessons so he could defend himself, a stupid move that got him beaten up several times.

James had tried to mentor him. He'd even taken him on a couple of fishing trips, but Noah showed little interest and kept his nose buried in comic books most of the time. To keep him off the streets at night, James recommended Noah for a janitorial job at the new Nerium Corporation. Unfamiliar with Noah's troubled history, they hired him. The company lead custodian reported that Noah did good work. James took this as a sign that Noah might make something of himself.

"I want you to take a little ride with me," James said.

Choki looked at him like he had a bad taste in his mouth. "I can't. I have to go to work."

"Nope, I told your boss you'd be a little late tonight. Get in the car."

Choki went around to the passenger side and opened the door, but didn't get in. "Where we going?" His hand shook as he picked at a zit on his chin until it bled.

James ignored the question. "How you been? Still going strong with your Judo lessons?"

"No, I quit." Choki turned his face away from James and seemed to show great interest in a flat open field beyond the manicured landscape of the Nerium plant.

"When?"

"A while ago." He whipped his head around to face James. In an agitated voice he said, "Why you asking all them questions?"

"That's right, Noah. *I* am asking the questions. Your job is to answer them. Why did you drop Judo?"

Choki looked back at the field and started to mutilate another zit. "I had a little accident."

"What kind of accident?"

"I don't remember. Nothing big."

James raised his voice. "You know what Noah, I think it was a big accident. I think you'd better get in and tell me about it."

Choki stared at James for an instant, his eyes wide like those of a deer startled by car headlights. Suddenly, he slammed the door shut and sprinted towards the open field.

James jumped out of his side of the car and shouted over the car roof. "Noah, stop. It'll be worse for you if you run."

Choki didn't look back. He vaulted over the low barbed wire fence and kept running through the knee-high grass. Hidden boulders and uneven ground made the field an obstacle course. He fell twice, scrambled to his feet and kept running.

James watched for a few seconds, but didn't bother chasing after him. He just shook his head at the futility of Choki's effort, eased back into the car and flicked his radio button. A voice crackled, "Officer Spitz. Go ahead."

"Sam, it's me. I got a juvenile on the run, Noah Pry. He took off from Nerium cross-country heading north towards Highway Thirty-Nine. He could be planning to hitch a ride out of town or more likely, he'll probably circle around toward his house. Send a car out to Thirty-Nine. Put Mary on the desk; Meet me at the Pry house."

"I'm on it. That kid sure is a pain in the butt."

James knew Spitz secretly enjoyed this assignment. He could barely tolerate Noah Pry and relished the opportunity to legally make his life miserable. Spitz had two well-behaved teenage daughters and had little patience with rowdy teenage boys. He had another reason for hating Noah Pry. Noah had given his fourteen-year old daughter, Ginny, a ride home from school one day and tried to force himself on her. She had jumped out of the car screaming and ran to the house of an acquaintance where Spitz picked her up. It traumatized her so deeply that her mother had to take her to school and pick her up for two weeks. Spitz had put Pry in jail overnight and warned him if he ever came near his daughter again he'd cut off his balls with a serrated knife. Ever since that incident, Spitz never passed up an opportunity to harass Noah. James also knew Spitz longed for a reason to put the kid in prison where he belonged. He probably hoped this would be his chance.

Chapter 17

The supper crowd had begun to clear out of the Sagebrush Café. Truck drivers in baseball caps and farmers in dusty, sweat-stained John Deere Tractor hats lined up at the cash register waiting to pay. Loud chatter, punctuated with snorts of laughter, amplified by a few beers, bounced around the room. In the corner, a teenage boy banged a pinball machine while a couple of pony tailed girls wearing thigh-high jean skirts and tight tee shirts broadcast each target hit with giggly squeals.

Lysi glanced around the still crowded restaurant trying to locate Pitt. She spotted Jade draped over the counter nearly nose to nose with a curly-haired muscleman. His short-sleeved Hawaiian shirt in a Hula girl print, stretched tightly over his torso. The Hula girls shimmied as his shoulders bounced to the fast-beat tune pouring out of the jukebox. Lysi headed toward Jade.

Jade pulled her gaze away from the hunk, cocked her head towards a table in a corner almost hidden behind an artificial palm tree, and immediately turned her attention back to the muscleman. Lysi grinned. Clearly, she does not want to be disturbed.

As Lysi approached the table, Bill Pitt looked up from his beer and managed a weak smile. Lysi didn't return the smile. She still smarted from Pitt's crude remarks at the reception two days earlier. Certain his sudden change of heart did not come from a newly developed sensitivity, but rather from fear of losing his job, she determined not to let him off the hook.

When she reached the table, he took off his Stetson, jumped up banging a table leg, and splattered some of his beer. With one hand he pulled out a chair for her and with the other he dabbed at the spilled beer with a paper napkin. A little taken aback at the clumsiness of his pitiful attempt at civility, she thanked him.

Lysi stared at his ruddy face and regretted having come. How many beers had he already downed? She drew a long breath that said, Get it done and get out.

She got right to the point. "What do you want to talk about?"

He tugged at his string tie and loosened the silver longhorn clasp. "I guess you're not in the mood for small talk, so I'll shoot from the hip. Sorry I acted like a jerk the other day. I know it's no excuse, but I'd had a little too much hooch and had trouble keeping my big mouth shut. You didn't deserve that stuff and I don't deserve forgiveness. Just wanted to go on record that I was out of line and I'm sorry." His conciliatory words sounded incongruous in his gruff, gravelly voice.

Lysi felt a fleeting pang of sympathy for Pitt. The feeling dissolved as the sad faces of Cristin and Denny floated through her mind. It seemed impossible to her that Cristin could have encouraged a man like Pitt even though she knew her partner's tastes weren't exactly refined when it came to one night stands. *I could be looking at the face of Cristin's murderer.*

"Forget it, Mr. Pitt. Now I have something else I want to discuss."

Pitt's alleged treatment of Denny Robbins appalled her. Figuring this was a safe place to confront him, she opened her purse and pulled out the packet of notes and pictures Denny had delivered to her. She spread them on the table and fired visual daggers at Pitt.

"These look familiar, Mr. Pitt?"

Pitt gave the papers a cursory glance. He dipped his head, but Lysi could see a little smile jiggling his mouth. Despicable. She considered an immediate exit. Only her promise to help Denny and her need to question him about Cristin kept her glued to the chair.

"Well?" she said.

Pitt slurped some foam off his beer mug; then looked up. "Okay, you caught me. We were just having a little fun with Denny Boy. Just messing with him. Where's his sense of humor?" He shook his head. "I swear, that kid's got the temperament of a wom—" He grimaced and gritted his teeth. "Oops."

"Don't say it," Lysi said, spitting her ending t's out like sharp needles.

She locked eyes with him. "You were sexually harassing Robbins."

"Sexually harassing! What are you talking about? He's not a woman! How could I harass him?"

Frustration shot through Lysi. Was his brain turned off during the seminar when I explained about male victims? She slammed her hand down on the bathing suit picture drawing a glance from two truckers at the next table wolfing down bacon burgers and fries. "You call this 'having fun?'"

Pitt stared at the bathing suit picture, winced, and jammed his hand under the table. Lysi guessed he probably imagined excruciating pain.

She waved the note about the paperboy's tip in his face. "You call this 'just messing with him'?"

He read the note and did one of those blinking head jerks people do when they see something weird. "We didn't have nothing to do with these two. They're not funny. We only did funny ones."

Pitt's light-hearted little prankster demeanor changed to confusion and disgust. Lysi had the impression he hadn't noticed the last two notes at first glance. His vehement denial gave her pause. Why would he admit involvement in all the notes and pictures except these last two? Is he lying? She studied the two scraps of paper. The writing and style of the last two bore little resemblance to the rest. Up until now, she hadn't considered any victimizers other than Pitt and his pals. But now...

"Funny ones!" Lysi said, the 'you idiot' implied. "Haven't you been paying attention the last couple days? I can't believe you sat through both my seminars and didn't grasp a word I said. Let me dumb the message down for you. It makes no difference whether your notes are funny or not, sexual harassment is a crime. It's against the law. Get it?"

Pitt's face flamed and he opened his mouth interject something but Lysi ignored his effort.

"I'm telling you right now I'm encouraging Denny Robbins to pursue this. You could end up with a high stakes harassment suit and probably a criminal charge against you." Her voice sizzled with anger.

"I know it. But we've stopped messing with him. I even apologized to him." He looked at her without rancor. He seemed sincere.

After allowing a few moments of heavy silence to pass, she decided to play her second ace.

"I understand you visited Cristin Holden at about 7:30 on the night of her death."

Astonishment flooded his face. "What? Who told you that?"

"Your company car was seen parked in her space."

His face now an outraged purple, he said, "No way! Not mine. Lots of people drive company cars. Most of the directors have them."

"Were you there?"

"No way! I wouldn't go anywhere near her. KiKi's so damn jealous she'd make my life a living hell if I even looked at another woman."

Lysi recalled Pitt's placating reaction at the reception when KiKi called him on his "hot little chili pepper" reference to Cristin.

Pitt leaned across the table, his pupils dilated. "Did someone tell KiKi they saw me parked outside Cristin Holden's motel room?"

She watched fear spread over his face and had to quell the urge to laugh at the vision of this big, macho male cowering at the possibility of being ragged on by poodley little KiKi Kavenaugh. But in all fairness to him, she did remember KiKi's venomous side at "sunch" the other day. Maybe Lysi might be scared, too—in his shoes. "I don't think anyone has gotten to KiKi—yet."

Pitt let out a slow breath through puffed out cheeks and sagged against the back of his chair.

Lysi furrowed her brow. *Jealousy is a powerful and not uncommon motive for murder.* What if someone did tell KiKi about Bill's secret soiree? Could wiry little KiKi be strong enough to strangle Cristin? Maybe. If Cristin had been drinking.

If Cristin moved in on Pitt, KiKi would have a lot more to lose than just a man. She'd lose a rich sugar daddy, her high-on-the-hog lifestyle, and maybe even a job—her livelihood. Yes, KiKi might well be a suspect.

Lysi raised her chin, looked blankly into space, and tried to imagine KiKi a killer. Doubtful. KiKi's too flighty. Could she plan and carry out a murder? Not likely. Besides, didn't James already have the suspect?

She frowned at Pitt. "If you weren't parked outside Cristin's room, where were you?"

Pitt glanced left and right then leaned over the table again. "Look, I was in Billings visiting my boy the night Miss Holden died. It was my day to sleep over. I go there once a month."

He looked at Lysi with big, round eyes and added, "Believe me, I don't tell KiKi about those trips, either. I tell her it's my poker night with the boys. One time I let it slip that I'd stayed all night at my son's house and she jumped to the conclusion I was doing his mother."

His face clouded. "Hell, Maggie wouldn't have me even if I tried."

Lysi saw regret in his face. Curiosity got the best of her and she asked how long he'd been divorced.

"I'm not divorced."

Pitt stared down at the table and tore a fringe around the edges of a paper coaster.

"Years ago, I made a hell of a mistake. I got my girlfriend pregnant. She wanted to get married, but I had big career plans that didn't include a wife and kids. She never forgave me for not marrying her—for not giving our Steve my last name."

"Steve is your son's name?" Lysi said.

"Yeah. Maggie picked out his name." He looked up at Lysi, his eyes bright with pride.
"You know, I loved that boy the minute I saw him. As soon as he was born, right there in the hospital, I changed my mind and begged her to marry me, but it was too late."

He lowered his eyes and said to the table, "I was so damn stupid. I've been asking her to marry me ever since."

His brows knitted as if in a quandary. "I don't think she hates me. She's always polite, but kind of cool. It's like...she just doesn't have any feelings for me at all. She's sort of neutral, like I'm…a doorman or something."

His words struck a chord in Lysi. She studied him. The boorish aggressor had become the victim. She saw in his face the same pain she remembered from her own shattered fairytale marriage so long ago. "Maybe her feelings are locked up and she's lost the key. Maybe you should try to find that key."

His eyes met hers and his face became a question.

"I mean, sometimes people are so hurt it's impossible for them to risk another try. They just bury all their feelings so deep even *they* lose track of them."

Lysi looked down at her hands. How well she knew about those hidden feelings. It seemed like yesterday that her marriage to a man she idolized had ended in unforgettable pain. She had tried for two years to hold her marriage together, until the day her alcoholic husband added physical violence to his ongoing emotional abuse. When she slammed the door on the marriage, she vowed never to risk emotional slaughter again. That was two master's degrees, a Ph.D. and thirty years ago.

The sound of Pitt's dejected voice snapped her back to the present. "There's not much hope for us. She won't even talk about marrying me."

"Don't give up. Keep telling her how sorry you are. Keep telling her how stupid you were. Keep telling her you've been living a half-life without her. Keep telling her you love her—Show her you love her!" Lysi's face reddened when she saw Pitt staring at her. She swallowed and looked away. "Well, that's my advice."

"You're right, Lysi. Can I call you Lysi?"

Lysi nodded.

"It probably won't work," he said, "but, hell, I've got nothing to lose by trying."

Lysi rose from the chair. "Good luck…Bill." His first name felt funny on her tongue.

Bill Pitt looked up at her. "I take back that remark about you being an ice cube. You're no ice cube. I bet, in the right hands, you'd be a hot little jalapeño yourself."

Lysi scowled at him.

"Hey, I meant that as a compliment." He looked as if his words would surely quell her anger.

"Wrong thing to say." She could hardly believe he considered his remarks to be compliments.

Pitt's mouth hung open as Lysi continued to rail.

"You need to work on yourself. Get rid of your Neanderthal ideas about what women want to hear. Start thinking of them as colleagues, equals–not play things." Lysi grabbed a breath. "And furthermore–"

Pitt held up both palms and leaned back from her. "Hold it, little lady." His fist flew to his teeth. "Oops! I'm sorry. I slipped. I *am* working on myself."

His face red with confusion, he sprung up, extended his hand and pumped hers in a hard masculine way. "I have to go now. Thanks for your advice."

He turned and hurried toward the door, shouting a quick goodbye over his shoulder.

Lysi couldn't suppress a smile. Again she felt a rush of pity for the futility of his efforts.

*

The restaurant had pretty much cleared out by the time Bill Pitt had made his escape. Now that Muscle Guy was gone, Jade looked expectantly at Lysi. "How about a quick coffee?"

Lysi moved to the counter.

Jade blew into her coffee and took a small sip. She giggled. "Bill looked as nervous as a long-tailed cat in a room full of rocking chairs."

Lysi poured cream in her coffee and looked serious. "Pitt denied he was here on the night of Cristin's murder. He has a believable alibi. Says he was in Billings, visiting his son."

"It's pretty possible. He goes there every couple of weeks." Jade nodded at a customer who signaled he'd left money for his bill on the table, then continued. "If you want my opinion, he probably didn't kill Cristin Holden. Fact is he's kind of an overgrown wimp."

"I still think I'll call James about Pitt's car being seen here the night Cristin died. He might want to check it out."

Jade raised one eyebrow and dipped her chin. "*James* is it now? I heard he took you to meet his mother and Nanny Namida. Sounds like something is developing here."

Lysi drew her gaze away from Jade, concentrated on pulling a piece of lint off her sleeve and said, hoping to end the topic, "He took me to breakfast to assuage his guilt. He's practically holding me captive here."

Jade persisted. "Better be careful. James never takes women to his mother's inn."

Lysi got up to leave. "Enough, Jade."

"One more thing I think you should know." Jade looked a little guilty. "The night I saw Bill's car outside Cristin Holden's room, I called KiKi Kavanaugh and told her Bill was here with Cristin."

Lysi dropped back down. "Jade, you didn't. Why would you do…Wait"–Lysi's mouth flew open as if she'd made a great discovery. "KiKi's the conniving little alley cat from the Cattle Rustler's Lounge. And Bill Pitt's the man she stole from you."

"You got it. I wanted her to feel as bad as I felt. You know as the Good Book says, we reap what we sow. I just added a little fertilizer. She probably hightailed it on over here and waited until he left, then followed him out. I bet she really gave him a ration of you know what." Jade roared with laughter.

Lysi pursed her lips. "I think KiKi may have a ration of you know what to fling at you. Better be prepared."

"Look Lysi, that'd be nothing new. I've known KiKi forever and she's always looked out for herself. Well, she's more or less had to; but she never cared who she hurt. Me and her, we were friends all through school. We both had family problems. What do you call it? Dysfunctional stuff. KiKi's been a survivor all her life. I'm the same; but I stop at hurting people."

The waitress took a sip of coffee and stared at the ceiling for a few seconds.

"Yeah, old KiKi learned early how to use her womanly wiles to get what she wanted from men. When she turned sixteen her dad called her a tramp and threw her out of the house. She moved in with my family until she finished high school then got a job as a waitress and moved into a small room above Clem's Cleaners here in Sage Deer. Yeah, KiKi had to fight hard her whole life."

"What about her family? Are things all right now between her and them?" Lysi said.

"Her mom and dad split. They left town and went their separate ways. KiKi doesn't know where they went."

Lysi could see why KiKi clung so tightly to Bill Pitt. She had no one else. "No wonder KiKi keeps a strangle hold on Bill."

Jade nodded and started talking again. "Me?" The waitress pointed her thumb at her chest. "I was raised on a cattle ranch. My mom wanted me to go to college. I could've, too. I was a good student and took hard classes in high school. In my senior year my mom died and so did my hope of going to college. I had to stay on at the ranch to take care of my dad and two brothers. But believe you me, the minute my dad died I was out of that place. I got a waitress job and moved in with KiKi. I took a couple night classes in computer over to the high school. Man, it was love at first sight for me and the Internet. I got me a computer and I been e-mailing all over the country ever since."

"I'm the same. I don't know how I managed before e-mail was invented. You were smart to take those tech classes. These days you almost have to be computer literate just to survive."

"A lot of good it's done me so far." Jade's mouth tightened. "But back to KiKi and me. Yeah, we had our share of battles, but we always stayed friends. Now we hardly speak."

Lysi slid off the stool. "Well, as I see it, you have two choices. Either make up with KiKi or move on in your life without her. Think carefully, Jade. Is a man like Bill Pitt worth ending a long friendship over?"

Chapter 18

A skinny crescent moon glowed in the sky as Lysi hurried across the dimly lit parking lot toward her room. She glanced left and right several times, keeping a lookout for Choki. Meeting a disturbed teenage boy in a dark, deserted parking lot would not be her idea of a fun evening. Only a few more yards and she'd be on the motel side of the tall privet hedge that divided the restaurant from the Big Sky then the police officer posted at her door would have a clear view of her. Even Choki wouldn't be stupid enough to try anything with a cop watching.

She hoped the cop hadn't taken another bathroom break. He'd been taking so many she'd begun to think he had a urinary tract infection.

Breaking into a slow jog, Lysi rounded the end of the hedge and her stomach did a somersault. No officer at her door. The slow jog changed to an unladylike sprint.

She reached her door, shoved the magnetic keycard into the slot and sighed in relief as the door opened. After tossing her purse on the desk, she dialed James's cell phone number and waited while the phone rang twice.

"Tennyson." He answered in a brisk, professional voice.

"James, it's Lysi Weston. Do you have a moment to talk?"

"Lysi, you must have read my mind. I was just thinking about you. I wanted to tell you how much I enjoyed our breakfast and walk this morning. I also wanted to let you know I'll pick you up for the Cheyenne Festival tomorrow at four o'clock."

"I'll be ready." Lysi smoothed her cheek with the hand James had kissed while in the gazebo, and recalled the unaccustomed rush of desire she experienced when his warm lips touched her skin. That moment had been popping into her mind off and on all day. "Yes, four is fine. I'll be ready." She repeated herself and felt like an idiot.

"Well, good," he said.

After a couple awkward seconds of silence, she remembered the purpose for the call. "I called to tell you I met with Bill Pitt this evening at the Sagebrush."

"Whoa, that's a surprise. I hope he behaved himself."

"Actually, he apologized for his behavior at the presentation." She decided not to mention his boorishness at the reception.

"That's an even bigger surprise."

"Well, since we're into surprises, here's another one. I got a call from Jade. She told me she'd seen Bill Pitt's car parked outside Cristin's room on the night she died. I confronted him and he denied it. He claimed he was visiting his son in Billings. I don't know what to believe."

"You confronted him? I thought we'd already talked about this. I'm the"—

"James, you said he wasn't a suspect. I wasn't interfering in the investigation since you already had your suspect. I just want to know what you think about all this."

James blew out a loud breath. Lysi imagined him shaking his head in frustration.

"Jade's pretty reliable," he said. "If you want to know what's going on in this town, she's your go to person. Better than a newspaper. If she says she saw Pitt there, she probably did."

"But how can we be sure?" Lysi said.

"Pitt does go and visit his son on a pretty regular basis. Whether he was there on Wednesday night is another question. I have to take a run to Billings tomorrow. I can easily check out his alibi since I know Steve and his mom."

"I have a feeling he might be telling the truth," Lysi said.

James's voice took on an official tone. "I'll determine his truthfulness based on evidence, not intuition."

Lysi caught the rebuke and suppressed an urge to challenge it. "Right."

His tone softened. "I'll see you tomorrow afternoon." After a couple of beats he added, "I hope you wear something lilac."

Lysi's eyes strayed to the silky lilac nightgown hanging on a bathroom door hook; the one she had worn the morning she saw James parked outside her window. She wondered what it would be like to feel James's warm hands stroking her through the thin gown. The image sent little charged particles careening through her body.

Not having much choice about what to wear to the Festival since she had only packed enough clothes for a couple of days, she'd already decided to wear a simple jacketed dress. She could have packed any number of pieces from the wardrobe of fashion designer clothing she had collected over the past few years. She just hadn't considered it necessary to bring anything more than casual sports and work clothes to a place like Sage Deer, Montana. Fortunately, the cool, cotton print in tones of lilac and grape would work for the festival. She would leave off the jacket and wrap a light shawl over the spaghetti straps.

With a critical eye, Lysi examined her reflection in the bathroom mirror and immediately started obsessing about her looks—neck too long, ears stuck out, hair always kinked into curls. *I guess I have more character than beauty.*

She turned away from the mirror and had just kicked off her shoes, settled down in a comfortable chair and opened a book when a sound distracted her. She barely heard the soft knock at the door. Thinking it might be Choki, she peered through the peephole. Denny Robbins' face filled her view. His creased brow and sucked in lips communicated fear.

When she opened the door, Denny began stumbling through a barely coherent sentence. "I booked a motel room for Thor, my partner, and now this has happened." He shoved a piece of paper into Lysi's hand.

"Come in, Denny. Slow down. I'm not getting everything. Your partner's coming to Sage Deer? When is he coming?"

"He'll be here Friday evening. I booked him into the Big Sky."

"Why? Don't you have enough room for him to stay with you?" Lysi thought she knew the answer to the question.

"I couldn't have him stay with me. I want to avoid trouble, not invite it. But I guess someone found out about him coming. Now things are worse than ever."

Denny brushed at fat tears gathering in the rims of his eyes. He caught them just before they tumbled down his cheeks.

"Look at this." He pointed to the paper he had given Lysi.

She read the note in her hand:

ONE FAG IS TWO MANY IN THIS TOWN. YOU BRING ANOTHER ONE IN AND THERE WILL BE 2 DEAD FAGS IN SAGE DEER.

Lysi stared at the capital letters written in the now familiar dark, heavy pencil strokes. At one point, a heavy stroke had torn the paper. The person who wrote this was angry and out of control. The person who wrote this is dangerous.

She motioned Denny to a chair next to her desk, sat down and reread the note. She narrowed her eyes and stared into middle space. A second later, her eyes focused on the wastebasket. She bent down, rummaged around in the can then pulled out a crumpled note. She placed it on the desk and smoothed the creases out with the side of her hand then laid Denny's note next to it and compared all the common letters.

Both notes were written with a dull pencil in all capital letters. There were clear similarities in letter formation. The author started his O's at the bottom instead of the top, an immature writing style. The bottom line of the E's didn't touch the down stroke. The points of the N's, M's, and A's didn't meet.

Lysi studied the two papers. "The writers of both notes have the same small motor problems. The writer is the same for both notes."

Feeling Denny's stare, Lysi looked up. "I know who wrote these notes."

Chapter 19

James watched the mist rise in silent wisps from the dew-soaked fields as the sun heated up the cloudless blue sky. In the distance, sandstone buttes painted in swirls of rust, gold and wheat, seemed to whisper of eternity. He loved the fresh, clean serenity of early Sunday mornings—no cars, no trucks, no motorcycles on the road.

He'd left Sage Deer after a quick breakfast, merged onto Highway 94 and taken his time driving the 100 miles to Billings. He put his car on slow cruise control, rolled down the windows and inhaled the sweet scent of mown hay.

James never missed an opportunity to visit Maggie Klein and Steven when he had to make a trip to Billings. But today would be a duty call. He considered carefully how he could delicately frame the questions he needed to ask to verify Bill Pitt's alibi. His warm regard for both Maggie and Steven would never allow him to hurt them.

He'd known Maggie Klein as far back as he could remember. She was an auburn-haired beauty with laughing eyes the clear blue of the Montana sky. When he was a high school senior, he fell helplessly in love with her. If things had been different he might have married her. But any plans he had dissolved when, at twenty, she fell in love with Bill Pitt who kept her dangling on a string for years until one night they slipped up and she became pregnant with Steven. That ended their courtship. By that time James had happily married his wife, Sally, and fathered two children. James never forgave Bill Pitt for getting Maggie pregnant and not marrying her.

He knew Pitt regretted his mistake and had always paid child support for Steven and visited him as often as Maggie would allow. Too little, too late, in James's opinion. Nothing Pitt could do would ever make up for his terrible treatment of Maggie. Over the years, James and Maggie had developed a close friendship, free of any romantic entanglements.

After two hours of driving, James turned down a tree-lined Billings street and parked in front of Maggie's one-story white clapboard house. He smiled at the bright yellow shutters that seemed to suit Maggie's upbeat personality. As he opened the picket fence gate, it scraped against the sidewalk. He made a mental note to reset the screws the next time he came to visit. He stepped onto the covered porch and knocked on the door. An adolescent voice from inside shouted, "I'll get it, Mom."

The door flew open framing a tall, gangly teenager with carrot-red hair and a downy red fringe under his nose. When he saw James, he grinned through a thick sprinkling of freckles. "Hey, Uncle James."

With all the determination of an I-can-do-anything teenager, Steven lunged forward to grab James's neck, but James grabbed him first and got him in a headlock. Steven wriggled like a fish on a hook and kept repeating, "No fair. I wasn't ready."

James started rubbing the top of Steven's head with the heel of his hand. "Stop whining! Just give up and I'll let you go."

Maggie came running to the door, her auburn ponytail tied up in a yellow ribbon. "Stop it both of you or get out in the yard. You're both acting like you were brought up in a barn." She pursed her lips, but her laughing eyes betrayed her enjoyment of their good-natured horseplay.

James released Steven. "Okay, Uncle James, you win this time. Enjoy it, because this is the last time."

James guffawed. "Yeah right. Didn't you say that when I got you two weeks ago?" He put his arm around Steven's shoulders and walked him into the living room. "I have to admit, it gets a little harder each time."

Steven's whole face glowed with pride.

"James, how nice to see you." Maggie took both his hands in hers, stood on tiptoes and kissed him on the cheek. "Come on into the kitchen. I made a fresh pot of coffee and I just finished a batch of those peanut butter cookies you love."

"Well, that's one of the reasons I'm here. I could smell those cookies all the way over in Sage Deer."

He sat down at a fifties chrome dinette table and watched Maggie pour two cups of coffee and fill a platter with warm cookies. Steven snatched half a dozen of them, grabbed his baseball bat and headed out the back door.

"I'll be back for lunch, Mom. Bye, Uncle James."

The screen door slammed and Maggie gritted her teeth. "Exactly when does the male of the species stop letting the door slam every time he enters or leaves a house?"

James chuckled and dunked a cookie into the coffee.

"Before you ask, the answer is yes. My mother still volunteers at the reservation preschool. I swear she's more Cheyenne than me. I may understand tribal language and customs, but she's embraced the tribal soul." James knew he owed his fervent pride in his Cheyenne heritage to his mother and grandmother. They never let him forget the blood of a noble people ran through his veins.

Maggie punched his shoulder. "Don't pretend to read my mind, you arrogant Indian brave. I was going to ask if your mother had talked Namida into dancing at the Festival tonight."

"You already know the answer to that. Will you be there to see her perform?"

"I wish I could. Steven's got a game tonight. Wish her luck for me."

James nodded. "Will do."

Maggie took a sip of coffee and looked at James with curiosity. "What brings you to Billings?"

For a moment, James's eyes fastened on a bulletin board covered with photos, game schedules, appointment cards and a grocery list. Then he looked at Maggie. "I came to see you, Maggie– kind of in the line of duty."

She examined him with the same inquisitive, but vulnerable eyes he remembered from childhood.

James looked down at the table and said on an outward breath, "Maggie, did Bill visit and stay over night here last Wednesday?"

"Yes," she said without hesitation.

"What time did he arrive?"

She frowned. "Why are you asking all these questions? Is Bill in some kind of trouble?" Her eyes clouded with concern.

James studied her face. Over the years, he'd often seen that expression at the mention of Pitt's name—a sad, empty look. He knew she would always love him.

"A witness says she saw him at the scene of a murder in Sage Deer. Bill claims he was here with you."

"Murder! In Sage Deer?" She seemed more amazed than upset.

James told her the victim had come to Nerium to present at a company-training seminar, and was found dead in her motel room.

"He wasn't here with *me*. He was here with Steven. He arrived about eleven. He always gets here late because he has to put in extra hours at work to make up for not returning to Nerium until late in the afternoon of the next day."

"Thanks, Maggie. That's what I needed to know." James reached for another cookie and asked about Steven's high school classes. He didn't tell Maggie that Bill Pitt could've murdered Cristin Holden and made it to Billings by eleven.

Chapter 20

"I'd love an espresso," Lysi said, squeezing the phone between her head and shoulder while she tied her shoe. "I didn't even know they had them around here. I'll see you in five minutes. Thanks, Carolyn."

She hung up the phone, ran a brush through her hair, dabbed on some makeup and hurried downstairs just as Carolyn pulled up.

Lysi scooted into the sporty red Mazda. "Carolyn, you saved my life. I had no idea what I would do with myself all morning. I finished my book. I even read the Sage Deer Weekly—Lori someone announced her engagement to Harold somebody; So and So will host a garden tea for the library fund; the grange meeting will address the best ways to store steer manure; high school football practice begins some time in August."

"Stop," Carolyn said, bent over with laughter. "You do sound desperate."

"And the stores are all closed today." Lysi groaned.

"I know. This place dies on Sunday morning and isn't resurrected until Monday." Carolyn's voice expressed the same frustration Lysi felt.

"Where is this Montana Starbucks?"

"It isn't a Starbucks, but they do have an espresso machine. It's a small coffee shop in a trading post on the Crow reservation about 40 minutes from here off Highway 212."

"I never thought getting a cup of coffee could be such an incredibly exciting adventure," Lysi said. "Let's go do it."

The highway seemed almost deserted. In spite of a 75 mph speed limit, Carolyn kept bumping 90. Her topic du jour for almost the whole trip consisted of singing the praises of Hank Jones.

"Hank has exquisite taste in clothes. Whatever he wears complements his unique good looks."

Lysi said, "Uh huh." Hank reminded her of Gordie, her former husband, a big, showy balloon full of hot air. She understood how Carolyn could see Hank as the most wonderful man in the world. She'd felt the same about tall, raven-haired Gordie, a young, upwardly mobile attorney she'd met during her first year of teaching. He seemed like a dream come true. When he proposed to her, she accepted immediately, thinking she would never find anyone like him again. Their hasty, fairytale marriage crashed when Gordie's Mr. Hyde personality surfaced—a braggart who couldn't hold a job and blamed everyone except himself for his problems.

"Hank has a kind of innate savoir-faire. I think it's his upper-class upbringing. I always feel so proud when I'm with him," Carolyn said.

"Uh huh," Lysi said. Jade's words echoed in her head. *There are only two men in this town worth looking at, Hank Jones and James Tennyson. Maybe Carolyn grabbed Hank because the choices were so limited.*

"I've known Hank since high school," Carolyn said. "Elizabeth has known him longer than I. They grew up like brother and sister. Her mom was sort of his nanny and cleaned house for Hank's mother. I think even back in high school, Hank and I knew we were destined for each other."

Now Carolyn had Lysi's full attention. So Carolyn and Hank have a long history. Lysi started to ask about marriage plans when Carolyn announced their arrival at the trading post. "Here we are. Best espressos in eastern Montana."

They pulled into a dirt parking lot in front of a two-story wood building the same color as the dry grass fields that surrounded it. Several benches crouched under a shaded porch surrounding the building. Joy filled Lysi's heart when she saw a large sign that had become very important to her since she had come to Montana—Air Conditioned.

They entered a large room decorated with paintings depicting contemporary and historical Native American life. The right half of the building housed a reservation store crowded with shelves full of every imaginable Indian souvenir—key chains, beaded Crow candles, carved wood buffalos and eagles, buckskin clothing, belts, jewelry, mugs. Lysi's eyes raced around the room trying to see everything.

Carolyn took her arm and nudged her under an archway into the other half of the building, a restaurant that reminded Lysi of an elementary school cafeteria with its stainless steel counter and long tables. As soon as they sat down at one of the wood tables, a black-haired kid with facial features similar to the Native Americans Lysi had seen in Sage Deer, brought them a menu.

"Hi Albert. Bring us two of your great espressos and we'll split a Fry Bread with honey butter."

Albert rubbed his hands on his clean apron and flashed a bashful grin. "Coming right up, Miss Norris."

In less than five minutes, Albert set two espressos on the table along with a hot, crispy, deep fried hunk of Fry Bread the size of a large dinner plate and beamed at Carolyn.

Carolyn tore off a small piece, spread it with honey butter, put it in her mouth and whispered, "This is to die for."

Lysi didn't taste her coffee right away, but sat with her eyes shut, nose close to the cup, inhaling the frothy steam. "This is Heaven on earth." She brought the cup to her lips and took a small sip. "Nectar of the Gods."

The two women laughed as they playacted ecstasy like a couple of teenyboppers then sat without speaking for a few moments sipping and chewing.

Seeing Carolyn so relaxed outside her office delighted Lysi. She felt she'd found a good friend in Carolyn. A friend in whom she could confide and whom she could trust.

Albert leaned over the counter, dark eyes resting on Carolyn. Before their cups were completely empty, he rushed to the table.

"Miss Norris, would you like another espresso and more Fry Bread?"

Carolyn seemed aware of his infatuation and patted his hand. "Why Albert, you're truly a professional restaurateur. Thank you for seeing to our needs so quickly."

A glowing smile spread across Albert's face revealing an endearing dimple in one cheek.

"I think we could manage two more espressos, don't you, Lysi?"

As soon as Albert bounced after the two espressos, Carolyn asked if there were any new developments in the murder case.

Lysi toyed with the last bit of fry bread. "As you know, at first I suspected Bill Pitt, but I confronted him last night in the Sagebrush Café. Now I'm not so sure. He claims he was at his son's house in Billings at the time of the murder. Detective Tennyson said he could easily check out his alibi."

"If his alibi checks out, what then? Do you have any other suspects?"

"Only one." Lysi didn't tell Carolyn that Hank Jones had made her personal list of possible suspects. Instead, she said, "Choki Pry. Do you know him?"

Carolyn's face twisted in disgust. "That little turd. He cleans the Nerium restrooms at night. He's supposed to start work after six when staff leaves. One time I was in a bathroom stall at about 5:30 and the little weasel walks right in and starts opening stall doors. He gets to mine, rattles it and says he's checking to see if everyone is out so he can start cleaning. I hitched up my knickers, walked out and gave him a word thrashing. I told him if I ever caught him in the women's restroom again before six o'clock, I'd have his sorry ass fired. He hauled right out of there and I haven't seen his face anywhere in the Nerium plant before six ever since."

Carolyn's eyes narrowed. "I'm convinced he saw me go into the bathroom and followed, planning to do God knows what." She stuck her finger in her mouth as if to vomit.

"I'm not surprised. That sounds like him." Lysi told Carolyn about Choki barging into her room with a master keycard.

Carolyn covered Lysi's hand with her own. "You poor thing. That would have scared me so badly I'd have run screaming out the door."

"I almost did, but something he said scared me more. He said, 'Why do you act so nice and then spit in my face? *You're just like her.*' It made me wonder if he'd done the same thing to Cristin."

A puzzled look spread across Carolyn's face.

"Carolyn, he could've gone to Cristin's room, and when she tried to kick him out, he could've strangled her."

"Strangled her! Is that how she died? Someone strangled her?"

Lysi nodded.

Carolyn stared at Lysi through a couple of beats. "I wouldn't put it past the little creep. I hope they catch him and put him away for good. She leaned forward and placed a hand on Lysi's arm. "In the meantime, Lysi, be careful. Be very careful."

Chapter 21

Bertha Pry scowled at Detective James Tennyson through the screen door of the old Skyline mobile home she'd inherited when her parents died. Wiry little Sam Spitz, behind Tennyson, averted his eyes to protect them from the glare of the sun reflecting off the silver metal of the trailer or maybe to avoid looking at Bertha. He told James he'd known her when she was young, a real knockout beauty and it depressed him to see how life had changed her.

"We know he's here, Bertha. Either you go get him or we'll get a search warrant and turn this place upside down," James said.

Bertha hesitated. She rubbed her fingers over the outbreak of eczema on her cheek then pushed a strand of hair behind her ear. She shifted her heavy body aside and opened the screen door.

"Why don't you leave him be? He hasn't done anything. He's got two jobs. He's trying to stay out of trouble. Haven't you got nothing better to do than chase after a kid?" Her voice broke and her eyes moistened.

James felt sorry for her—all the frustration, helplessness and guilt she must have experienced over the years. Raising a kid alone is difficult enough, but raising a kid like Noah must be a real heartbreaker.

"Now just calm down, Bertha." James stepped into the trailer. The stale air made him feel a little queasy. He cringed at the flies lighting on the unwashed breakfast dishes, still on the table. The strip of sticky flypaper hanging from the ceiling had captured so many flies that its usefulness had ended days ago. A stringy haired dog of dubious ancestry lay under the table. It groaned and rolled onto its side, stretched its legs out and then retracted them. It glanced at the two intruders then its eyelids fell shut.

"Just go get him for me and we'll get this over with," James said. He looked around the room; his eyes lighted on Noah's *Judo Kid* hat.

"I tell you, he's not here. He…he went over to visit my sister in Billings." She swiped at her cheeks with the hem of her apron.

James walked over and picked up Noah's hat. "Without this?" He knew Noah never went anywhere without the hat.

Bertha sighed. She looked toward an accordion door in the rear of the trailer and yelled, "Choki, you come on out here."

A couple of seconds later, Choki banged the accordion door open, stomped out and fired an ugly look at his mother. "Great, my own ma gives me up to the cops."

The dog jumped up and ran to Noah. Without taking his eyes off his mother, Noah scratched behind the dog's ear. When he stopped, the dog reached up and licked his hand. Noah resumed scratching the dog's ear.

"You left your damn hat on the chair. It's your own fault, stupid. I've had it with you." Her voice cracked. She turned her back to them, slumped over the sink and stared out the trailer window.

"Noah, we're going to take that little ride I promised you yesterday," James said. "You can do it with or without cuffs. Take him, Sam."

The dog attempted to follow Noah but stopped when Noah said, "Stay, Lob, stay. Good boy." He gave him a last ear scratch and patted him on the head. The dog whined softly.

James figured the dog must be the only creature in the world that showed unconditional love to Noah.

Bertha didn't turn around when they left.

*

Choki didn't talk at all during the fifteen-minute drive to the police station. He just stared straight ahead, his eyes as empty as the barren landscape outside the car window.

James parked in the gravel lot behind the police station and took Choki by the arm and steered him through the back door into a short hall that led to the interrogation room. He shoved him into a chair on one side of a wooden table and sat across from him.

Bright light from high transom windows reflected off the gray enameled walls of the bare room, creating a glare from all directions. Choki squinted.

"Tell me about Cristin Holden," James said.

"Who?"

James waited.

Choki's eyes raced around the room as if searching for an escape.

James spoke again. "I think I already know what you did to Cristin Holden. I'm giving you a chance to tell me your story."

"I didn't do nothing to her. I don't even know her. I only saw her a couple of times when she picked up her room key."

In a cold, patient voice, James said, "Let's go back to the night of the murder. Where were you between nine and eleven-thirty?"

Choki swallowed. "I was…working the desk for my mom's break."

"For two and a half hours? I don't think so. Your mom's break lasts about forty-five minutes."

Beads of sweat gathered on Choki's upper lip. "She took longer than usual."

"Why?"

"I don't know. She just did."

"Did Cristin Holden pick up her key while you were working the desk? Is that when you talked to her?"

"I don't remember. I didn't talk to her."

"What time did you say your mom returned?"

"Around ten."

"Not eleven-thirty?" James waited for an answer then continued. "You know what I think? I think you strangled Cristin Holden. Maybe you didn't mean to do it. Maybe it was an accident."

James spoke in a supportive voice, but his hard stare delivered a different message.

Choki opened his mouth as if to protest then, his expression signaling resignation, dropped his head to the table and buried his face in his arms. In a plaintive voice, muffled by his arms, he said, "I didn't mean to do it."

"Get your face up and look at me, Noah," James shouted. Choki raised his head. Fear filled his eyes.

"Now talk," James said.

Choki slipped into a nervous falsetto. "It was an accident. She was just supposed to go unconscious and then wake up. This would never have happened if she hadn't acted like she wanted me."

James dropped down on a chair across from Choki, folded his hands and spoke in a restrained voice. "Slow down, Noah. Let's start from the beginning."

"That lady, Cristin, she kept stopping by the desk and acting all nice to me. She was all smiling and winking at me. So I figured I'd give her what she wants."

It disgusted James to watch Choki change as he told his story. Now Choki spoke in the present tense. His voice became more animated and his lips curved into a salacious grin as if he were reliving his fantasy.

"So I wait until my mom gets back to the desk and I go off duty. Then I go to her room and knock on the door. She answers it all dressed up in her fancy nightgown. She's kind of weaving a little bit—like she had a few. I figure she's ready for me so I go and try for a little kiss. She makes a big deal about jumping back and yelling at me to get out. I figure it's just an act to get herself–you know–in the mood. So I push her down on the bed. Well, all of a sudden she starts screaming and calling me names."

The excitement on his face changed to humiliation. "I had to shut her up so I could get out of there. So I gave her a little Judo choke."

The whimper returned to his voice. "I didn't even hurt her. Nothing was supposed to happen to her. She was supposed to wake up. I tried to rub her neck to wake her up. I didn't mean nothing to happen to her. It was an accident."

James stared at Choki, trying to comprehend his extreme self-delusion. A real sickie.

He shoved a yellow pad and pencil across the table. "Noah, write that story down."

Choki picked up the pencil with trembling fingers and began to write.

Chapter 22

James drove slowly toward the Big Sky Motel, hoping to time it so he'd knock on Lysi's door right at four. A small bouquet of dried Montana wild flowers—geraniums, wild hyacinths and asters—tied with a satin ribbon lay on the passenger seat next to him. He looked at them and tried to recall the last time he'd given flowers to a woman. Maybe to his wife on her last birthday before the accident. Maybe he'd had some delivered to Maggie when she got her new job. He really didn't remember. He just knew it'd been a long time and now he felt pretty uncomfortable with the whole idea. When the postman delivered the bouquet with a note from his mother instructing him to give them to Lysi, he'd balked at the idea; then decided to do it, telling himself he didn't want to offend his mother who'd done such a nice job assembling the bouquet.

He pulled into the Big Sky parking lot and waved at Jade, who had leaned over the counter to peer through the Sagebrush Café window at him. He knew Jade would be on the phone reporting his activities even before he got out of the car.

When Lysi opened the door to his knock, he had to force himself not to stare. He saw no trace of the stiff businesswoman ready to take on all comers. A soft cloud of femininity had replaced her. First he noticed the bare shoulders then the full-skirted dress that accentuated the curve of her waist; finally, the heady floral scent of her perfume wafting through the air. She was drop-to-your-knees beautiful.

"You look nice," he stammered. Instantly, he thought of ten much more creative things he might have said. "I don't mean you look nice. I mean—well I do mean that, but what I really mean is—you look…fabulous."

She flushed. "Thank you. You look pretty good yourself."

"Thanks," James mumbled, self conscious about his new shirt, haircut and aftershave cologne.

"Are those for me?" She pointed to the flowers he held pressed to his chest like a timid bridesmaid.

"Oh…yes. They're from my mother's garden. She thought you might like them. *I* thought…you might like them, too."

She took the bouquet from him and surprised him with a peck on the cheek. "They're lovely. Thank you."

He cleared his throat. "About dinner, you have a choice. We can dine at a restaurant or we can sample Cheyenne food at the festival. You might find the Cheyenne food a little unusual, but I guarantee its authenticity and quality."

She picked up a crocheted shawl and a small handbag. "I'll take my chances with the Cheyenne food."

As they got into the car they both waved to Jade, who still leaned over the counter watching, except now she had a phone to her ear.

*

As they snaked along the oiled county road to the Festival, Lysi listened with interest to James's descriptions of Cheyenne history and culture.

"Five thousand Cheyenne live on the reservation," he said.

"Five thousand! How big is the reservation?" Lysi stared through the windshield at the bleak, mono-colored landscape—flat fields strewn with rocks, boulders, juniper and sagebrush framed by bland rolling hills. Not wanting to offend, she didn't ask her real question—how could anyone survive in such a dry, miserable place?

"About 700 square miles," James said. "They used to live on the Missouri River where they practiced agriculture and handicrafts. They lost those arts when enemy tribes drove them out onto the plains where they had to live in skin teepees and follow the buffalo to survive."

Lysi studied James. Now his Cheyenne characteristics were so obvious—sculpted features, high cheekbones and straight black hair. She admired his fair skin and dark blue eyes, gifts from his English mother.

She found herself drawn to this man, so different from herself. Where could a relationship with a man like James go? Nowhere. Maybe she should just take Cristin's advice and hop on this streetcar for a short fun ride. No expectations. No complications.

When he glanced at her, she quickly said. "I knew the Cheyenne lived on the plains, but I had no idea they had once lived on the Missouri River. How did they end up here in Eastern Montana?"

James smiled at her interest and went on retelling the stories his grandfather and Nanny Namida had told him.

"They had migrated into Montana, but the government resettled them in Oklahoma where the conditions were so intolerable that about 200 staged an escape in midwinter. We're talking below zero temperatures, harsh winds and snowstorms. Only about 60 made it back to Montana. The U.S. government assigned them this piece of land."

Lysi shook her head. "What a sad end for a noble people."

*

The sun burned lower in the sky and sent its rays shooting through the windshield. Lysi squinted at the faded Cheyenne reservation road marker. The reservation was a conglomeration of rundown commercial buildings and government pre-fab houses, bleached and weathered by the extremes of Montana's merciless winters and summers. It seemed as if every small house had old broken down cars parked helter-skelter in its packed-dirt yard.

James parked the car in the festival parking area, a sun-dried field of wild grass teaming with little flying and creeping creatures—grasshoppers, beetles, dragonflies. They continued on foot to the performance area, each step releasing a dusty cloud of chaff and insects.

As they trudged along, Lysi's dress clung to her in the intense heat. She blotted at her face with a tissue and marveled for the hundredth time how people could tolerate Montana summers.

At the entrance to the festival grounds, Lysi saw a light blue flag suspended over a tall weathered wood gate. On the gate post a hand lettered cardboard sign set the behavior standards for the day. WELCOME. NO DRINKING. NO ROWDY STUFF.

Lysi asked James about the white emblem in the center of the blue flag. He told her the glyph of the "morning star" had been used for ages by the Cheyenne in their art and religious ceremonies. "The great chief, Morningstar, was the man who led his people from the Oklahoma reservation and eventually back to Montana."

Inside the gate, Lysi surveyed the crowd, a mix of locals and tourists. Children scampered after teens and adults. Dark-skinned elders sat fanning themselves in shade near craft canopies and under faded umbrellas. The Native Americans intrigued her—their sun-bronzed skin, dark eyes, angular features and aquiline noses. Many had donned traditional costumes for the festival—deerskin clothing decorated with intricate beading and symbolic headdresses.

Lysi relished the medley of sounds and scents that filled the air: drum cadences, barbecued meat, tinkling bells, candied apples and laughter that seemed to come from every direction. As James pulled her along, she forgot about the heat and kept switching her head left and right, trying to take in everything at once.

They passed long tables crowded with vividly painted pottery, woven baskets, rainbow-colored blankets and other craft pieces. A table loaded with necklaces and earrings captured Lysi's attention. She jerked to a stop and read the sign above the table: *Native jewelry made from tinted porcupine quills and glass beads.* James explained the dyes were all natural—bright blues from larkspurs, yellow from fox moss, red from cochineal. She pointed to a necklace made of porcupine quills with violet beading and told James she would purchase a piece like it after the program.

When they reached the performance area and sat down on a front row bleacher, Lysi's eyes swept over the arena and halted at a giant Nerium banner on the opposite side of the dusty parade ground.

She lowered her gaze to the Nerium group seated beneath the banner. Elizabeth Scot, the quiet director of Information Technology, sat next to Denny Robbins. KiKi Kavenaugh clung to Bill Pitt like a Siamese twin. Hank Jones had his arm draped around Carolyn Norris. Interesting interface among business colleagues, Lysi mused.

James interrupted her thoughts. "The program begins in about an hour. Sorry I rushed you, but I wanted to make sure we had good seats before the place filled up. We'll have time to visit the craft booths after the show."

"I'm going to hold you to that."

James looked pleased. "I promise, you'll get to shop 'til you drop. Right now you must be starving. Save the seats and I'll go grab a couple of food platters."

"A Montana tiger couldn't get these seats away from me," Lysi said.

He laughed and hurried off, shouting over his shoulder, "No tigers in Montana."

A steady drum cadence drew Lysi's attention. She searched the festival grounds trying to locate its source. Her body swayed to its primal rhythm and she had just closed her eyes when a voice made her jump.

"Hey Lysi. Don't sit by yourself. Come join us. I promise to make KiKi behave." Elizabeth Scot smiled down at her, looking overdressed in a brown pantsuit and practical oxfords.

"I'm not here by myself. I'm with James Tennyson…and Namida. She's going to dance." Lysi decided she'd better add Namida's name so Elizabeth wouldn't start asking questions about James.

Elizabeth slumped down beside her. Lysi noticed her eyes glued to the Nerium crowd. Just to make conversation Lysi said, "How are things going with the new management information system?"

Elizabeth looked at her distractedly. "Everyone is still having a tough time with it. Seems I'm always being called to undo some ridiculous mistake. It's overwhelming because there're so many computers and only one me. I've put in for a tech trainee, but so far no luck. I input a universal password for everyone and they're supposed to change it to their personal password. They're not even secure enough to do a simple thing like that."

Lysi recalled Jade's wish to get out of the waitress business, her night school computer classes and her love affair with the Internet. "Elizabeth, have you considered a local person for that tech trainee position? Nerium might be willing to hire someone who's already here. I'm thinking of Jade Green, the waitress at the Sagebrush Café. She's a hard worker and seems very intelligent. She's computer literate and probably more of a techie than most of the people at Nerium. I'll bet she'd do anything to get a job at Nerium."

Elizabeth didn't look skeptical. "I know her. Actually, I like her. I didn't know she knew computers. It's a possibility." Lysi expected a more enthusiastic response from Elizabeth. She sounded unfocused like she had more important matters on her mind.

Lysi watched Elizabeth's gaze trail back to the Nerium crowd.

After a few seconds, Elizabeth said, eyes still on the Nerium group, "I had to bale out Hank Jones the other day. He was having a problem with his e-mail. When I went into it, I saw something that might just interest you."

"What's that?" Lysi couldn't imagine why she would have any interest in Jones's computer, but she did have an interest in his possible connection with Cristin.

"Well, what I see in the computers is confidential. But the universal password isn't because everyone knows it. The universal password is 'change-it'. I'll just say his computer holds some information you should know. Maybe Detective Tennyson could get a search warrant to access Hank's computer." Elizabeth kept her eyes trained on the Nerium crowd.

"A search warrant?" Lysi said. Knowing James had no grounds for a search warrant, she put that idea out of her mind. But curiosity about the information on Hank's computer branded itself on her brain. She would have to find a way to access that computer. She would think about a plan later. For now, she would enjoy the festival.

Two young boys followed by a thin little girl raced past Lysi and Elizabeth. The little girl dropped her cotton candy in the dust and her big brown eyes clouded with tears. One of the boys came back, picked it up, picked off the dusty parts and handed it to her. She wiped her eyes and all three hurried to their seats a few sections over. Lysi wished her problems were as easily solved.

Lysi recalled Elizabeth's discomfort in the boisterous crowd at the Cattle Rustler's Restaurant and decided to rescue her from a repeat performance here at the Festival. "Looks like they're having a rollicking good time over there. Why don't you sit with us during the performance? That way you won't have to traipse back across the parade ground again."

"I'd love to, but I don't want to leave Denny alone with KiKi and Bill."

"Hank's there. He seems to be able to handle Bill."

"Hank's got a new love. He'll be busy lavishing all his attention on her." Elizabeth tipped her head towards Hank and Carolyn. Hank nuzzled Carolyn's ear.

"I see."

"I'm worried about Carolyn," Elizabeth said. "I think she's falling for Hank. Not good. He'll be charming and attentive until the next conquest comes along. She could get hurt."

"You seem to know a lot about Hank," Lysi said, her interest mounting.

Elizabeth surprised Lysi with a candid reply. "I was in love with him. I guess I've loved him for as long as I can remember. Early on, my mother warned me not to set my heart on him, but of course I did."

"Then you knew him before you came to Sage Deer?"

"Oh yes, my mother kept house for the Jones family for years. She started before I was born. When I turned five, she started taking me along when she cleaned. Hank and I would play together. My mother never thought much of Hank. Then at about fourteen, I told her I'd fallen in love with him. It really upset her. She told me he was just a beautifully wrapped box with nothing but junk inside. She told me he'd been a cute, smart baby, born to a mother who worshipped him. His mother loved him more than she loved his father; more than she loved husbands two and three. Mother said in elementary school his teachers adored him and let him get by with things they would never allow other kids to get away with."

"You grew up together, then?"

Lysi smiled at the little brown-eyed girl who had tired of her cotton candy and now walked the bench toward her trying hard to keep balanced. As she got closer, Lysi extended a hand to help her balance. The little girl giggled, quickly turned and scampered back to where her brothers sat.

"Not exactly," Elizabeth said. "When I started private school, I still kept track of him through my mom's negative comments. I think when he grew up, he realized he couldn't manipulate men and decided he needed power to control them, so he started climbing the management ladder."

Lysi thought Elizabeth had pretty good insight into Hank's character. "Is he a long-time Nerium employee?"

"He worked about five years in the L.A. office. I met him again when we both ended up working for Nerium Montana. He said he took the Montana job because it was far away from corporate headquarters and the micro managing, upper-level executives. Here he was king among the directors."

"He seems to fit in pretty well at Nerium Montana," Lysi said. *Basically he's just another pile of hot feces out here in the cow pasture.* Lysi smiled and thought of Cristin who would've put it much more graphically.

"When we got together again here in Sage Deer, we fell in love—or maybe I did. He acted like I was his heart's desire and I bought it. When I found out he'd cheated on me I hated him and I hated her."

"Hated Hank and who?" Lysi said, remembering the Nerium car Jade had seen outside Cristin's room. Could it have been Hank, not Bill? Could Cristin be the person Elizabeth hated?

Elizabeth shook her head as if to say she just couldn't continue this bout of pain. "It doesn't matter now. He's had so many women. I don't hate any of them anymore. It's too late. Hank's going to the highest bidder—Carolyn. She can give him a lot more than I can."

Lysi's curiosity piqued. "What do you mean?"

"I guess you wouldn't know this, but Carolyn's father is a top executive at Nerium headquarters, Los Angeles."

"Really." Lysi looked across the dirt festival ground at Hank and Carolyn. So that's his game.

Lysi turned back to Elizabeth. "At the reception Carolyn mentioned you two have been friends since school."

"We weren't actually friends; we just attended the same private school. She came from a rich family and...well, my mom cleaned houses.

"Between you and me, Carolyn wasn't a good student. Her family actually purchased a private college education for her with generous alumni contributions from her mother who had graduated from the same private college.

"She was a big disappointment to her father. He provided her a private tutor who taught her how to dress, speak and behave like a professional; then hired her as director of staff development and placed her way out here. My mother told me she overheard Mr. Norris say he wanted his daughter as far away from headquarters as possible."

"Do you think Carolyn's happy here in Montana?" Lysi already knew the answer to her question, but she wanted to learn more about Carolyn and Hank.

"She hates it here. All she talks about is marrying Hank and moving back to L.A. I know Hank's not the marrying kind, but I guess it could happen because she has everything Hank wants—looks, money, connections."

Elizabeth removed her glasses, took out a tissue and rubbed a fine layer of dust off the lenses. "You know, I'd take him back in a heartbeat. Am I crazy?"

Before Lysi could answer, Elizabeth stood. "Well, I'd better head back. Enjoy the Festival."

Lysi watched her start across the parade ground then switched her gaze to the Nerium group. Bill Pitt seemed unresponsive to KiKi's pawing. Maybe he decided to drop her and put all his energy into getting his son's mother to marry him. Lysi hoped it wasn't too late for him. She hoped his alibi checked out. She hoped—she almost knew—he hadn't murdered Cristin.

Lysi shifted her eyes to Hank who now had his face buried in Carolyn's neck. Although it sickened her, she knew at a visceral level how a woman could fall for a Hank Jones with his movie star good looks and Casanova charm, ignoring his Marquis de Sade scruples. There were moments when even she felt a stab of animal attraction to him. She gave herself a hard mental kick and tried to trash the feeling by conjuring up an image of James's sky blue eyes.

The scent of food caught Lysi's attention immediately. She turned her head toward James who had just arrived with two overflowing platters. He handed one to her.

"You're about to taste staples of the traditional Cheyenne diet." He pointed to each food. "Roasted buffalo strips. Wild berries. Batter bread. Indian tacos. Pemmican."

He tore off a piece of pemmican and offered it to her. "Pemmican's always been a very important staple. For centuries, the Cheyenne prepared this jerky-like food for home and travel. It's made of dried meat and berries."

Lysi tasted each food, savoring the unusual flavors. "It's different, but good."

After she'd cleaned her plate, James opened a bag and pulled out two caramel apples. "Since you were such a good girl and ate all your dinner, you may now have dessert."

"Yummy, Papa." Lysi took a big bite of apple.

A symphony of jingling bells signaled the opening of the festival show. The program began with the Grand Entry. A line of dancers marched to the center of the dusty parade ground in sync with the beat of a single drum. The parade formed a colorful circle around a lone, silent drum and continued to march in place.

"The drum is the heartbeat of the people and respected as a spirit," James said, his eyes bright with excitement.

Abruptly, the drums ceased. The audience grew quiet. James pointed to a high wooden archway on the far left side of the parade ground. "The Festival Princess."

Erect posture and an understated smile suited the quiet dignity of the princess who rode by on a high-stepping mustang looking as though she'd been born to ride. To Lysi she looked just like the maiden in the mural at Sage Deer City Hall. Her ebony hair hung down her back in two braids sparkling with beads the blue color of the Cheyenne flag. The princess gazed at the crowd through almond eyes framed by thick lashes. The white buckskin dress she wore made her tawny skin glow.

Lysi saw her look directly at James as she passed. James tilted his chin to her.

"Her name is Ominotago. It means beautiful voice. She has a rare crystalline quality when she sings, like the sound of the wind passing through an icy canyon."

"She carries herself so regally," Lysi said.

James told Lysi that Ominotago was Namida's grandniece. He said the princess had earned her self-confident air. Now a senior, she'd been a straight A student throughout high school. Three leading universities had accepted her. "You may recognize her. She's the Cheyenne maiden in the mural you admired in city hall."

"Of course. She's beautiful."

Lysi noticed a single fine line on the princess' smooth forehead along with a shadow of sadness in her face that seemed to hint at an inner conflict. "She looks so serious."

James explained that Ominotago faced a very big decision for her young age. She had to make a choice between her desire to attend a university and her love for a Native American boy.

"The boy has begged her to make a life with him on a small piece of arid land he purchased with money he'd earned working on a large cattle ranch after high school graduation."

James waved at a raven-haired boy, slouched in a gelatinous teenage fashion in the front row of bleachers about ten seats from them. "That's the young man, Honehe, over there."

The boy straightened up and waved back, a smile crinkled the corners of his deep-set eyes. The same kind of thick lashes as Princess Ominotago's softened his chiseled cheekbones.

"He has a proud look about him," Lysi said.

"He should be proud. Not many youths his age own land. He's already finding ways to get water to it. I think he's a fine, hardworking kid. Namida knows this and hasn't refused permission for Ominotago to marry, but she's advised her to finish university and then make a decision," James said.

Lysi started to reply when the touch of James's hand on her shoulder silenced her. A hush fell over the whole arena as total attention rested on Ominotago. From somewhere, the soft slow pulse of a lone drum cut through the silence then escalated to a feverish beat that filled the arena. The pounding seemed to hypnotize the audience.

Suddenly, Ominotogo's mustang streaked to the far end of the parade grounds, halted, and stood like a statue as the princess slid off its side.

The drumbeat stopped.

In silence the princess made a complete circle, greeting the audience with the same Cheyenne sign of friendship—clasped hands—with which Namida had greeted Lysi in the Wild Flower Inn.

At the roar of multiple drums, the princess broke into a run and raced to the circle of dancers.

The Gourd Dance began.

To a low chant, performers wearing orange and green ribbon shirts and buckskin leggings, moved around the circle slowly dancing and shaking their gourds. As the chant changed to a louder, stronger beat, the dancers stopped in place and lifted their heels as they shook the gourds harder, tapping their beaded moccasins.

After the dance ended, the next group of performers tiptoed to the center of the grounds.

A soft tinkling heightened into a beautiful sound, made by hundreds of small cone-shaped metal pieces sewn to multicolored dresses. The sparkling cones resembled falling droplets of rain as the women honored the princess with the optimistic Jingle Dress Dance.

Several more dances followed. James explained that the Native dances all have special meanings and are symbolic of many different creatures such as the butterfly, bison, horse, and eagle. The dances' colorful names describe them—Slippery Dance, Sun Dance and Galloping Buffalo Bull Dance.

Lysi listened to James as if she were a freshman in awe of an esteemed college professor. This man may be part English, but in his heart he's all Cheyenne.

The sinking sun transformed the western sky into a kaleidoscopic flurry of scarlet and coral. Namida appeared and led a line of women onto the parade ground to perform what James called a traditional women's dance. As she danced, the foot long fringe on her buckskin dress sleeves swayed with her. The beads on her skirt sparkled red, yellow and blue, catching the waning light at every turn.

James nudged Lysi and pointed toward the dancers. "Watch their feet. The Women's Traditional Dance reflects woman's close connection with Mother Earth because the dancers never allow their feet to completely leave the ground."

Lysi watched the gentle steps of the dancers move in perfect time with the drum. "Namida is an extraordinary dancer."

Suddenly, amid a loud drum roll and much whooping, Namida opened her arms to the spectators. Lysi watched as the audience merged onto the parade ground.

"It's the Round Dance." James leapt to his feet and extended his hand to Lysi.

Lysi hesitated. "I don't know how to do this dance."

"It doesn't matter. Everyone, young and old, Native American or not, unite in this friendship dance."

He led her into the rhythmic circle and with a light touch guided her through the simple movements. His closeness dissolved her tension and she soon swayed as one with all the other dancers.

The Round Dance ended the performances.

As James and Lysi headed toward the parking area, they passed Honehe, the young Native American boy. He jumped to his feet and held out his hand to James.

James shook his hand and slapped him on the back. "Lysi Weston, meet Honehe, an excellent horseman and the owner of a fine piece of land."

With a proud smile Honehe extended his hand to Lysi. "James always calls me by my Native American name. You can call me Jake. Nice to meet you."

Lysi took his hand. "Which name do you prefer?"

"Either, I guess."

"Then I'll call you Honehe."

"I'm sorry about your friend." Honehe looked away.

James studied Honehe's face as though he sensed the boy might be hiding something. "What is it, Honehe?"

"Nothing, or maybe a little something. It's about Choki."

James's face reddened. "I told you not to hang out with Noah Pry."

"I know. I'm sorry. I do it because his mother sometimes lets him use the car and we can go someplace. He got the car on Saturday night and we just went for a hamburger."

"What about Noah?" James decided to deal with Honehe's disobedience later.

"He said some things I didn't like." Honehe stared at the fine dust on the desiccated ground.

James looked frustrated. "You can talk in front of Miss Weston. What did he say?"

"He said that lady, Miss Holden, was a tease. He said she invited him to her room and then when he showed up, she tried to kick him out. He told me he taught her a lesson she would never forget." He turned his head to Lysi. "He said he needed to teach you the same lesson. I'm sorry, Miss Weston."

Lysi's mouth went dry. So Choki not only killed Cristin, he bragged about it. Now he's threatened to come after me.

James seemed to sense Lysi's fear. He put his arm around her shoulders. "Don't worry, I've got him right where he belongs."

He turned to the boy. "Thank you, Honehe. You did the right

thing telling me." He punched Honehe on the shoulder and added,

"Don't go with Noah again or I'll skin your ornery hide."

*

When they started for the Festival ground gate, James remembered a present he had purchased for Lysi. As soon as they reached the shelter of a grove of cottonwoods, he took her arm. "Wait a second.

He pulled an envelope from his pocket. "This is for you."

When Lysi opened the envelope she caught her breath at the finely crafted necklace of purple porcupine quills with violet beading, the one she had pointed out to James.

"It's lovely."

"I thought it looked like you."

He took the necklace from her and fastened it around her neck. The flowery scent of her hair made his knees weak. He let his hands drop to her bare shoulders. At the feel of warm skin, he stopped breathing.

She turned to face him.

He took a step closer and could feel her body against him. He lifted her chin, leaned slowly down and kissed her. The kiss was unplanned. The intense feelings it evoked astonished him. When she put her arms around his neck and returned the kiss, his body hungered for more.

After a moment, cold fear of what Noah Pry might have done to Lysi invaded James's consciousness. He drew her even closer and swore to himself he would go to any extreme to keep her safe.

Chapter 23

James gazed out his office window at the vacant lot on the east side of the police station. His eyes softened at the sight of ground squirrels scurrying in and out of their holes in the thirsty summer grass. He hated sitting behind a desk, but he had finally squeezed in a few moments to complete a progress report on the Cristin Holden case and knew he had to force himself to concentrate. It galled him that the Chief of Police had instituted a new policy of written Case Progress Summaries that replaced the less time-consuming oral summaries required by previous administrators. It already took too much time away from investigations to do final summative reports, let alone progress updates. Sometimes he felt more like a clerk typist than a detective.

James's head shot up when a folder plopped onto the desk accompanied by a loud snort and the scent of Vicks VapoRub. He looked right into the bloodshot eyes of the Billings forensic pathologist who had just entered the room.

"Dr. Goldfein…I didn't hear you come in. Have a seat."

Dr. Goldfein pulled a handkerchief from his pocket and swiped at his pointy, red nose then folded it with care and returned it to his pocket.

"I can only sit a minute. I have an exhausting schedule today. Just wanted to get this report to you."

While James opened the folder, the short fine boned doctor perched on the edge of the chair like a scrawny sparrow ready to take flight at any second. He looked at James with an expression that said: *Get to it man. I don't have all day*. He kept scrunching his eyes shut then forcing them as wide open as possible. Finally, he pulled a small plastic bottle labeled eye drops from his shirt pocket, tipped his head back, squirted two drops in each eye and blinked several times.

James flipped through the report and scanned the main points. After a moment he raised questioning eyes to Dr. Goldfein who now kept a steady rhythm of impatient toe tapping on the floor. "Cause of death was *not* strangulation?"

"Nope. I assumed it was when I saw the condition of her neck, but the autopsy indicates cause of death was poison. The carotid artery was wide open. I found traces of toxic glycoside in the blood."

Dr. Goldfein popped a white tablet into his mouth. "Dyspepsia. I shouldn't have eaten those spicy links this morning."

Damn, I arrested the wrong man. The fact exploded in James's mind. He picked up a pencil and circled the phrase— "cause of death: poison." He knitted his brow and looked up at Dr. Goldfein.

"The autopsy states cause of death was poison, but I've got a man in jail who *confessed* to strangling her."

Dr. Goldfein leaned across the desk so he could see the report. His finger raced down the page and halted at the paragraph that described the bruises. He tapped his finger on the paragraph.

"There were bruises indicating attempted strangulation. That's true. But by the time choking occurred, the poison had already started to take effect. She would've died whether strangulation had occurred or not."

James recalled Noah's words. *She's kind of weaving a little bit, like she had a few*.

James stared at the Case Progress Report he'd started. He'd planned to declare the case closed, but now he had nothing. He believed Noah was where he should be, in custody. But now his confession didn't solve Cristin Holden's murder. He wadded the report into a tight ball and tossed it into the waste can across the room making a clean basket.

"Nice one," Dr. Goldfein said and stood.

"Thanks," James said in a distracted tone. His thoughts shifted to what he needed to do to keep Noah in jail. Clearly, Noah didn't murder Cristin Holden, but he did assault her. He would have assaulted Lysi if he figured he could've gotten away with it. He had to get that kid into some kind of facility where he could get help before he did murder someone.

He decided to hold Noah on sexual assault, trespassing and resisting arrest.

Dr. Goldfein interrupted his thoughts. "I'm on my way. Give me a call if you have any questions."

The detective watched the doctor position his gray felt Bowler squarely on his head. The downy red feather tucked in the grosgrain-band fluttered. James had always considered it quite remarkable that in a state where wide-brimmed Stetsons were the norm, Dr. Goldfein wore his Bowler everywhere—summer and winter. He told James he wore it to honor his membership in the Orange Order, a protestant group originating in Northern Ireland. James had never asked the fine doctor how a nice Jewish boy named Goldfein had managed to become an Orangeman, but he certainly was curious.

James liked Dr. Goldfein. The doctor's perpetual motion reminded him of the skittering little squirrels he'd watched in the woods as a child. Even his words seemed to skitter from his mouth. James always felt like he had to listen fast to keep pace with the conversation.

Just before Dr. Goldfein reached the door, James stopped him. "One quick question before you leave. Where does toxic glycoside come from?"

Dr. Goldfein halted and whipped his head around to face James. "Where *doesn't* it come from?" He sniffed and pulled out his handkerchief again. "There are several sources. It occurs abundantly in medicines like warfarin, coumarin and certain antibiotics; medications used in the treatment of congestive heart failure; some condiments and spices like saffron; plants, like foxgloves, hyacinths; nuts like almonds; vegetables like lima beans. You want me to go on?"

"No, no. I get it. It'll be pretty tough to trace."

Dr. Goldfein used his teeth to nip a hangnail on his thumb then scraped if off his tongue with his pinky. "There are different kinds of glycosides. Our lab can at least determine the kind of glycoside. That'd narrow the possible sources down a bit. It'll take a little time, though. There's quite a backup right now."

"I'd appreciate that information as soon as possible," James said.

"I'll let you know. Regards to your mother." The door swung shut.

Chapter 24

Lysi cracked open the door to the Sagebrush Café, but stopped short when she heard female voices shouting inside. She peered through the window in the door. The last of the breakfast crowd had gone. The café was empty and the Cheyenne busboy had already cleared most of the tables. Head bent to his work, his black eyes darted to Lysi, then returned to the mustard colored cleaning bucket.

KiKi Kavenaugh stood at the counter, stiff as a board, her back to Lysi, black spandex pants stretched embarrassingly tight across her caboose, a patch of skin exposed below the hem of her tank top. Jade faced her, slouched on the opposite side of the counter supported by her crossed arms, a smug grin on her luminescent red lips. A mug of coffee sat on the counter between the two combatants—in a sort of no man's land.

It occurred to Lysi that the two women must have the same hairdresser because their platinum blond curls dangled about their faces in exactly the same style, KiKi's secured by a red velvet ponytail clip; Jade's caught up in a ring of silk roses.

"You jealous slut, you lied to me," KiKi yelled at Jade. "I don't know why I believed you."

"Hey, I saw what I saw. Your precious Bill looked real satisfied limping out of Cristin Holden's room."

Jade's embellishing the story a bit, Lysi thought.

KiKi slammed her fist on the counter. Droplets of Jade's coffee splattered on the counter. "I'll tell you what you saw. You saw Hank Jones getting a freebie, not Bill."

Lysi sucked air. *Hank Jones*! The number on the white envelope zipped into her mind's eye. Maybe Hank's phone number on that paper wasn't just business related.

Jade jerked back in feigned terror. "My... my... KiKi, you do need to find your happy place."

"Me? You're the bitter old spinster. You've been jealous of me ever since high school when guys started dumping you for me. Why can't you get it? Men always take filet mignon—me," she jabbed at her chest with her thumb, "instead of warmed over chopped liver—you." She flipped her middle finger at Jade.

"Hey, you're still p.o.ed because I made cheerleader and you didn't. High school's long gone. Get over it!" Jade said.

"*I* had to study. Besides, everyone knew only morons went out for the cheerleading squad."

Jade's mouth flew open, ready with a comeback verbal punch.

Lysi stood stark still, listening at the door, debating whether to enter the fray or quietly retreat. She'd missed breakfast and had hoped for an early lunch. The aroma of fresh coffee mingled with the left over scent of fried hamburger and onions flooded through the crack in the door triggering insistent rumbles in her empty stomach. Hunger and curiosity won out.

Before Jade could throw her punch, Lysi jiggled the restaurant door several times to make the bells jangle louder and longer.

The two women jerked their heads toward the harsh metallic noise.

"Hi, Ladies." Lysi entered with caution. "I hope I'm not interrupting anything."

Jade and KiKi stared at her like two junior high girls caught in the school bathroom dissing their best friend.

Lysi closed the door. "Am I too early for lunch?"

"No, no." Jade's voice tightened. "What'll it be?"

"Cheeseburger and fries with a small OJ," Lysi said. She did not add, "Unless you happen to have a nice bowl of gazpacho and fresh sourdough."

Jade called the order to the fry cook who grumbled back, "Little early for lunch, ain't it?"

Lysi slid on to the barstool next to KiKi and managed a plastic smile. Jade swiped at the spilled coffee with a well-used sponge, barely missing KiKi who jumped back out of Jade's target area a split second before the sponge could baptize her pale pink tank.

Lysi cast an expressionless glance at Jade then KiKi. She had the impression these two had started battling it out in high school and, like an old married couple, had grown comfortable with continual bickering. She ventured, "I'm sorry, but I couldn't help overhearing a bit of your conversation."

Her words seemed to hang in the heavy atmosphere of the room for a long moment. Jade and KiKi exchanged hostile glares. Then, as if the gong for round two had clanged, the fighters reentered the ring.

"I'm not surprised, what with Thunder Mouth here." KiKi had forgotten she'd been the one yelling just before the doorbells jangled.

Lysi ignored the outburst. "KiKi, did I hear you say you saw Hank Jones here on the night of Cristin Holden's death?"

"Yeah, I came over because the mouth here—" She cast a venomous look at Jade. "—told me Bill was cheating on me with Holden, the visiting slut. I decided California Girl needed a little lesson on Montana etiquette."

Jade put her finger to her head, made circles and mouthed "crazy."

Lysi drew a controlled breath at KiKi's coarse reference to Cristin, although she'd noticed KiKi using that term almost as often as she blinked.

KiKi showed no embarrassment at having planned a jealous spectacle. In fact, she seemed to relish sharing the details of her plan.

"Right after Big Mouth called, I hauled on over here to see for myself. When I pulled into the lot, I spotted the Nerium car, so I parked behind the restaurant and waited for Bill to come out. But who comes out?" She paused, lifted her chin and bobbled her head from side to side, her springy tendrils almost twanging. "Little old Hanky Panky Jones."

Lysi remembered Hank nuzzling Carolyn's neck at the Festival. "At the Pow-Wow, it seemed Hank was pretty much enamored with Carolyn Norris. Are you sure it couldn't have been someone else?"

"Oh, it was Jonesy Boy all right. I saw him with my own eyes. I was right there watching because that gossipy, low class, greasy-spoon witch had called me on my cell and told me I'd better get over here because Billy had a new girlfriend. Not!"

Jade didn't say a word, but raised her eyebrows and tucked in her chin as if to say don't-be-too-sure.

Lysi stared at KiKi. If Hank and not Bill had made the late night visit to Cristin then KiKi's motive for murder had just evaporated into thin air. She crossed KiKi off her mental list of suspects.

"Shut up, Jade." KiKi looked like she wanted to smack Jade.

Jade howled with laughter. "I didn't say a word."

Lysi studied Jade for a long moment. She'd noticed Jade's head shifting back and forth between KiKi and her, as if watching a tennis match, waiting for a big score. *She's loving KiKi's tantrum.*

"I've always said Hank Jones is poison," KiKi continued. "He won't stick with one woman for long. He's probably had a piece of just about every good looking woman in this town." She jutted her chin in the direction of Jade. "He doesn't bother with the ugly ones."

"I don't believe he's had a piece of you," Jade said in a calm, irritating voice.

"I said close it, Jade!"

KiKi leaned closer to Lysi. "Anyhow, it's common knowledge that Carolyn's daddy bought Hankie for her."

"Bought him! What do you mean?" Lysi felt the trail of motives growing more tangled.

"Carolyn's father is a big shot at Nerium Corporate headquarters in California. The word is he's suddenly taken it into his head to promote Hankie Boy to Corporate Manager of Nerium Montana. I think we all know who put that bee in his bonnet. Hank owes Carolyn big time."

"Why would Hank risk all that for a one night stand?" Lysi asked.

"He figured he wouldn't get caught." KiKi shot Lysi the 'duh' look.

Lysi was beginning to feel like a rat in an endless maze. Every lead she got seemed to open more possibilities. She had yanked the lid off a Pandora's box. Needing time to sort things out, she asked Jade to pack her order to go and left the restaurant amid the hot cadence of KiKi's continuing verbal whipping.

*

Back in her room, Lysi sat at her desk and nibbled at the burger, her brain a whirlpool of unanswered questions. Clearly, she needed to tell James about Hank right away. She picked up her phone and punched in his cell number. When he answered, she blurted out the information with barely a hello.

"Hold on, Lysi. Are you telling me KiKi actually *saw* Hank Jones leave Cristin Olsen's room on the night of her death? I mean, not just his car, but Hank himself?"

"That's what she said."

"Could be she's covering for Bill," James said.

"I don't think so. If she'd caught Bill leaving Cristin's room, she'd have clawed him to pieces by now."

"I hear you. I appreciate the info. I'll follow up with KiKi."

Lysi started to ask about the suspect James had mentioned earlier. "How's your interrogation of the sus—

"Sorry, Lysi. Got to hang up. There's a call on my office line. Call you later."

Later didn't feel good to Lysi. She needed to do something now. Too many loose strings. Every time she thought she had one tied up, another one unraveled. She needed some structure, some organization. Chaos made her crazy.

She grabbed a pencil and scribbled names of possible suspects in a column on the left side of a yellow pad then labeled a second column: *Possible Motives*. The bottom half of the page she labeled: *Action Items*.

She tapped the first name on the list with the point of her pencil and pondered for several seconds. Noah Pry. He seems like a sad kid who would have stepped way out of his league if he tried sniffing around Cristin. Lysi recalled how he'd backed off at her raised voice when he came to her room the other evening. He probably would've reacted the same if Cristin told him to get lost.

Yet… he bragged to that Cheyenne kid, Honehe, that he'd taught Cristin a lesson. And, hadn't he had the colossal gall to barge into Lysi's room? She pictured the anger on his face when he said, *"Why do you act so nice, then spit in my face? You're just like her."* After a moment, Lysi wrote "humiliation" in the motive column next to Noah's name. Under *Action Items* she wrote: "talk to Noah."

She moved her pencil down to Bill Pitt's name.

Bill Pitt didn't do it. Lysi felt certain of that. She figured he had enough trouble trying to dodge KiKi's tantrums without igniting her temper with another woman. Besides, KiKi said the driver of the Nerium car outside Cristin's room wasn't Bill Pitt. Would she lie to save face?

Yet…Lysi underlined his name, he might have gotten drunk and followed Cristin to the motel after the reception. Maybe she threatened to file a sexual harassment complaint and put his job at risk. That would have struck fear in his heart. Lysi remembered the scared look on Bill's face when she told him she would help Denny Robbins file a complaint that could get him fired.

Bill's got a bad temper when he's had too much to drink. Could he have gotten so mad he…? Under *Possible Motive*, she wrote: "fear of losing job." Under *Action Items* she wrote: "ask James if Bill's alibi stood up."

Lysi stared at Elizabeth Scot's name and recalled her sad disclosures at the Festival—she loved Hank and hated the woman with whom he'd had an affair. Could Elizabeth have discovered Hank was involved with Cristin? Lysi paused then shook her head. *Elizabeth Scot would never hurt anyone.* She drew a line through her name then thought better of it and wrote under *Possible Motive*: "jealousy" and under *Action Items*: "ask Elizabeth Scot where she was on the night of the murder."

Lysi poked a couple of cold fries into her mouth and eyed the next person on the list. She wiped her fingers on a napkin then drew a hard circle around Hank Jones's name. She dropped the pencil on the desk, leaned back in the chair, locked her fingers behind her neck and stared at his name.

Hank's the kind of man who'd attract Cristin like a magnet. She'd have targeted him the moment she saw him. KiKi swears she saw him leave Cristin's room. It's likely he would have spent the evening with Cristin. But murder her? Could he have been afraid she would say something to Carolyn and jeopardize his promotion? Under *Possible Motive* she wrote: "to save promotion." She moved her pencil to the Action Item column, then dropped it and snapped open her cell.

Clearly she needed to know more about Hank Jones—and soon. She picked up the phone, dialed Hank's Nerium number and made an appointment with his secretary to meet with him in his office at 4:00 p.m.

Chapter 25

Lysi paused outside large mahogany doors and read the brassy four-inch letters—Human Resources. *Why is everything so excessive around here?*

She took out a compact and did the primp thing, then snapped it shut and gave herself a mental slap for giving a rat about how she looked for a meeting with a man like Hank Jones.

A take-charge approach was what she needed. She'd greet Hank then immediately take command of the discussion not allowing him to sidetrack her with his blatant flattery, a skill he'd probably mastered as a child. She'd confront him with questions about his relationship with Cristin, demand to know why he'd visited her on the night of the murder, maybe even accuse him. Then make a quick exit.

The antique brass doorknob felt cold in her hot hand. She took a resolute breath and pushed open the heavy door. The smell of new carpet, sparkle of glitzy lighting and drone of elevator music fell far short of Lysi's idea of elegance.

A porcelain-skinned brunette who could have just stepped out of a page in *Vogue* magazine, looked up from behind a glossy desk. A single crimson rose in a crystal vase shared one corner of the desk with a green marble nameplate on which the engraved letters spelled out "Paris Spyer, Administrative Assistant." The rest of the desktop was clear. Lysi saw no evidence of work in progress. Could Paris Spyer's function simply be eye candy in an already ostentatious office? This lady is almost too perfect. Just the kind of woman you'd expect Jones to hire.

Ms. Spyer's needle-sharp eyes inspected Lysi as if she were a prize heifer. "May I help you?" she said in a buttery alto voice. Her impeccably painted lips curved into a well-practiced smile.

"I'm Lysi Weston, here to see Mr. Jones." Ms. Spyer's cover girl perfection made Lysi feel like a reject from *Extreme Makeover*.

"Of course, he's expecting you." Spyer moved, graceful as a puma, to the door of Hank Jones's office and held it open for Lysi.

"Mr. Jones will return in about fifteen minutes. He said to have you wait in his office."

Jones's cavalier disregard of a four o'clock appointment with her annoyed Lysi.

With an elegant sweep of her hand Spyer motioned towards a chair in front of the desk. "Please make yourself comfortable. May I offer you a drink?"

"No thank you." Lysi caught the scent of expensive perfume when she passed by Paris Spyer to enter Hank's office.

Lysi glanced around. The office seemed to exude machismo. She stared at a replica of Manet's *Olympia* framed in antique gold on the wall above Hank's oversized faux leather swivel chair. It struck her that the French masterpiece of a reclining nude woman wearing only a black ribbon around her throat and a voluptuous pink hibiscus behind her ear was little more than Hank's version of a truck driver's girlie calendar. Her eyes wandered to a marble-topped credenza on which three cut-glass decanters filled with liquors sparkled in the sunrays streaming through a large octagonal-shaped picture window. She walked over and read the labels: bourbon, scotch and vodka. Strong medicine for a mama's boy.

Lysi started toward one of the shiny hardwood chairs facing Hank's mahogany executive desk, but stopped short when she heard a bubbling sound coming from the computer behind it. Her breathing increased when she remembered Elizabeth's words at the Festival, *There's something in Hank's e-mail you should see…. universal password…* change-it.

Licking her lips, she turned and squinted at the closed office door. Hank would return in fifteen minutes. That's long enough to check out a computer.

She slipped quickly behind the desk. An aquatic screensaver scene of listless tropical fish floated across the monitor.

A click of the mouse brought the computer to life. Hoping Hank had not input his new password, she moved the mouse to the Mail menu and typed *change-it* on the password line. The Mail Inbox popped up. A quick visual scan of the first page turned up Cristin Holden's name. Interesting.

Lysi highlighted the *From* column heading. Two seconds later her eyes widened in surprise. At least ten e-mails labeled Cristin Holden filled the screen and more appeared as she navigated downward.

Her eyes narrowed as she scanned the list. She had just started to open one message when she heard a sound. Her fingers froze on the keyboard and her eyes jerked to the door. Stark still, she waited.

Nothing.

Drawing a nervous breath to slow her runaway heartbeat and still her shaking hands, she turned back to the computer and opened a recent e-mail dated August 15th, one day before Cristin left for Montana.

Hi Hank, I'll arrive on Tuesday. Can't wait to see you. We'll have our usual private,

***hands-on* practicum after the seminar. Cristin**

Lysi stared at the screen. Cristin knew him *before* she came to Sage Deer. She had a history with him. Why hadn't she ever mentioned him? Is he the reason she pushed so hard for this assignment?

More curious than ever, Lysi opened Hank's Sent window and scanned for his response.

Panic halted her fingers in mid air when she heard the voices of Paris Spyer and Hank on the other side of the closed door.

Hands trembling, she hit command Q and the mail window disappeared. She sprinted from behind the desk, landed on one of the wooden chairs, and whispered a silent prayer that the fish screen saver would kick in before Hank went behind his desk.

An instant later, the door opened. Lysi bounced to her feet, a little too quickly and turned around as Hank spoke.

"Lysi, how nice to see you."

Hank stood at the open door. The statuesque Miss Spyer stood next to him, her hand on the knob, sharp eyes glued to Lysi. Pearls of sweat percolated onto Lysi's upper lip. Does Spyer suspect something? How long can it take those damn fish to start gurgling?

In as casual a tone as she could manage, Lysi said, "Hank, I didn't hear you come in. It's a pleasure to see you again, too."

Trying to keep up the small talk so Hank wouldn't notice the absence of the screen saver's bubbly sound, she rambled on. "I know how busy you are. You have such a demanding job. Such a big corporation. How do you do it? I promise not to take much of your time."

An overly sweet smile of relief spread across Lysi's lips as the bubbly sound of the aquatic screensaver gurgled up.

"Take as much time as you like. It's always a delight to meet with an attractive woman." He looked at her in a way that made her want to check to see if she'd forgotten to button her blouse. "Please sit down."

Lysi sat on one of the chairs in front of the desk, expecting him to join her, but he strode to the couch instead.

"I was just admiring your computer. It's the latest Mac, isn't it?"

Hank flashed his disarming smile, dimples dancing, eyes fawning. "Yes, the company takes good care of me." He seemed not to suspect her of snooping. "But I'm sure you don't want to bother your pretty little head with boring old techie guy stuff."

Lysi gritted her teeth and swallowed a thorny comeback. She executed a cute little sideways tilt of her head. "Hank, you do indeed understand us little women, don't you?"

Hank beamed. Lysi could hardly believe he didn't see right through her sarcastic comment.

He sank into the overstuffed couch. "Won't you join me over here? It's more comfortable." He patted the cushion as though she were a pet cocker spaniel expected to bound onto the couch next to him and put her chin on his knee.

"I'm fine here." She turned her head towards the masterpiece turned girlie calendar. "I see you're a fan of Manet."

"I'm a fan of Olympia," he said, an artificial hoarseness in his voice, eyes caressing the young woman's body. He inhaled.

"Please, I insist you join me. I sit at that desk all day long. At least allow me a few moments respite with a charmingly beautiful woman. Come." He patted the cushion again. "Actually, my painting is better viewed from further away."

Lysi got up and sat down next to him. No harm sitting on the couch. May as well quell his whining and get down to business.

"Now what's this big, important topic you needed to discuss with me?" He put his hand on her shoulder, ran it down her arm and squeezed her hand.

Paris still stood at the door watching the action on the couch. When Hank looked up at her with an irritated expression she said, "Will there be anything else, Mr. Jones?"

"No thank you, Paris. Please close the door on your way out and hold all calls." He looked back at Lysi, hand still cupped over hers.

Hank's momentary distraction gave Lysi a chance to gather her thoughts. She looked down at his hand and forced a laugh that came off too loudly. "I see my seminar didn't help you any."

He jerked his hand away. The dimples disappeared. Eyes turned metallic. Voice turned icy. "What did you want to talk to me about?"

This man cannot tolerate any kind of rebuff, Lysi mused. "How well did you know Cristin Holden?"

With the ease of a snake slithering through grass Hank lied. "I met her for the first time in Staff Development on Tuesday when she reported for duty." He raised his eyebrows and grinned. "She was quite a woman."

Lysi paused before her next question. He's an expert liar. But why is he lying?

"Why did you visit her on the night she died?"

"Who told you that?" His smile vanished and his eyes hardened again.

"You were at the Big Sky. You were seen leaving her room."

Hank stood and started toward the door. "I don't have to answer to you or anyone else about where I go and what I do on my own time. Now if you'll excuse me, I have another appointment."

Lysi hadn't expected such a strong reaction. She stared at him, wondering why he had responded so vehemently.

Then she knew.

She stood and looked hard into his eyes. "Congratulations on your promotion. I'm sure it means a lot to you. You'd probably go to any extreme to avoid jeopardizing it."

"What are you getting at?" A muscle beneath his eye started to twitch.

"Come on, Hank. It's common knowledge Carolyn's father is promoting you. It would be a big problem for you if Carolyn found out about your little tryst with Cristin and told Daddy all about it."

Hank raised his voice and his anger rocketed to rage. "Are you implying I murdered Cristin Holden to keep her from talking to Carolyn? That's ridiculous! Cristin didn't even know about the promotion arrangement. She planned to fly out Thursday without returning to Nerium."

Lysi lowered her voice and spoke in slow, concise words. "All she had to do was pick up the phone and call the right person. Your hope of promotion would have evaporated."

"You're not hearing me. Cristin knew nothing about any promotion and even if she did, she wouldn't give a damn. She—" Hank clamped his mouth shut as though he realized he'd already said too much. He yanked out a handkerchief and swiped at his wet forehead.

"Go on, Hank. She what?"

"Look lady, I'm no murderer, but if I was, Cristin Holden wouldn't be the kind of woman I'd pick for my victim." He shot Lysi a fiery look, sending a clear message that she'd qualify as his victim of preference.

"Good day, Ms. Weston." Hank Jones had his hand on the knob of the inner office door.

Lysi sauntered toward him. She knew she'd struck a tender chord and decided to deliver another blow.

"Oh, just one more thing. Why would Cristin have your direct telephone number on her bed stand in the motel?"

He blinked and opened his mouth but didn't speak. His hand dropped from the knob.

Heady with success, Lysi pressed her advantage. "Why would she have your personal e-mail address in her laptop?"

174

Lysi didn't know if his address was in Cristin's laptop because it had been confiscated as crime scene evidence, but she had seen Cristin's name on the sender line of several e-mails in Hank's computer.

The color drained from Hank's face. She decided to let the brew she'd created ferment a bit and walked silently from Hank's office leaving the door wide open. As she passed Paris Spyer's desk she turned back to Hank and said in a throaty voice for the benefit of Paris, "Bye, Hank. Until later." She smiled, puckered her lips in a little air kiss, raised one eyebrow and jiggled three fingers at Hank's reddening face.

Lysi felt Paris's stare stabbing her in the back as she crossed the large outer office to the main door. She glanced over her shoulder at Paris who quickly dropped her eyes to the computer screen.

*

Lysi sat in the Nerium parking lot and thought about Elizabeth Scot's access to all Nerium's computers. She probably read the e-mails. She must have known Cristin was the woman who had stolen Hank from her. Cristin was the woman she hated. Now Lysi could see Elizabeth had a strong motive for murdering Cristin. *But, why would she incriminate herself by telling me about the e-mails?*

Lysi picked up her cell phone and punched in the Nerium number. The voice of the receptionist purred, "Nerium Telecommunications. How may I direct your call?"

"Elizabeth Scot, Information Technology, please."

A second later a tired, stressful voice answered. "Nerium Corporation Information Technology, Elizabeth Scot speaking."

"Elizabeth, this is Lysi. You were right. What I found in Hank Jones's e-mail did interest me. I didn't have the chance to read the messages, though. Did you get a chance to read them?"

"No. I don't read e-mails. I just thought it strange to see Ms. Holden's name so many times in the From column. Do you think you can get a warrant to read them?"

"Maybe," Lysi said.

How strange that Elizabeth would try to dig herself in deeper by involving the police. None of this makes sense. She decided to come right out and ask Elizabeth about her whereabouts on the night of the murder. "Where were you on last Tuesday night, Elizabeth?"

Lysi listened to a long pause on the other end of the line.

"Elizabeth, are you there?"

"Sorry, Lysi. I'm just so shocked that you'd ask that question; that you'd suspect me."

"I don't suspect you," Lysi lied. "I'm trying to prevent you from becoming a suspect in case the word gets out that you had a previous relationship with Jones and that Cristin might have infringed on that relationship."

"I see."

Lysi could hear the hurt in Elizabeth's voice.

"I was with Denny Robbins in the Sagebrush Café trying to convince him to talk to the sexual harassment seminar leader, you, about the terrible abuse he'd been experiencing. Jade Green was there. She can vouch for us. We were there past her shift. She even stayed over time so we could finish talking."

Lysi felt terrible. "I'm sorry if I hurt you. It's just that I'm driven to find out who did this horrible thing to my partner. I have to follow every lead. I like you, Elizabeth. You can't imagine what a relief it is to me to know you have an alibi."

Again there was a long pause on Elizabeth's end of the line.

Finally, Lysi said, "I hope you understand. Goodbye."

Lysi leaned her head back against the car seat and closed her eyes. She hoped Elizabeth understood she has to consider everyone a suspect. Suddenly her eyes flew wide open. Does Carolyn know about Hank and Cristin? Should she add her to the list of suspects? No, Carolyn is a much smaller woman than Cristin. She wouldn't have the strength to strangle her. Besides, Lysi was sure KiKi hadn't told Carolyn about Hank's night visit to Cristin. First, KiKi would've bragged about it if she had. Second, she wouldn't risk her job at Nerium by upsetting the CEO's daughter.

Chapter 26

James woke up Tuesday morning with a sour feeling in his stomach thinking about a current case involving a disagreement between a Cheyenne woman and her white husband over two children. Having no place to go when the husband forced her out of their family home, the wife had moved back to the reservation. Her husband refused to allow her to take the two children. James had the unpleasant job of picking up some custody dispute documents from the Billings 13th District Court.

James hated being involved in divorce custody cases between Cheyennes and whites. They always ended up in messy court proceedings. Deep down, he thought in this case the children would be better off with their mother on the reservation, though he could never express that opinion.

He glanced out the bedroom window at a couple of kids and a black dog ambling along a field path at summer-vacation speed. The sun shone softly through a thin cloud cover, promising a moderately warm day. He wished he could amble along with them.

A woven Cheyenne basket on his bedroom bureau reminded him of the Dance Festival last Sunday and how much he enjoyed taking Lysi.

Since he had some free time after his court visit, he decided to invite her to ride along to Billings. He could show her some of his favorite Montana spots, get to know her a little better, reveal a little more about himself.

When she picked up the phone he said, "I have to make a trip to Billings. Do you think you could take time out of your busy day to join me?"

"Very funny. The highlight of my crowded daily agenda's rereading the Sage Deer Weekly—Thanks to you detaining me."

James forced a laugh, not sure how to take her last comment.

"I'd like to show you some of the local sights tourists often miss, like Pompey's Pillar and the Pictograph Caves. I thought we'd get off the main road and see some of the countryside." Before she could refuse, he quickly added, "I'd really like you to see the Montana I love."

"I've heard of Pompey's Pillar. That's where Lewis, or was it Clark engraved his name in the stone, isn't it?"

He felt more confident when she showed interest. "Whoa, I'm impressed you know about our famous Pillar. Not everyone does. William Clark carved his name there when he passed through the Yellowstone Valley on his way back to St. Louis."

"I knew it was one of them."

His gaze returned to the window. It framed a field of the silvery green sagebrush he loved. He guessed sagebrush couldn't compete with the lushness of a San Francisco garden like Golden Gate Park. But since he'd already invited her, he decided it would be worth pressing a little anyway. "Well, what do you say?"

"Thanks. I'd really love a little off-the-trail tourism."

*

James didn't take the interstate to Billings, but instead followed a network of secondary roads. They drove through rolling hills of rust-colored grain past isolated farmhouses shaded by stands of cottonwood and aspen trees. Black Angus cattle gathered at waterholes and colts scampered after sleek mares. Lysi asked questions about everything.

After they had traveled several miles, she turned to James. "Now tell me the things you love most about Montana."

"Easy. I love the clean air, changes of seasons, room to move around, people who go out of their way for you, and—the sunsets."

Lysi laid a hand on his. "Montana means a lot to you, doesn't it?"

Her touch stirred passions that had long lain dormant. A rush of feelings tumbled through James's head. He wanted to tell her how she'd resurrected his dead emotions. Emotions he had buried in order to survive the death of his wife. He wanted to tell her how he'd lived from day to day before he met her, but now looked forward to a future. He wanted to tell her he might be ready to try to love again— to risk loving her. Instead, he pointed to a well-aged windmill. "That old mill's been there for over a hundred years and still works."

Lysi admired the windmill and James admired Lysi.

*

James had appreciated Lysi's interest in the 2100 year-old Pictograph Cave with its collection of Stone Age artifacts and paintings. The cool cave had felt comfortable out of the heat of a Montana summer day.

It was quite another story at Pompey Pillar. When he saw perspiration running down her face and wet hair sticking to her brow, he almost wished he hadn't taken her on the hot hike up the winding path to the top of the Pillar.

Back in the car, Lysi mopped her brow with an already-damp tissue, flipped the air conditioner on high and directed all the fans towards her sweltering body. "I'm not used to this heat," she gasped; then gulped down a full pint of bottled water.

"Montana summer heat is tough on the natives. It must be unbearable for someone from foggy San Francisco. I'm sorry." James tried not to stare at the sweat-soaked bodice of her silk dress clinging tenaciously to her breasts. Another kind of heat stirred his body and he self-consciously glanced at his lap.

Lysi surprised him when she grabbed another bottle of water and turned a scarlet face toward him. "I'll have my revenge. Watch your backside."

He laughed and started the drive back to Sage Deer.

*

After Lysi's core temperature had moderated to below boiling, she broached the topic of the investigation. "Did Bill Pitt's alibi check out?"

"Pretty much. It's possible, but unlikely Pitt would've had time to see Cristin before he went to visit his son."

"What about Noah Pry? Is he still a suspect?"

James furrowed his brow. "It's strange. Noah confessed to choking Cristin but"—

"I *knew* it was Pry," Lysi said.

"Lysi, I haven't finished. But…the Billings forensic report states poison as cause of death not strangulation. Now the case is a little more thorny. I—"

"Poison! What about the first report you told me about? There must've been indications of strangulation. Are you saying she was strangled *and* poisoned?" Lysi spoke in a higher pitch than usual, hands flying, eyes blinking rapidly.

James touched her shoulder. "I know this is hard for you. You want this to be over. So do we."

"If it's unlikely that Noah Pry or Bill Pitt committed the crime, then you have no solid suspects." Lysi looked bewildered. "If neither of them, then who?"

"We don't know yet. Here's what we do know—Noah Pry came to Cristin's room and attempted to assault her. When she resisted, he tried to quiet her with a Judo choke."

"Judo choke. What's that?"

"A kind of hold to induce unconsciousness. The bruises from that choke made us conclude strangulation caused her death. Led us to Pry. The Billings report blew strangulation out the window. Now we know the cause of death was poison. I'm waiting to find out the kind and source. From that I'll trace the person who had access to the poison and from there, the murderer. We have no solid suspects right now."

"What about Hank Jones?"

Lysi's voice sounded desperate as she told James what she'd discovered on Hank's computer and that she'd told Hank a witness had seen him leave Cristin's room on the night of her death.

It surprised James when Lysi told him about the computer, but it shocked him to hear she'd confronted Jones with KiKi's accusation of having seen him leave Cristin's motel room on the night of the murder.

An image of the handsome sophisticated Hank Jones flooded his brain. Alarmed and irritated, he pulled the car over to the side of the road, stepped hard on the brake and skidded on the gravel, causing them both to lurch forward. A cloud of dust settled behind the car. In a tautly controlled voice, he lectured her in a way he knew might jeopardize their friendship, but he had to make her understand the dangerous game she was playing.

"You put yourself at risk by interrogating a suspect. Once a murderer has killed, he has little to lose by killing again."

He hoped to close the subject once and for all by adding, "I am the detective. I am trained to take risks—*paid* to take risks—not you."

Lysi looked like he'd slapped her face. He figured his words had hit home.

She glared at him as though he had deliberately insulted her intelligence. "I'm not stupid. I didn't go to some deserted place to talk with him. I was in his office and his secretary was right outside the door."

"You put the investigation at risk."

"How?"

"You alerted Jones that he might become a suspect. Now we've lost the element of surprise. Now he's got time to work up an alibi. Look Lysi, I'm trying to investigate a murder. I can't be chasing around trying to keep amateur sleuths from getting themselves killed. I don't want to say it again—Stay out of this case!"

James knew part of his intense reaction had its roots in his growing feelings for Lysi, his desire to shield her from possible harm. He also knew that his barrage of harsh words might have damaged their relationship. What choice did he have? He had to stop her meddling.

Lysi stared at him without speaking, hot color flooding her cheeks, eyes burning. He could not read her expression. Anger? Hurt? Humiliation? Defiance? When she turned her head away to the window, he wondered if he'd come across more angry than professional. He wanted desperately to mend fences, but his mind went blank. He didn't know what to say or do. He considered getting out of the car and slamming his head against the hood. That idea seemed neither practical nor productive, so he just started the car and drove.

*

The sun drifted toward the horizon casting long shadows over the low hills. Lysi had not spoken since he'd pulled back on the road. He glanced over to see if she might have dozed off. She seemed to be gazing out the car window at the passing panorama of colors, muted by the gradual dimming of the sky.

The steady motion of the car in the quiet countryside seemed to have lulled her into a calmer state. Her hands lay open in her lap, no longer clenched in tight fists. He wanted to apologize for his harsh tone, but decided this was not the right time.

After an hour of silent driving, he pulled into the Big Sky Motel parking lot. Before he could get out to open the car door for her, she grabbed the handle, opened the door and jumped out.

"Thanks for the tour." She closed the door before he could say a word.

Her anger didn't surprise him. She's not the kind of woman you can command...too sensitive...unreasonable...stubborn. He should be glad he discovered her real character before they got further involved.

"Fine!" He backed the car out of the lot and sped away from what might have been a new beginning for him.

*

Lysi sat on the bed staring out the window at the hypnotic progression of bright headlights alternating with red taillights streaming by on the highway. James's words pounded in her head—*I can't be chasing around keeping amateurs from getting killed. Stay out of this case. Don't want to say it again...Stay out...Stay out...Stay out.*

How dare he speak to her as though she were an errant child. What he said was bad enough, but his tone was unforgivable—curt, irritated and final.

She got up and tried to pace, but there wasn't enough free area in the small room for her long stride. Frustrated, she plopped onto a chair. It upset her that she had no one to talk to about his arrogant behavior. If only she could pick up the phone and call Cristin. Cristin—her colleague, her confidant, her friend. How is it possible that James didn't understand her need to find her friend's killer?

The phone rang. She jumped then stared at it for a moment. Could James be calling to apologize? Well, she would accept his apology and cooperate with him to find Cristin's killer, but that's all. Forget everything else.

"Hello."

"Lysi, you left your shawl in the car. I'll bring it by tomorrow morning on the way to work." James clipped his words.

"Thank you for letting me know. Just drop it at the reception desk."

"I can do that. Bye." His voice was cold.

"Bye." *Good. I think he got the message.* Her chest felt empty.

Then James's words returned. Not the same words as before. Sensible words—*trying to investigate a murder...You alerted Jones...lost the element of surprise...gave him time to work up an alibi.* Concerned words—*You put yourself at risk...murderer has nothing to lose by killing again...put yourself at risk...at risk.*

Now it all made sense. James was scared for her, not just worried about his case. He wanted to find Cristin's killer as much as she did. How could she have misunderstood? She wasn't listening. She was wrong. He was right.

Now it was too late. He got her message alright—"We're finished."

Chapter 27

Lysi stood outside the door of the motel reception area and watched James pull into the lot and park. As he got out of the car, she hurried over and opened the passenger door. She noticed the look of confused surprise on his face.

"You must really be in a big hurry to get this shawl back."

He handed her the neatly folded shawl and crossed his arms tightly over his chest, his expression aloof.

"No. No that's not it. Look, you're on your way to work right now. This is a bad time, but I'd really like to talk to you. Any possibility of meeting somewhere for a drink when you're off duty?"

He unfolded his arms. "I guess. I'll call you when I leave the department."

She watched his car move into traffic and disappear. His lack of enthusiasm had disappointed her. What did she expect? She'd stung him with callous words. She hoped she hadn't stepped over that onerous line that would take tons of work to cross back again.

*

Hours later, Lysi choked the phone with an angry fist as she waited for James's explanation for contacting her at ten p.m. Did he think she wanted to crawl back to him?

His voice sounded tired.

"Trouble on the reservation. Three Billings guys mixed it up with some reservation boys. I had to go."

"You could've called."

"I did call. Twice. I left messages both times."

She started to insist he hadn't called when she remembered she'd turned her mobile phone off so she could have a short rest before meeting with him. How could she have forgotten that? Why didn't she check her messages? Why hadn't she given him the benefit of the doubt? She had to get out of Sage Deer before she fell completely apart.

"I'm sorry. I had my phone off. I guess all this is getting to me. We can talk another time."

After a long pause he said, "Whatever you want. But if it's not too late for you, I'd like to hear what you have to say."

"You mean come tonight? What time would that be?"

"I'm here right now. Look out your window."

She went to the window. He'd turned on his interior light and sat looking at her with his phone to his ear. The thought crossed her mind that he seemed pretty self-assured. This was the second time he'd taken it upon himself to just show up. She thought of all the reasons she should say no—Ten o'clock is late. She's tired. He's presumptuous.

"Okay," she said.

*

Lysi slipped into James's car and closed the door but didn't speak immediately. Strains of Kenny G's mellow saxophone floated from the car stereo. James leaned back in the seat, stretching out his long legs. He turned toward her but seemed to have nothing to say. Maybe he was waiting for her to begin.

She inhaled and decided to test the water. "I could sure use a cup of coffee. How about you? The Sagebrush is still open."

Seeing him hesitate, she reasoned that he must be tired after his long day and wanted to get to bed. She could understand that. Still, she wanted to tell him she overreacted yesterday. Apologize. Make him understand her stress level. "I hope the case closes soon, so I can return to San Francisco."

He turned disappointed eyes toward her. "Is that what you wanted to tell me?"

"I do need to get home as soon as possible. I know Cristin's death will mean big changes for me, both in my job and my personal life." Her voice sounded distant, as though her mind had already traveled back to San Francisco.

He grasped the door handle. "It's late. Coffee probably wouldn't be a good idea."

She touched his arm. "That's not what I wanted to say." She swallowed hard. "I wanted to say…I understand you're upset about me poking into your job, that…you don't need me making your job harder that…I'm sorry I flew off the handle…I—"

He reached over and took her face in both hands and kissed her forehead. "I should have been more understanding about what you're going through."

The kiss lifted a ten-ton weight off Lysi's shoulders. She could hardly believe he forgave her so easily—even took part of the blame. She wanted to throw her arms around this man and never let him go. Instead, she smiled. "Thank you."

After a moment she said, "You're right, it is too late for coffee. I never take caffeine after eight at night unless I'm behind on a job with a deadline the next day. But—"

James opened his door. "I agree. Coffee wouldn't work for me either. Thanks for meeting with me. If you're okay with it, I'll call you tomorrow. I think we have more to talk about."

As he started to slide out of the car, Lysi tapped him on the shoulder and finished the sentence he had interrupted. "But…I do enjoy a small liqueur after a big day. It helps me unwind and relax. Any place we might get one?"

A grin spread across his face but quickly changed to a frustrated frown. "I wish there was. Here in Sage Deer, everything closes early on week nights."

Then he raised one eyebrow and said, "I do know of a small place that'd stay open all night for you. Interested?"

"Sure. I guess so."

"I call it James's Joint. The owner stocks a pretty good variety of liqueurs."

"How far is James's Joint?" she asked with a twinkle in her eye.

"It's about twelve minutes from here."

"Let's do it," she said without hesitation.

*

James couldn't hide the flood of feelings as he slammed the car door, switched on the ignition and plowed out of the parking lot thinking, I haven't had an adventure like this in years. I don't know where it's going, but I'm ready for anything.

He drove without speaking, eyes straight ahead, enjoying the moments. She seemed comfortable with her own reflections. He was glad she didn't ask him what he was thinking. When a woman did that, it always threw him off balance because most of the time his thoughts were random. He was particularly glad she didn't ask him at this moment because his thoughts weren't just unfocused, they were roaring around and crashing into each other, filling his head with ambivalence. Why did she accept an invitation to his place so easily? Maybe she's into one-night stands. She travels a lot. Maybe she's got guys all over the country.

He glanced at her. She's not acting seductive. She's acting like a friend. Granted, she looks seductive with that lacy shawl slipping off her shoulder and those strands of hair curling on the back of her neck. Maybe a one-night stand would be an experience. On the other hand, she probably knows I'm not an instant intimacy kind of guy. Women are perceptive about that kind of stuff. Besides, she's talked to Jade who knows everything there is to know about me. Maybe she feels pretty safe. I guess if something happens, it happens.

He grinned.

*

James pulled into the driveway of his two-story house. "Here we are."

He parked the car in front of a small, detached garage. When they got out of the car, a motion sensor switched on a light at the top of a tall pole, revealing a cobblestone path that traversed an informal wild flower garden. The path ended at two steps leading to a front porch that extended the full length of the brown-shingled house. They followed the well-lit path to the porch.

He opened the door and invited her into a pine-paneled living room. He motioned to a tan leather couch opposite a ceiling-high, river-rock fireplace with tall bookcases on each side. "Have a seat."

"James's Joint is pretty classy," Lysi said.

James grinned at her reference to his earlier attempt at humor. "I bought this house because I needed a place to quarter my two daughters when they come to visit and because it's close to my job. It's really more space than I need: a master bedroom and three guest bedrooms not to mention a formal dining room I never use."

Lysi looked around. "Very nice."

James picked up a lacy envelope from the coffee table and handed it to her. "My mother asked me to give this to you. I meant to bring it along yesterday but I forgot. It's an invitation to tea. She was quite taken with you."

"She's charming. I'm delighted she invited me."

Lysi pointed to a photo on the wall. "That looks like an old photograph."

"Those are my maternal grandparents. I spent several summers in England with them when I was growing up. My mother believed I needed some civilizing to balance my Wild West upbringing."

He placed two liqueur glasses on the dark oak coffee table, then opened the cut glass doors of a well-stocked liquor cabinet. "What can I offer you?"

Lysi spotted the long-necked, fat-bottomed, amber bottle of her favorite liqueur, immediately. "Grand Marnier would be delicious."

He poured her a Grand Marnier and himself a cognac then settled down next to her on the couch. "To a great evening." They clinked glasses and took a sip of their drinks.

Lysi set her glass on the table and turned a serious face to James. As she spoke, he forced himself to listen without comment, determined not to repeat his earlier mistakes.

"James, are you aware of the Denny Robbins' sexual harassment issue?"

James considered for a moment. "Not really. I've heard a few disparaging remarks about his being homosexual, that's about all."

"He's been receiving ugly notes and pictures. Some of them came from Bill Pitt."

"Why am I not surprised?" James set his drink on the table.

"The last two notes were death threats. They didn't come from Pitt. I'm almost certain they came from Choki…Noah Pry."

"Has Robbins reported the threats?"

She shook her head. "Only to me and Elizabeth Scot, a woman he works with." She hurried on before James could interrupt. "From what I gather, Noah has some pretty serious psychological problems. If he's capable of threatening Denny, I think he's capable of murdering Cristin. He could have poisoned her."

"It's possible. Certainly Pry needs long-term treatment," James said.

Choosing his words carefully, James tried to end the discussion. Listen Lysi, we can't even discuss this until we get the information on the poison. When we know that, we'll work on tracking down the person who had access to it."

He picked up Lysi's drink and handed it to her. "Can you put your sleuthing on hold until we have more information?"

She took her drink and nodded. "But just one more thing about Cristin's murder—I can't help thinking there are some pieces of the puzzle missing. I—"

James took the drink from her hand and set it back on the table. "Lysi, the last thing I want to talk about right now is work."

He put his arm around her and moved closer. He felt her sharp intake of breath and knew she wanted him as much as he wanted her.

He smoothed his big hands over her warm shoulders and let his fingers slip under her dress straps then leaned over and pressed his lips to hers. He felt her rising response and parted her lips in a deep kiss. An intense need consumed him and he tightened his embrace.

Suddenly, breathing hard, she pushed away from him, leaving him confused, his heart pounding with unfulfilled desire. For a moment he could only stare at her as she left the couch and stood in front of him.

A heat, like whiskey, surged through his veins when she unbuttoned her dress, and let it slip to the floor. He caught his breath as her inviting body filled his senses. When she slid into his arms and returned his kiss, his body jerked as the sensation from her tongue shot through him. She let herself fall back on the couch, her breathing deep and uneven. He pressed himself against her, kissing her neck and shoulders; tasting, touching, exploring every part of her. He thought only of satisfying an insatiable hunger as their bodies dissolved into each other in a frantic, rhythmic, grasping for pleasure.

*

The next morning, Lysi woke to the flutelike warbling of meadowlarks in the field behind James's house. She rolled over in the cool sheets and gazed at the hollow in the pillow next to her. She reached over and smoothed the back of her hand over it. Contented as a cream-fed cat, she replayed last night's lovemaking in her mind. This was one great streetcar ride. A rush of desire ignited a heat wave that navigated upward, setting fire to her face.

When the bedroom door opened, Lysi jumped.

James walked in with a full breakfast tray—boiled eggs, little sausage links, scones spread with lemon curd, and a teapot covered with a blue and white striped tea cozy.

"Hey, Sleepy Head, it's about time you woke and—" A lascivious smile spread across his lips as he took in her flushed face. "Maybe we should skip breakfast and—"

Slightly embarrassed she said, "No way. I'm starving."

"Yes…but for what?" James set the tray on the bed stand and studied her face. He reached under the sheet and smoothed his hand over her breasts. "For what? Hmmm?"

After a sharp intake of breath she said, "Food, I'm starving for food."

In a smooth, lingering motion he slid his hand back across her breasts and out from under the sheet. "Alright. I can see your priority is your stomach."

After she scrambled into a sitting position, James picked up the tray and set it on her lap. "I know you liked the Cowboy Bonanza Special at the Sagebrush Café, so, here's the English version."

He took a bite of link sausage. "Mmm! Good, if I do say so myself." He held it so Lysi could take a bite, handed her a fork, and they both nibbled at the scones.

"It's wonderful, but I shouldn't eat too much. I have to watch my girlish figure."

James let his eyes wander over the outline of her body under the sheet. "You eat. I'll watch your figure."

When they finished, James took the tray and set it on the bed stand. "This is a great morning after."

Looking at her with a different kind of hunger, he slid between the sheets.

Chapter 28

James dropped Lysi at the Big Sky Motel on his way to work. Lysi noticed Jade leaning across the Sagebrush Cafe counter, watching. "I see we have an audience."

"Right," James said. "Jade's hobby is knowing everybody's business." He touched Lysi's hand. "I'll give you a call after I get off work. I'd really like to continue where we left off this morning." He raised both eyebrows a couple of times and a contented grin captured his face.

Lysi felt her cheeks redden. She could see from James's expression that he noticed. "I think I can work you into my schedule." She squeezed his hand.

Lysi darted into her room.

Giddy as a teenager, she studied her crimson face in the mirror and relived James's insistent kisses. She crossed her arms, massaged her shoulders and recalled the smooth texture of James's skin and his strong arms locking her close to him.

She had turned away from the mirror and was trying to prolong her intense feelings a little longer, when Denny's envelope of abusive pictures, still on the desk, caught her eye. She remembered James saying Denny had to report his sexual harassment problem himself.

She knew James was right, but down deep she also knew Denny wouldn't report for fear Bill Pitt and his cronies would heap even more misery on him. She picked up the envelope and stared at it, trying to think of a way to help Denny. She'd almost reached frustration level when an idea struck her. She clicked open her cell phone, called Pitt and set a meeting with him for seven p.m. at the Sagebrush.

After the call, she tried to take her mind off recent events. She slipped off her shoes, stretched out on the bed and picked up the novel she had purchased in Billings while James was in the courthouse.

The insistent warbling of the motel phone interrupted her reading. Who would call her on that phone? Choki? She considered not answering, but curiosity got the best of her.

Hank's tense voice sounded conciliatory. "Lysi, I need to clarify a few things, but I can't do it over the phone. Could you come to my office for a few minutes?"

Lysi checked her watch. She'd accepted the invitation for afternoon tea from James's mother and needed to be at the Wild Flower Inn by three o'clock. She didn't want to be late, but the urgency in Hank's tone convinced her to meet with him. "I can be at your office at one."

"Fine. Thank you." He hung up.

When Lysi heard the dial tone, her mind filled with misgivings. She knew James would object to her continuing to investigate the murder. Wait. Why did she think Hank's call had something to do with the murder? After all, she really had no idea why he wanted to see her. Isn't it just as likely he wanted to debrief on the seminar? That's probably it.

She sunk into a functional armchair and read a few more chapters of her novel. After a quick sandwich at the Sagebrush she returned to her room. She slid open the mirrored closet door and looked at the two dresses she had packed for the trip.

"Like there's a choice," she said. She had already worn the yellow sundress to breakfast at the Wild Flower Inn. So after a shower, she slipped into the lilac dress she'd chosen for the festival and covered the spaghetti straps with a matching jacket. She twirled around in front of the mirror. *This looks like a prim and proper tea ensemble.*

The instant she opened the motel room door, a blast of midday heat engulfed her and sent rivulets of perspiration cascading down her body. She peeled off her jacket to keep it from turning into a wet dishrag. Once in the car, she laid the jacket on the back seat, turned on the cooler full blast and drove to Nerium.

When she entered the staff development office, Paris Spyer's appraising eyes swept over her. Lysi's ego soared. Could it be this gorgeous young woman might envy her appearance? But her self-esteem took a serious dip as she followed Paris's stare to her spaghetti strapped bodice with its inappropriately revealing décolletage. She had left her prim little jacket in the car.

Paris raised a disdainful eyebrow as if to say, "We dress for business here, not barhopping."

Oh God, I bet she thinks I wore this dress for Hank. Lysi considered explaining she had dressed for the 3:00 tea and had worked this meeting in, but decided she didn't owe any explanation. She watched Paris levitate from her chair and float to the inner office door. "Mr. Jones is expecting you."

Hank unfurled from his desk as though lifting a heavy load. His face was drawn, eyes red. He swallowed and in a thick voice thanked Lysi for coming.

Paris stood with her hand on the doorknob scrutinizing Hank's every move.

"Please join me on the couch."

At first Lysi was going to balk, figuring Hank wanted to get her to the couch so he could charm her out of suspecting him of murder. But something in his expression changed her mind, and she sat down.

Paris's perfectly smooth face hardened into a deep frown. It flitted through Lysi's mind, with some satisfaction, that she might be jealous.

Sinking down on the couch next to Lysi, Hank motioned Paris out with a wave of his hand. "That'll be all, Paris."

Hank waited until Paris closed the door. He blinked several times and seemed to grope for words. Finally, he whispered on the exhale, "Lysi, I'm not going to beat around the bush."

"Good." Lysi looked at her watch and mentally calculated how long it would take her to get to the Wild Flower Inn. "I don't have time for chitchat, either. Just say what you want to say and I'll get on my way."

"You asked how well I knew Cristin Holden."

He paused and let his eyes drop to his lap. "Very well. I knew her very, very well."

He looked up at Lysi and detonated the bomb.

"I was married to her."

Lysi's jaw fell open. Her vocal chords locked. She stared at Hank. After a long pause she croaked, "Did you say married?"

Hank nodded. "We met shortly after she graduated from Fresno State University. She'd come to Los Angeles in June to find her dream career. While waiting for the right position, she took a job with a small start up company—electronics."

Lysi tried to picture Cristin in the technical world. It did not compute.

"I was the one-man human resources department for the company. I interviewed and hired her the same day to be the sales promotion person."

Lysi nodded understanding. She glanced up at the nude figure of Hank's Olympia painting. Of course, she knew the only qualification Cristin needed for him to hire her was a hot body.

"As you can imagine, almost every purchasing manager she contacted suddenly needed our product," Hank continued with a sad grin. "I fell for her like for no other woman."

Carolyn's joyful face flashed through Lysi's mind. Thank God Carolyn isn't hearing this. His words would break her heart.

"We got married two months after we met. Cristin wanted an open marriage arrangement. She said she needed her freedom. I agreed to it. I would have agreed to anything to have her." Hank took a hard breath. "It didn't work. We divorced before the year ended."

Lysi finally found her voice again. "Let me tell you, Hank, it's a rare woman, indeed, who can handle this type of marriage." Truthfully, Lysi figured this kind of marriage arrangement would have been Heaven-sent for both Hank and Cristin.

"Oh, Cristin did fine. *I* couldn't handle it. In the beginning I tried seeing other women, but I had no interest. All I could think about was what Cristin might be doing. How I compared with her other men. She assured me I was the only man she really loved, but I still felt fearful even though I knew she always wore my ring. I never saw her without it."

"You mean you're the one who gave her that beautiful diamond and ruby ring?"

He nodded.

"Hank, she treasured it! She rarely took it off her finger. She showed me how you engraved her initials on each side of a little heart."

His eyes softened. "Not her initials. Those letters stood for Cristin and Hank. I guess it seems a little corny to you, but at the time I had it made, I was so much in love with her I couldn't think straight."

"When did you last see the ring?" Lysi said, careful not to tell him it was missing, but needing to know if Cristin's murderer had actually stolen the ring.

"Wednesday night, the last time we were together. I never wanted it back. I wanted her to keep it. I wanted to keep *her*, but I guess my ego was just too weak. I couldn't risk her coming to me one day to say she'd found someone better. Stupidly, I decided to end it before she could. Strangely enough, she was okay with the divorce and wanted to keep the relationship going. So, that's what we do—did. We'd meet two or three times a year, have a hell of a good time, then go our separate ways."

Lysi tried to assimilate what Hank had just told her. She saw pain and resignation in his face not the kind of anger and revenge that would lead to murder.

"About Carolyn." Hank's eyes lost the passion they had when he spoke of Cristin. "Yes, her father's promoting me. Yes, I owe Carolyn. Yes, it'd be a catastrophe if she found out about Cristin. But no, I did not murder Cristin to shut her up. First of all, as I told you before, Cristin knew nothing about Carolyn and me. She wouldn't have cared anyway. Second, even if she had known, she would never say anything to compromise my future—I like to think it's because she still cared—cared for me in her own way. Finally, I still have feelings for her and always will. I could never hurt her." His eyes moistened. "A part of me died with her."

Lysi stared at Hank, stunned into silence once more. She tried to speak, "I…" but stopped.

"You don't have to say anything. I just needed you to know. I figured you'd have found out soon enough anyway. I wanted you to hear it from me." His voice cracked.

It struck Lysi that he might have internalized his grief because he had nowhere else to turn.

She took his hand in hers. "Hank, I can't tell you how sorry I am for your loss. I understand how you feel because I loved her, too. I lost a dear friend."

They sat in silence.

Suddenly the door burst open and Paris appeared. She stopped with one spike heel comically in mid air, her mouth a perfect O. She stared at Hank and Lysi's entwined fingers.

Paris watched while they separated and smoothed their clothes. The tone of her words dropped the room temperature several degrees. "Mr. Jones, your 1:30 appointment is here. Shall I show him in?"

As Lysi left Hank's office, it struck her as strange that Paris had barged in without knocking instead of announcing the appointment on the intercom.

Chapter 29

The medicinal perfume of sage and goldenrod wafted through the open car windows as the tires crunched along the gravel lane to the Wild Flower Inn. The breeze off the lake lightened the heavy heat of the day.

In the cool living room Namida grinned at her from behind the antique registration desk, her hands clasped in the Cheyenne greeting.

Lysi clasped her hands in response. "Namida, your performance at the festival was unforgettable—so graceful, like an eagle gliding on currents of air. Truly, I'll always remember it."

Namida's face blossomed into a broader grin that puffed out her round cheeks. "I don't deserve such praise. Thank you for your nice words."

Deborah Tennyson stood in the dining room doorway, tall and straight, chin held high, the carriage of an aristocrat tempered by a gracious demeanor. Lysi could easily picture her in a tweed suit, standing at the entrance to an English manor.

"Lysi, so nice of you to come. Thank you for your lovely words to Namida. We always tell her she's a wonderful dancer, but it's good for her to hear it from someone else."

Deborah hooked arms with Namida. "Come, dear. Join us for our tour of the garden."

Deborah led them down a brick path, under a white arbor dotted with red roses, into an informal flower garden enclosed in a meticulously clipped hedge. "This is my English cottage garden."

Lysi's eyes darted from one patch of flowers to another. "It's charming. My mother had a garden like this—foxgloves, delphiniums, Canterbury bells, mums."

"You certainly know your flowers," Deborah said.

Lysi pointed toward a ceramic frog sitting in a circle of blue and yellow pansies next to an ornate concrete bench. "I grow pansies and violas on my deck throughout the winter months in San Francisco."

Deborah crisscrossed her arms over her heart. "I would love to have flowers blooming all year round."

Lysi could not quite picture Deborah hoeing and planting in the killer Montana heat. "Your gardener is certainly talented."

"Oh, Heaven's no." Deborah put her arm around Namida. "We don't allow any hands but our own to touch our little piece of paradise."

Namida's face shone with pride. "We patterned our English garden after a celebrated one in Worcestershire—Eastgrove Cottage Garden."

"My mother would've adored this garden." Lysi wished her mother were alive to see it. A stroll through the yard had been part of every visit to her mother's home. Lysi always had feelings of emptiness mixed with regret when she thought of her mother—how much she missed her, how she should have spent more time with her, how her mother always had time for her.

Her mother had been the anchor in Lysi's life. It was Cristin Holden who became the anchor during the dark period after her mother's death. Now Cristin was gone, too.

A sudden cacophony of chirping grabbed Lysi's attention. Several birds exploded from a small birdbath. One of them flew into a blue and white birdhouse a few feet from the bench.

"Oh, hush now." Deborah shook a finger at the indignant flurry of feathers. "Don't mind them. They scold whenever anyone disturbs their bath. One of them has a nest in the birdhouse and is trying to frighten us away." All three women laughed as the cross little birds ruffled their feathers, puffed out their chests and continued their vehement protest.

Deborah put her arm through Lysi's. "Come, let's leave them to their afternoon toilette."

When Namida went to set the tea table, Deborah led Lysi down a path toward a sun-drenched corner of the garden. Overhead, cottonwood seeds floated in the air like tiny snowflakes. Insects buzzed. A light breeze off the lake ruffled their skirts.

"These are my Montana wildflowers." Deborah strolled among the plants. "Each flower serves a practical purpose—the berries of the Nootka rose make rather good jelly and wine; you can boil the taproot of the oyster plant and it tastes quite like oysters; the tiny bitterroot, Montana's state flower, scatters its seeds helter skelter about the garden. I never have to plant a bitterroot. Of course, sage is an herb." She pinched a silvery green leaf and gave it to Lysi to sniff.

"This is my most carefree garden. It minds itself. That's why I planted my drive with the same wildflowers."

Deborah took Lysi's arm again. "Well, I think our tea is ready. Let's have it straight away."

The three women sat at a table on a shady corner of the deck.

Deborah spread a napkin on her lap. "The English have loved their tea since the 17th century, but the afternoon tea ritual is rather a recent tradition, you know. Anna, the Seventh Duchess of Bedford, is credited with having started the tradition during the early part of the nineteenth century. Today we're having what is called a Cream Tea. It consists of a pot of tea," Deborah pointed to the sunflower-print cozy keeping the teapot hot, "and some fresh warm scones spread with homemade raspberry jam and thick cream."

Deborah removed the quilted tea cozy from the pot. "Milk?"

"Yes, please," Lysi said, remembering that milk with tea is often labeled "the English way."

Deborah poured milk and tea for Lysi and Namida. She gestured with an open palm to the tray of scones. "Please, try my homemade scones and jam."

Lysi watched as Deborah helped herself to a scone, cut it in half, spread jam on each half, and topped it off with Devonshire cream. Then she carefully followed her lead.

Deborah took a bite of her scone and a sip of tea. "James is really quite something, wouldn't you agree?" She held up the scone. "Rather nice, don't you think?"

Somewhat taken aback, Lysi nodded yes to both questions and took a bite. "Absolutely delicious."

Deborah took another bite. "James has taken quite a fancy to you. He's in love with you, you know." Without a pause, she pointed to a full plate of scones. "You must try the apple scone."

Lysi coughed to keep from choking. "I will. Thank you." She swallowed. "He said that?"

"Oh, heavens no. But he didn't have to. I saw it in the way he looked at you during breakfast the other day. The more important question is: How do you feel about him?"

"I think he's quite something," Lysi said and took a big gulp of tea.

"Yes?" Deborah elongated the word.

Lysi licked her lips. "There are so many obstacles. Things are complicated. I live on the West coast. I have a job."

"Of course. I understand perfectly. I lived across the Atlantic in London when James's father and I fell in love. I had family. I had a good job. I had never been to America. I pondered all the possibilities. In the end, I realized I had a one-time opportunity. I had to make the right choice. So I left my brolly and the long queues forever, and took a giant leap in the dark. I've never regretted it. Mind you, I almost made the wrong choice."

"Uh…uh… What's a brolly?" Lysi stuttered the irrelevant question and immediately felt like a klutz.

Deborah ignored the question. "It's probably best if you don't tell James about our little chat. He would throw quite a wobbly. We always have a bit of a row when I approach the subject of marriage with him."

Namida leaned over and whispered, "It's an umbrella."

Lysi took another bite of scone and another gulp of tea. *James…love…marriage…* She turned to Namida and said, as though the definition of a brolly had given her a whole new outlook on life, "Oh, really."

As quickly as Deborah had opened the subject, she closed it. She slapped her hands together and said with great enthusiasm, "How about a refreshing ice lolly. I can offer you a frozen orange or lemonade."

A half hour later, Deborah walked Lysi to her car. She gave her three rosebuds in an Indian vase. When Lysi leaned through the car window to say a last goodbye, Deborah patted her arm. "I'm not asking you to leap out of your life into James's. I'm simply suggesting that you ponder possibilities."

*

Back in her room, Lysi placed the vase of flowers on the desk. Her spirit soared, remembering the bouquet James had given her the night of the festival. She looked in the mirror and fingered the necklace he'd placed around her neck. Deborah Tennyson's words kept running through her mind—*I realized this was a one-time opportunity; I had to make a choice; Mind you, I almost made the wrong one.*

James was the first man for whom Lysi had had any real feelings since she'd left her husband. There may never be another one. She touched her lips, remembering his kisses, reliving the excitement of his caresses, the safety of his arms.

Lysi tried to imagine life in San Francisco with James. Would he ever consider moving to her city? Could she possibly live in Montana? Deborah Tennyson made the transition from London to Sage Deer. What if they lived part of the year in San Francisco and the other part in Montana? Yes, that would work. Wouldn't it?

Chapter 30

When Lysi left her room to meet with Bill Pitt she counted fourteen semis and doubles in the Sagebrush Cafe truck lot, their chrome sparkling in a rainbow of reflected colors. Must be trough time for truckers, she thought. The other morning at the Sagebrush, she'd watched more than one trucker put away a fat-packed breakfast consisting of a six-egg omelet complete with a half platter of hash browns, at least a half pound of artery clogging sausage and several slices of butter-drenched toast. Where do they put all that food? She knew if she ate like that she'd make one of those huge Montana bison look like a stick bug compared to her voluminous physique.

Homey scents of sizzling meat and apple pie poured out of the restaurant when she opened the door. The supper crowd had already filled most of the tables and boisterous truckers were hurling wisecracks around the room.

A couple of long haul truck drivers emerged from the trucker's lounge in the rear of the café wearing clean plaid shirts and wet slicked-back hair, looking as though they'd just finished showering. The room howled with laughter when a bearded road warrior the size of a house yelled at them, "Now ain't you two pretty."

Jade moved from table to table, scratching orders as customers pointed at the two specials posted on the wall: The Belly Buster, an eight piece chicken platter and the "Eighteen Wheeler", a 32-ounce steak. Both dishes came with mountains of mashed potatoes—yellow with butter—and buns. She had already delivered several overflowing platters.

Lysi spotted Bill Pitt. She joined him at a table by the window and ordered a house white. Everything smelled delicious, but certain she'd already gained ten pounds since coming to Montana, she refused Bill's offer to buy dinner. Instead, she took a sip of wine and got down to business. "I think I know who made the death threats to Denny Robbins."

Bill's lips parted and he wrinkled his forehead.

"Noah Pry."

Disgust washed over Bill's face. "That little prick. I'm not surprised."

"I reported my suspicions to Detective Tennyson and he told me Denny has to report the threats himself."

"I vote for that." Bill took a swig of his beer and wiped his mouth with a small napkin.

"Denny's afraid to do it."

"What, afraid of that jerky little piece of sh—" He slapped his hand over his mouth. "Sorry."

Lysi stifled a laugh. For some reason she found Pitt's clumsy efforts at self-improvement very funny. "No, he's not afraid of Pry. He's afraid of you and your cronies. He insists you and Noah both want to get rid of him."

Bill's face reddened and he slapped the table. "Me and Pry! I don't even talk to him. Why I'd squash that miserable little cockroach if he got anywhere near me. Robbins got to be out of his gourd. What's his problem?" He took another big gulp of beer and slammed the mug on the table.

"I need you to talk with Denny. Encourage him to report the threats. "

Bill leaned forward and lowered his voice. "Hell, I've already apologized to him. Besides, I had nothing to do with the death threats. What does he want from me? I swear, that kid's as impossible to figure out as wom–," He slapped his hand over his mouth again, "Oops."

This time Lysi's eyes ignited and burned into him until he finally breathed a frustrated sigh. "Alright, I'll do it."

"Thank you." She rose to leave just as Jade plopped a "Belly Buster" in front of Bill and hurried after another order.

Bill looked down at the plate with a lost-my-appetite expression.

"Be assured, you won't regret your decision," Lysi said, hoping Bill got the message that Denny would probably withdraw the complaint against him.

Jade raised her head from behind the counter long enough to wave as Lysi went out the door.

*

Lysi decided to sit out by the pool before returning to her room. The sound of tiny chirping crickets and the vastness of the clear navy blue sky sprinkled with brilliant stars, trivialized her worries. Thoughts of James quickened her pulse. Excited about their plans to meet this evening, she decided to call him to firm up the time and picked up her cell. Before she could dial, a voice said, "Hi Lysi, it's Carolyn."

"Carolyn, the phone didn't even ring. Great to hear from you."

"I just called to check on you. Being a California girl myself, I can imagine you must be bored silly being stuck in this suburb of hell indefinitely."

Lysi snickered at Carolyn's apt description of Sage Deer. "Thanks for thinking of me. I'm definitely ready to get back to San Francisco, but I can't really say I'm bored. I've kept pretty busy."

"I wonder if our cowboy detective might have something to do with that?" Carolyn laughed.

Normally Lysi didn't talk much about relationships, but she felt comfortable with Carolyn. They'd established a sort of instant intimacy like the kind that sometimes occurs on a long train or plane trip with a fellow passenger you'll never see again.

"He might." Lysi couldn't keep the smile out of her voice.

Actually, there was no need for James to detain her in Sage Deer. He no longer considered her a suspect. Interestingly though, he hadn't brought up her going home. And that was all right with her.

"Why am I not surprised? He's hot. If I didn't have Hank, Tennyson would be my next choice."

Lysi reddened. "I guess he's okay for a Montana boy."

"You guess? Lady, that cowboy rocks!" Carolyn clicked her tongue a couple of times.

"Anyway, I called because I figured you might be feeling a little cooped up. God knows there's zippo to do around here. I'm taking the day off tomorrow because I need a little R&R. Why don't I pick you up in the morning say about 10:30, and we can spend the day together? I'll fix you a California brunch and you can tell me all about your adventures with that foxy Detective."

Ten thirty seemed like a reasonable time, given the fact that she would probably be out late with James. "I'd love it. See you at 10:30."

Clearly Carolyn had suffered in the transition from cosmopolitan Los Angeles to provincial Sage Deer. Spending some time together would be good for both of them.

Lysi hung up and dialed James's number. The sound of his voice sent delicious little electrical surges coursing through her. Could Deborah be right? Is James Tennyson really in love with her?

"Hi, James, I just wanted to tell you what a lovely time I had at your mother's tea. She's so charming."

"You went?" James's voice sounded cool.

"Of course I went. Why would you ask that?"

"I just talked with Paris Spyer." James sounded as though no further explanation was needed.

Lysi had to think for a moment before she recalled the name. "Oh, yes, Hank's secretary."

"Yes, *Hank's* secretary. Well, I'm glad you were able to make the tea."

"Han—James, what is it?" Lysi's joy evaporated.

"Look Lysi. I know about your little meeting with Hank Jones. Paris filled me in on the whole scenario when I called to follow up on KiKi's claim that Jones had visited Cristin Holden on the night of her death."

"I had planned to tell you about the appointment with Han— Mr. Jones."

"All right. Explain."

Lysi took a breath. "I went because he telephoned and asked me to come. Said he had something important to tell me. You'll never believe this."

"Try me."

"Hank Jones used to be married to Cristin."

The long pause on the other end of the line told Lysi James probably needed a few minutes to digest this bit of information. Since he didn't make further comments, Lysi added, "There's more."

James sighed. "Go on."

"Turns out they've been carrying on a long distance affair since the divorce. Jones was with Cristin on the night of her death, but I don't think he killed her because he's still in love with her."

James barely kept his voice below a shout. "It's not up to you to determine who is or is not a suspect. Lysi, your amateur meddling is making my job ten times harder than it should be. If I can't get a conviction in this case, it'll be because of you."

"You don't understand."

"No, I do understand. I need to convince you that I mean business when I say keep your nose out of my case. As for Paris Spyer's interpretation of what she saw between you and Hank Jones, you're an adult and can do what you want. Maybe I misunderstood...things...us. It's no longer any of my business."

Lysi swallowed a hard lump in her throat. Confusion, then anger and finally hurt brought tears. "James, I—" She stopped in mid sentence as an icy riptide of pain tore through her.

Memories of her disastrous marriage and her debasing attempts to revive it brought home to her the futility of trying to explain. She dragged in a breath, exhaled hard, then pressed the off button on the phone.

Back in her room, Lysi sat on the bed and stared out the window seeing nothing but her mistakes. She should have told James right away what Elizabeth said about Hank's computer . She should have checked with him before she went to see Hank at all. She should have called him when she found out Hank and Cristin had been married. But she didn't and now it was too late.

Not only had James's words cut into her heart, his lack of trust and vile opinion of her character crushed any feelings she might have had for him. Lysi let herself fall back on her pillow and choked back tears.

Seconds later, anger replaced pain. She hoisted herself up and sat on the edge of the bed, head in hands. How could she have been stupid enough to even consider caring about another man?

She took a deep breath, jutted her chin and said in a firm voice, "Pull yourself together, girl. He's nothing to you. Just another streetcar!"

She went to the mini bar and pulled out a double Reese's Peanut Butter Cup, her comfort food of choice. "So much for finding that special streetcar."

Chapter 31

All morning James had buried himself in work, painstakingly forcing images of Lysi out of his mind. Now he leaned back in his chair, locked his fingers behind his head and tried to analyze his interview with Hank Jones.

Jones had admitted visiting with Cristin Holden Wednesday night. He insisted that when he left at 9:30 she was still alive. Sure, he'd been married to Holden and claimed he still loved her, but James bet Jones loved himself more. Maybe Holden became an inconvenience.

James stared at his interrogation notes. Something didn't fit. He concluded that it wasn't what Jones said; it was what he hadn't said. He judged Jones as the kind of joker who would enjoy boasting man to man about his conquests. But the guy had revealed nothing about what went on in Cristin's room. Something was out of kilter—something in his face, his eyes, his voice, choice of words—James couldn't pinpoint it. Something's out of sync with that bastard's true character. He jabbed the point of his pencil into Hank's name on the yellow pad.

When the phone rang, James picked up after the first ring. He tried to squash a nagging hope that Lysi might be calling with an explanation. He still clung to a possibility, however remote, that she cared about him; that this was all some big mistake. Deep down, he knew his outburst had destroyed any chance of reconciliation. "Detective Tennyson."

"James. Dr. Goldfein. I've got some specifics on the poison."

"Great, Doc. I've been waiting to hear from you. What've you got?"

The doctor cleared his throat. "Let's see here." He began reading some information. "It's a cardiac glycoside, a plant product found in members of the Apocynaceae or dogbane family. By the way, there are about 3700 species of plants in the group. It's similar to the Digitalis we get from foxgloves. You know, the med we use to regulate the heart rate. But it's toxic. It plays havoc with the heart. Makes it slow down, speed up or beat erratically. Death can occur within a few hours after ingesting this stuff. It can be pretty nasty."

James grabbed a pencil. "Can you spell Apocynaceae?"

"Sure. I'll fax the Cause of Death information and the list of antidotes to Dr. MacKinnon."

After Dr. Goldfein spelled Apocynaceae twice, James thanked him, hung up and did a computer search on cardiac glycoside. He skimmed a couple of descriptions that were pretty much the same as those of Dr. Goldfein's, then skipped down to the source of the poison. He discovered most of the toxic plants in the dogbane family would not survive at temperatures below 50 degrees. He figured it'd take only one Montana winter to kill them off.

He read further trying to connect this new information to what he already knew about the case. *All parts of these plants are poisonous. People have died from ingesting the flower, chewing leaves, and from honey made by bees using the plant for nectar.* He squinted into middle space. None of this is relevant unless the plant in the Apocynaceae family can be found in Sage Deer where the temperature sometimes dips to 38 degrees below zero. James knew how to find out.

*

A small wood sign tacked to a seventy-year old cottonwood tree marked the Juniper Berry Nursery on the outskirts of Sage Deer.

James parked in the shade of the tree and strode into the weathered-pine nursery building. Shelves, crowded with bulbs, seeds, pots, planters, plant foods, pest controls and yard tools lined all four walls of the one-room garden supply shop. The smell of various potting soils always reminded James of the many trips he'd made to the nursery with his mother when he was a kid.

He looked around for seventy-eight year old Ben Tot, who had started the business in a small fruit stand and nurtured it into the kind of nursery that attracted people from as far away as Billings. The real popularity of Juniper Berry stemmed from Ben's plant expertise. He liked to say, "Ask me any plant question you got. I'll probably know the answer. If not, for sure I'll get it for you."

At the sound of a loud grunt. James stepped out the back door and zigzagged through a variety of plants in one and five-gallon containers until he found the nurseryman unloading a shipment of clay pots onto a low shelf perched against the back wall of a lean-to by the rear fence.

"Hey Ben." James grinned when the short, wiry gardener turned around, stretched, and massaged the small of his back with the heels of his hands.

"Jamie, good to see you, boy."

"How's the knee?"

"Pretty good, pretty good. I only wish I'd replaced it years ago." Ben squatted down and got back up again. "Not bad for an old guy, huh?"

"Not bad at all. Looks like the plant business is doing okay, too."

"Yeah, yeah. Maybe a little slower this time of year. The heat you know."

James wiped his brow with the back of his hand. "Tell me about it."

"Come on in. I got a couple cold beers in the ice chest."

"I'd sure like to, but I'm here on duty. Had any orders for dogbane lately?"

Ben rubbed his fingers over his mustache, as if trying to smooth out the bristly, salt and pepper hairs.

"You're talking about hundreds of plants in that Apocynaceae family or dogbane in common English. Nope, I don't really carry any of them because most of them aren't hardy enough to withstand our cold winters. I could order some for you, but you'd have to keep them in containers in some sort of sheltered but sunny environment like a greenhouse. What kind do you want?"

"I don't really know. Do you know of anyone who cultivates them around here?"

Ben scrunched up his eyes and tightened his lips over his teeth as if doing a Google search of his vast horticultural memory bank. "Nope, can't say as I heard of anyone."

"But if someone were to be growing one around here, they'd have it in a container, right?"

"Right. In the ground them plants would die long before our temperatures hit zero."

Ben turned and walked towards the back of the nursery. "Hey, Jamie. Come here for a minute." He pointed lovingly at a deep blue hydrangea. "I bet your mom would like this."

James slapped him on the shoulder. "I'll take it. Tag it for me. Her birthday's coming up."

James had almost gotten to the nursery gate when Ben called out to him. "Jamie, wait a second. You know, I did have some plants in the Apocynaceae family come through here. Hold on."

He shuffled into the nursery shop, opened a black order book, licked his thumb and flipped through the pages.

"Yep, right here. About ten oleanders got shipped through me around four months ago. I had the job of delivering them to that new Nerium Corporation. They got some big greenhouse in one of the top floor offices. Oleanders are real pretty plants, but they're poisonous you know. You'd have to be pretty hungry to eat them; they're kind of bitter." He shrugged his shoulders. "I guess somebody had to try them to know they're poisonous. Heck, some people eat snails and grasshoppers." He shook his head. "It takes all kinds."

James knew about the oleander plant. He'd seen it growing in abundance in California when he was at the university. It grew in yards and down the middle of streets and even along freeways. He did not know it was poisonous and figured not too many other people around Sage Deer knew it, either.

"Who placed the order?"

"Let's see. A guy in the Nerium L.A. office, Bob Schram."

"Who signed for receipt of delivery at our Nerium plant?"

Ben moved his finger down the order page. "Chuck Paul. He's a custodian up there." Ben paused. "You know, that boy was valedictorian of his high school class. Who'd a ever guessed he'd end up sweeping floors?"

"Yeah," James said. "You never know where life's going to put you." He slapped Ben on the shoulder again. "Thanks, for checking on the order. I got just what I needed to know."

*

As James drove along the two-lane road towards the Nerium plant, he reviewed the people who might have access to the Nerium greenhouse. Noah Pry's name popped into his mind. He has pretty much free run of the building since he cleans restrooms. James knew Cristin hadn't died from Noah's Judo choke, but that didn't mean he couldn't have poisoned her. Doesn't add up. Pry probably didn't even know about the toxicity of oleander. Or did he? Could've overheard someone at Nerium talk about it.

Bill Pitt's face filled James's head. He quickly dismissed him as a possible suspect. Not likely. He's lived all his life in Montana. He wouldn't know an oleander from a palm tree.

James considered Hank Jones the most likely suspect. He admits to seeing Cristin on the night of her death. He probably knows about the toxicity of oleanders, having come from Los Angeles. But what about motive?

*

James pulled up to the Nerium plant entrance gate. He inserted the guest card he'd been given to attend the seminars. The heavy iron-gate yawned open. He parked in front of the building and entered through the gigantic main doors. A thirty-something receptionist raised her chin. She looked up through thick lashes, recognized him and curved her luscious red lips into a flirtatious smile. "Detective Tennyson, it's a real treat to see you again."

He picked up a pen and bent over the sign-in sheet. "Nice to see you again too, Ms. ..." he quickly glanced at the name plate, "Golden."

"Really." She lowered her lashes and purred, "I'll bet you say that to all the girls."

At another time, James might have enjoyed this playful exchange, but not today. He needed to get on with his investigation. Ms. Golden seemed to sense his mood and her smile faded. "Whom did you wish to see?"

"That depends. I actually came to see the oleander garden."

The receptionist grinned. "You want Staff Development on the fourth floor. Ms. Norris is out and won't be back today, but her secretary is used to showing people the garden. It's become quite a tourist attraction. I'll let her know you're on the way up."

"Thanks," James said and turned toward the elevator.

"You're welcome." Ms. Golden flipped her straight, shoulder length hair behind her ear and called after him. "Stop by again when you can stay a little longer."

*

James exited the elevator on the fourth floor and followed the direction signs to the staff development office. When he opened the door the no-nonsense secretary looked up from her computer and peered at him over her spectacles. She didn't have to point out the garden. James stared through the floor to ceiling glass wall at several plants in large containers, sprinkled with red, pink and white blossoms. That's when it hit him. Why hadn't he made the connection before?

He turned to the secretary. "Where's Ms. Norris today?"

The secretary looked down her nose at James. "I'm not at liberty to discuss Ms. Norris's whereabouts with just anyone. Would you like me to tell her you called?"

James flashed his badge. "Tell her Detective Tennyson, SDPD, called. Now where is she?"

The secretary swallowed hard. "She took the day off. She didn't say where she was going. May I ask what this is all about?"

"I'm not a liberty to discuss Ms. Norris's business with just anyone," James said as he walked out the door.

Chapter 32

The late morning traffic on Highway 39 was light. As they drove, Lysi tried to keep her mind on Carolyn's endless chatter about the joys of living in Los Angeles and how she planned to return as soon as possible. Visions of James kept eroding Lysi's concentration. Still smarting from the shock of his angry outburst, she could only manage to insert occasional one-syllable responses.

"I plan to go back to Los Angeles, settle down and raise a family," Carolyn said in an almost dreamy voice. "Maybe I'll work at Nerium L.A. until the first baby comes."

Lysi felt a pang of sympathy for Carolyn as Elizabeth's words at the Festival echoed in her mind—*Carolyn's father sent her way out here...wanted her as far from corporate office as possible.*

After a while Carolyn glanced at Lysi. "Are you all right? You seemed in such good spirits this morning, now your aura seems to be drooping."

Carolyn didn't wait for a response. "Is everything okay with you and your detective?"

Lysi looked down at her hands and twisted the amethyst ring on her finger. She started to tell Carolyn about James's phone call, but recalling his sharp words brought a lump to her throat. "No, not really. I hope you'll understand if I can't talk about it right now."

"Of course." Carolyn patted Lysi's hand.

After a few moments, Carolyn said, "I guess you know Hank and I are engaged to be married."

Lysi felt Carolyn's eyes on her waiting for a response. She wanted to tell Carolyn not to waste her time on a man like Hank, that he would never bring her happiness, only heartbreak. A woman like her could do so much better. But she didn't know how to word it, so she said, "Congratulations! I wish you the very best."

"Thank you, Lysi. That's such a nice thing to say. I hope things work out for you and Detective Tennyson. I hate seeing you so down."

"I think James and I are history. Actually, it's better. Fewer problems." She forced a smile. "Lunch with you will brighten my day."

She felt grateful for Carolyn's consideration and friendship. She decided she needed to at least try to warn her about Hank. "Carolyn, you know I've grown quite fond of you. You've been a real comfort to me since I came to Sage Deer. May I tell you something as a friend?"

"Of course. Go for it."

"It's about Hank."

Carolyn shot her a tight glance.

"It doesn't seem to me that Hank is the type to settle down and have a family and live in the suburbs. He's a nice enough guy, but he's…he's…flighty."

"I don't know what you mean—flighty."

"He just doesn't seem like the type to stick with one woman."

"Lysi, you don't know what you're talking about. You don't even know Hank. I'm surprised you'd disparage his character like that."

Lysi glanced at the speedometer. Carolyn had increased her speed to an unsafe 80 miles an hour. *What is it with her and speed?* "How about slowing down a bit? I get carsick at high speeds," Lysi lied.

Carolyn's voice had a slight edge to it. "No problem."

"Look Carolyn. I shouldn't have said anything. It's just that I don't want to see you hurt. It's none of my business."

"I know you wanted to help. It's just that everyone jumps on Hank. No one knows the real Hank like I do."

"You're probably right. Let's forget it, okay?"

"Forgotten."

*

After about twenty minutes, Carolyn turned off the highway onto an unpaved road bordered by gray fence posts linked by broken barbed wire. The road curved through rocky ridges, blotting out more and more of the view of the main highway as they juddered over gravel and potholes.

Ten minutes later Carolyn slowed and maneuvered the car into a narrow dirt lane. Lysi didn't see the lane until the actual turn because it was shrouded by a dense stand of cottonwoods. Thick branches scraped both sides of the car. Up ahead a small cottage came into view, half hidden behind what seemed like a forest of trees fighting for space. Its unpainted board siding aged to dull silver was barely visible among the shadowy green foliage of overgrown arrow-wood shrubs and more giant cottonwoods. The gentle shaded play of light and shadow through the tall trees seemed a refuge from the harsh, sun-scorched land they had just passed through.

Lysi stepped out of the car onto a spongy leaf-covered path. She could hear the sound of a trickling stream somewhere and the insistent call of a loud-mouthed jay. She breathed in the moist scent of arrow-wood and recalled quiet morning strolls on the shaded paths of Golden Gate Park.

"Carolyn, it's beautiful here. So different from the typical Montana landscape."

They crossed a sagging porch spotted with gray-green moss and Carolyn unlocked the front door of the deeply shaded, one-room cottage.

"Welcome to my hideaway." She switched on a lamp and opened a window. Fresh air rushed in, displacing a musty, closed up odor.

Lysi crossed her arms and shivered. "I can't believe the drop in temperature."

"Nice isn't it?" Carolyn said. "Have a seat." She motioned toward a large gray leather sofa. "I'll just put water on for tea."

After setting the picnic basket on a braided rug next to a knotty pine coffee table, Carolyn stepped into a small galley kitchen. She filled a teapot, set it on a hotplate next to the sink then opened the compact refrigerator and took out a box of tea leaves. "The old clunker doesn't work anymore but it's a good place to keep things like sugar and tea. The varmints can't get into it."

Lysi recalled the light airy décor of Carolyn's office and concluded the cabin didn't seem compatible with her personality. In fact, it didn't seem to suit a woman's taste at all. It had the stark, utilitarian look a hunter might prefer. An Australian sheepskin rug in front of a plain metal stove, imparted a trace of warmth to the Spartan room.

Lysi waited on the couch watching the leaf shadows shimmy in the meager light that streamed through one small window. As she relaxed, she began to appreciate the restful seclusion of the cabin. "You know, this is a terrific get-away. No phone. No nosey neighbors. No TV. It's a place where you can let it all hang out—sweats, no blow dryer, no makeup—just lie around and read racy novels. Do you ever get lonesome here?"

Carolyn looked over her shoulder as she reached into the cupboard for a china teapot, cups and saucers. "I'm never lonesome here. This is where Hank and I come to be alone. You might call it our little passion nest."

Lysi reflected on Hank's ongoing love for Cristin. Now that Cristin's gone, maybe he'll marry Carolyn. She questioned whether the marriage would work. Hank cheated on Elizabeth and had already cheated on Carolyn. A leopard doesn't change its spots. He'd cheat on Carolyn again. Lysi sighed. She'd already tried to talk to Carolyn about Hank in the car and it was futile. It amazed her that Carolyn could be so trusting, so optimistic, so blind. She almost wanted to grab her and shake some sense into her, but knew anything she said would fall on deaf ears, anger Carolyn and spoil the lunch.

When Carolyn came back to the couch, she reached into the picnic basket and pulled out two lemon yellow placemats and matching napkins. Then she lifted out two covered plates and set them on the placemats. Her face lit up. "Are you ready for a little California treat?"

She removed the covers from the plates revealing an avocado and kiwi fruit salad on a bed of baby lettuce garnished with grape tomatoes. Next she pulled out a sourdough baguette and made a circle in the air with it. "Ta-dah!"

Lysi laughed. "Where did you find all this ambrosia of the gods?"

"I made the salad myself. You can find the ingredients around here if you look hard enough, although I did have to go all the way to Billings for the kiwi. As for the bread, whenever my mother comes to visit, I have her pick up several loaves of sourdough for me at the LAX Boudin Bakery/Café. I freeze it. It's not as good as fresh but it's better than you can find around here."

Lysi scooped a bite of avocado and kiwi salad into her mouth. "Absolutely delicious."

Carolyn sawed off two pieces of the crisp sourdough and passed them along with butter to Lysi then served herself. As they ate the carefully prepared lunch Lysi felt their relationship warm into what might become a permanent friendship. *I'd love to show her San Francisco.*

The teapot whistled and Carolyn went to the kitchen alcove to prepare the tea. Lysi leaned back on the couch and blocked out all thoughts of James.

Chapter 33

James decided to grab a bite of lunch at the Sagebrush Café before returning to his office after his Nerium stop. When he entered, he nodded at a couple of truck drivers seated at tables near the window.

"Hey, Tennyson. Catch any bank robbers or mass murderers today?" one of them yelled. The other one slapped his knee and howled and snorted.

"Not today." James flashed a good-natured smile. "But I heard there's a couple of smart-mouth truckies disturbing the peace at the Sagebrush. I might haul them in and have them dust the cobwebs out of the jail cells."

Laughter rang out again.

As soon as he sat down at the counter, Jade rattled off the specials; then took his order for a steak sandwich with a side salad and coffee.

After a couple of bites of his sandwich and a sip of coffee he said, "Jade, how well do you know Carolyn Norris?"

"Not well. I know her by sight because she's been in a few times with Elizabeth Scot. They both work at Nerium. Most of what I know about her I hear from KiKi."

James noticed Jade's contemptuous look when she mentioned KiKi's name. He guessed they were on the outs again.

"Yeah?" he said, knowing that's all it would take to get Jade to rattle off a trainload of information.

Jade glanced around the tables. All the customers were served and eating. No one needed her immediate attention. She splashed coffee in her mug, folded her arms on the counter, raised her eyebrows and leaned closer to James. "My personal impression of Carolyn Norris? She's not bad looking and has a nice personality. But KiKi has a real different opinion of her."

James nodded. "I've only seen her twice. She introduced Lysi at the two Nerium seminars I attended. I agree with you. She's attractive and very personable."

"KiKi says Carolyn's got it bad for Hank Jones."

James cringed at the sound of Jones's name.

"She says Carolyn got her daddy, a big kahuna at Nerium, to give him a promotion. Words out, Carolyn wants to marry him. According to KiKi, Hank's not the marrying kind."

"Interesting." James brooded over what Paris Spyer had said about Lysi's romantic interlude with Jones. His rational side told him it was an unlikely scenario, but his emotional side told him there must have been something going on. Paris would have no reason to make up such a wild story. He realized how important Lysi's happiness had become to him and he didn't want to see her hurt, especially by that good for nothing gigolo.

Jade sniffed her coffee and wrinkled her nose. "I wish that cook would stick to his stove and keep his hands off the coffee maker." She reached for the sugar. "Anyway, KiKi says she saw Hank sniffing around Cristin Holden Wednesday night. She just couldn't wait to get on her cell and tell Carolyn all about it. According to KiKi, Carolyn gets real hot when she sees Hank look at another woman."

As Jade spoke, James kept his eyes glued to her face and tried not to betray the connections beginning to bubble up from deep inside him. "Is that so?"

Jade took a sip of her coffee and added two more heaping tablespoons of sugar. Stirring the thick brew, she added, "I guess Lysi and Carolyn might be getting to be good buddies. I saw her get into Carolyn's car about an hour ago."

James almost dropped his fork as an image of Carolyn's oleander garden shot into his head accompanied by the receptionist's words. *Ms. Norris won't be back today.* He looked at his watch. "That would have been about 10:30."

"Yeah, I think so," Jade said.

In as casual a voice as possible, he said, "Did she tell you where they were going?"

"No, but they headed east on 39."

James frowned. "There's nothing on 39 between here and Colstrip."

He slapped some cash on the counter and got up. "Keep the change."

Jade picked up the money. "Thanks."

"Wait," she called as James bounded out the door. "That's a twenty dollar bill."

*

After James left the Sagebrush Café, he sat in his car a few minutes and tried to think who might know where Carolyn would be taking Lysi on Highway 39.

He watched two muscular teenage boys climb out of the Big Sky pool and begin smearing suntan lotion over their buff physiques. James decided they were city boys who probably lifted weights in a gym, not bales of hay in a field. No respectable Montana farm boy would spend time greasing himself up lying around a pool. Pretty boys.

Speaking of pretty boys. Hank Jones's magazine model face appeared in his mind. The image stung like a wasp. The possibility that Lysi might be drawn to a shallow creep like Jones tormented him. His gut ached when his imagination spewed unwanted pictures of Jones holding Lysi in his arms the way he had held her; Jones caressing her where he had caressed; Jones kissing her. Could he have misunderstood her feelings? When they made love, she seemed to want him as much as he wanted her. He almost wished she'd never come to Sage Deer. Never turned his life upside down.

But a stronger feeling knotted his stomach. Lysi might be in danger. Jones might know where Carolyn had taken her. No matter how he felt, he had to reach Jones. He rummaged around in the glove compartment until he found the Nerium main number on the seminar schedule he'd been sent and punched it in. The operator answered.

"Hank Jones, please."

"One moment, sir. I'll transfer your call."

A feeling of helplessness struck him when he heard the voice mail kick in. "You have reached Hank Jones, Nerium Corporation Director of Human Resources. I am either away from my desk or on another line. Please leave a—."

James disconnected and redialed the Nerium main number. When the operator answered he said, "This is Detective Lieutenant James Tennyson. I am investigating a homicide. I want to speak to Hank Jones. I don't want his voice mail. I want *him*. Now!"

The receptionist sounded a bit nervous. "Yes…Of course…I'll find him immediately. Please hold, Detective Tennyson."

A moment later, the oily voice of Hank Jones oozed into James's ear. "Detective Tennyson. Hank Jones here. I really hope this is important because you pulled me out of a critical planning meeting."

"A murder investigation trumps your meeting."

James thought the only critical planning Jones did was deciding what to wear for the day. "I need to know where Carolyn Norris would be going headed east on Highway 39."

"I wouldn't have the slightest idea. Sorry, can't help you. Now if that's all, I really have to g—"

"I don't think I made myself clear. Let me try again. Carolyn Norris picked up Lysi Weston this morning and has taken her someplace off highway 39. Ms. Weston may be in danger. I think you had something to do with it." James paused a moment to let this sink in.

Hank started to say something. James interrupted. "I promise you, if Ms. Weston is harmed in any way and I find out you're involved, I'll put you away until you're an old man."

Hank's voice went up an octave. "Why would Carolyn harm Ms. Weston?"

The line remained silent for a long moment. James waited.

Finally, Jones exhaled a frustrated breath. "Look, I may know where she might have taken her. If I tell you, you need to keep it confidential. I've got a promotion pending and this could jeopardize it."

"Don't try to bargain with me, Jones. Just tell me where she is." James felt his muscles tighten and his face burn with impatience.

"It's ridiculously funny to think Carolyn would harm Lysi. They're friends." Hank forced a shallow laugh.

"Where is she?" James could hear the desperation in his own voice.

"All right. She's probably headed to a little cabin. About ten miles out of town there's a gravel road that takes off to the left. You have to watch for it because there's no street sign. It's a pretty rough road. The cabin's at the end of a dirt lane that takes off to the right about three miles up the road. It's hidden in trees; hard to find."

"That won't be a problem because you're going to show me."

"No, I can't. What about my meeting?"

"I'll pick you up outside the main Nerium gate in fifteen minutes. If you're not there, I'll come into your office and drag you out in handcuffs."

When James hung up, he realized he'd been shouting. He sat still staring straight ahead, eyes focused on nothing, trying to slow his thundering heart.

*

As they approached the Nerium gate, Officer Sam Spitz whom James had picked up on the way, pointed to a tree by the side of the gate. "There he is. Kind of looks like he's trying to hide behind that tree." Sam scratched his grizzly, red beard and raised his bushy eyebrows. "He sure looks pretty in that spiffy suit."

James pulled up to the gate. Sam got out of the car and opened the rear door. "You just hop right into the backseat there, Pretty Boy."

Sam slid into the front seat of the car and watched with an incredulous expression, as Hank adjusted his trousers and ran his shiny, manicured fingers over the creases.

Sam coughed, rolled down the window and fanned himself with his open hand. "What's that perfume you're wearing, boy?"

Hank had started to reply when James revved the engine and squealed into a U turn that threw Jones against the door. "Hey, watch it," Hank said, fumbling to buckle his seatbelt.

"Hank, you're the navigator," James said. "Tell us when we come to this mystery road of yours."

"It's not my road. Besides, you said this would be confidential. Why's he here?" He glowered at Sam.

"Well now Hank, you've gone and made me feel real bad. Sort of unwanted," Sam said. "Hey James, maybe you should drop me off at the Sagebrush and I could tell all the guys about Hank's secret cabin." He laughed. Hank squirmed.

James felt anger rising in his throat. "You don't worry about Officer Spitz. Just watch for that road."

"I shouldn't even be here. This isn't my problem." Hank centered his tie knot.

James hit the brakes and the car screeched to a stop, throwing Hank against the front seat. James leaped out and jumped into the back. "Take over driving, Sam. Hank needs a little reality check."

"Sure thing, Boss." Officer Spitz took the driver's seat and drove. His tense brown eyes watched James and Hank in the rearview mirror.

"Lysi isn't your problem? You're not worried about her?" James's eyes bored into Hank. "What kind of animal are you?"

Hank looked at James, his mouth hanging open in confusion. "I'm concerned about her like I would be about any business associate. But I hardly know her."

James's eyes narrowed to dagger sharp points. "You're lying. You know her all right—intimately. To you, she's expendable. Now that Carolyn's launching your puny career, you don't dare risk the excess baggage of an affair with another woman."

Hank's face registered terrified shock. "Affair! Hey, you got this all wrong. I swear. I only had a business relationship with Lysi Weston. Nothing else!"

James grabbed him by his perfect tie, tension strangling his words. "You lie to me again and I'll rearrange your pretty little face."

Officer Spitz raised his voice from the front seat. "Detective Tennyson, you better take over driving. I'm not sure where we're going."

James didn't take his eyes off Hank. He knew Sam Spitz wanted to step in to avert an intimidating or abusive interrogation, but he just needed a minute more. "Not now, Sam."

He yanked Hank's tie tighter, pulling his face so close it almost touched his own. "Paris Spyer saw you on the couch with Lysi. She said you practically had Lysi's clothes off and would have if she hadn't interrupted you to announce your next appointment."

Sam swerved to the side of the road, opened the car door and jumped out.

Hank gulped and looked like he couldn't quite grasp the meaning of James's words. His mouth moved before he spoke. Suddenly the words poured out like an avalanche. "Paris said that? She's a lying little bitch. I never touched Lysi Weston. I'm seeing Carolyn Norris. Even if Carolyn wasn't in the picture, Lysi Weston isn't my type. She doesn't even act like a woman. She's cold. She's frigid. No, no." He shook his head vigorously. "You're dead wrong."

It was James's turn to look astonished. *Oh my God, he's telling the truth?*

Slowly, he released Hank's tie and gave it a motherly pat. He leaned back against the car seat and watched Hank straighten his tie, pinch his pant creases, and smooth his fingers through his disheveled hair.

"This is police brutality," Hank said in a hoarse whisper.

Sam looked at him with distaste. "Police brutality. What are you talking about? I didn't see anything out of the ordinary. We're just taking a nice pleasant drive in the country." He slid back behind the wheel, shifted the car and pulled smoothly back onto the highway, whistling an off key version of "She'll be Coming Around the Mountain."

Plagued by uneasy feelings, James barely noticed the blur of yellow fields pocked with boulders streaming past the car window. His mind struggled with flimsy threads of facts loosely knitted together with a multitude of maybes.

Fact: Cristin Holden died from cardiac glycoside poisoning. Maybe the origin of the poison was oleanders growing in the staff development office.

Fact: Several people with motives had access to the oleanders in that office. Maybe Noah Pry, his ego bruised…Maybe Jones, his promotion at risk.

Fact: Jones and Carolyn are a twosome. KiKi told Carolyn about Hank's little affair with Cristin. Maybe Carolyn decided to eliminate Cristin, the competition. Maybe Paris told Carolyn about Hank's dalliance with Lysi. Maybe Carolyn has plans to poison one more competitor.

James squeezed his temples hard between his thumb and fingers as one more chilling fact blasted into his brain. Fact: Carolyn Norris has Lysi—alone in an isolated spot.

Chapter 34

Carolyn set two cups on the coffee table and filled each from the china teapot. "You'll like this tea. It's Mother Norris's special herb mix for whatever ails you."

Lysi laughed. She lifted the cup to her lips, took a sip and scrunched up her face. "I'm afraid it's a little too bitter for my taste."

"I'll get you some sugar." Carolyn jumped up and covered the few steps to the old refrigerator in an instant. Lysi watched her. *She is so considerate and eager to please. I wish she could see Hank for the taker he is.*

Carolyn returned with an old fashioned Mason canning jar of lumpy sugar and set it on the coffee table. "I know the first taste is always kind of a jolt. This should sweeten it up a bit."

She unscrewed the jar lid and scooped out a teaspoon of sugar, dropped it into Lysi's cup and swirled the spoon around until the crystals dissolved.

"There, try a couple more sips. It mellows. Believe me, the lift you get is well worth a little bitterness."

Lysi took a cautious sip and coughed. Her eyes watered from the acrid drink. She gritted her teeth. "I don't know. I think the cure is worse than the disease."

Carolyn laughed. "Hang in there, girl. Mother Norris knows best."

They both giggled each time Lysi took a gulp and wrinkled her nose at its acidity.

231

Something about that pungent scent seemed familiar to Lysi. Unable to put her finger on where she'd smelled it before, she just let it fade from her mind.

Carolyn seemed like such a caring person and so positive about the future. Lysi just couldn't believe this charming, intelligent woman had pinned her hopes on a self-centered man like Jones. She deserves better.

Lysi looked at Carolyn with compassion. She decided, as Carolyn's friend, she should try one more time to share her concerns about Hank. "KiKi told me about Cristin and Hank. I'm sorry."

A shadow passed over Carolyn's face. It quickly disappeared under a forced smile while her eyes remained cold. "KiKi Kavenaugh? Why Lysi, no one pays any attention to trash like her." She looked at Lysi as if waiting for a response.

The cruel comment came so unexpectedly and seemed so out of character that it took a moment for Lysi to digest it. "You mean you think she might have made up the story?"

This time fury ignited Carolyn's face. "Of course she made it up. That ridiculous specimen! KiKi's nothing but a high-paid hooker—empty headed and stupid. I wouldn't believe her if she yelled fire and the flames were licking at my feet."

Lysi's eyes widened. She hadn't seen this kind of vitriolic reaction in Carolyn before. She tried to hide her consternation with a weak comment. "Idle gossip, I suppose."

Carolyn didn't acknowledge her, but raced on spewing more venom. "I didn't need KiKi's dribble to know the history of Hank and Cristin. My father did a thorough investigation of Hank before considering him for the promotion. That's how I found out he'd been married to Cristin. I thought it was over between them until Paris told me about the e-mails and calls on his direct line."

"Paris Spyer? Hank's secretary?"

"Paris Spyer answers to me," Carolyn said.

So that was it! Paris Spyer is a direct pipeline to Carolyn. Paris saw the e-mails between Hank and Cristin on Hank's computer and told Carolyn about it. Carolyn *knew* about Hank's plans to meet with Cristin in her motel room. She must have been devastated.

At that moment, a cold reality hit Lysi. Carolyn had a compelling motive for killing Cristin. She thought Cristin stood in the way of her plan to marry Hank.

Still, Lysi didn't want to believe it.

Random thoughts, like puzzle pieces, began to flow together to form a picture in Lysi's brain. Out of nowhere, her mind floated back to the conversation in Carolyn's office after the first presentation. She replayed Carolyn's words. *I really respect you going through with this presentation today. It must have been terribly difficult so soon after the death of your partner.*

At the time, Lysi hadn't questioned the kind words. But now—how had Carolyn known about Cristin's death only a few hours after it happened, even before the media? Pretty certain Carolyn didn't move in the same social circles as Bertha Pry or Jade Green, Lysi decided they were not her information source. Could one of the officers at the crime scene have told her? Or James? Or Choki? She could have heard it from anyone. Word travels like the wind in a small town.

"Carolyn, how did you know Cristin was dead before it came out in the newspaper?

Carolyn smiled. "Why Lysi, honey. Think. You already know how I knew, don't you?"

Lysi caught her breath. All doubt was gone. Why had she been so blind. The evidence had been there all the time.

"Surely you must see why I had to kill Cristin." Carolyn seemed to want Lysi to understand.

Lysi could only stare at her. She couldn't speak. Shock had frozen the words in her throat.

Carolyn's words poured from her mouth. "I saw it the first day she walked into my office. I remembered the way Hank's eyes devoured her. When I saw the way she looked at him I knew they still had something going."

Carolyn paused and swallowed as if the words were choking her. "I went to see Cristin, just to get some things straight with her. When I got to the motel I saw Hank's car. I knew he was with her. I waited until he left, then I went to her room. She opened the door wearing that black nightgown." Carolyn's mouth twisted. She swept a strand of hair off her forehead, took a breath and continued.

"When I told Cristin Hank and I were getting married she said she didn't care if he was married or not. She said he could be mine on paper but she would still have him whenever it suited her. Anyway none of it matters now. *Now* that Cristin's dead."

Lysi started to get up from the couch but her legs felt spongy.

"Oh, one more thing." Carolyn reached into her purse and pulled out a crumpled tissue enclosed in a small plastic bag. She opened the bag and dug into the tissue, revealing a ring set with rubies and a diamond. After slipping it on her finger she held her hand so Lysi could see the jewels sparkle in the light from the window.

"Do you like it? It's my wedding ring. Hank even had it engraved with our initials on each side of an adorable little heart—*C* for Carolyn and *H* for Hank. Wasn't that sweet? So…Hank."

Lysi stared at Cristin's ring. *Find the ring, find the murderer.* Lysi felt anger rise in her throat. How dare Carolyn touch Cristin's ring. "That's not your wedding ring."

"Why Lysi, you've seen this ring before, haven't you? You described it to me, didn't you? What was it you told me? 'Find the ring, find the killer.' Wasn't that it? Well, here's the ring." Carolyn's eyes seemed to fill with pain. "That little bitch had the nerve to take it off her finger and flaunt the engraving."

Rubbing the diamond with her thumb, Carolyn mimicked Cristin, "'See. Cristin and Hank will always be bound together with love; this ring is a testament to that.' Then she laughed and offered me a drink."

"Give me the ring, Carolyn." Lysi reached for the ring.

Carolyn seemed not to hear Lysi. "I decided to fix little Cristin a very *special* drink." Her smile broadened but ended before it reached her eyes. "Now Cristin is no longer the problem, is she Lysi?" She jabbed Lysi in the chest. "You are!"

"Me! What are you talking about?" Lysi had trouble speaking. Her tongue felt like it had grown too big for her mouth.

"Oh please. Don't play innocent with me. Paris told me you went to Hank's office half dressed. She saw you on the couch with him. She saw him pawing you. She saw the way you looked at him. So now you're trying to take Cristin's place with Hank, aren't you? Well I won't let that happen."

Lysi remained transfixed as Carolyn's words whirled in her head.

"Why Lysi, you look pale. Isn't the tea helping? Take another sip."

Lysi stared at the mixed message on Carolyn's face—a false smile, bitter eyes. Her gaze moved to Carolyn's cup. She hadn't touched it.

Carolyn picked up Lysi's cup and refilled it from the teapot. She held the cup out to Lysi. "Here, dear. It'll do us both good."

Lysi shook her head and took a deep breath through her nose, trying to steady herself. At that moment she caught a strong whiff of the acidic scent again.

That's when she remembered. She'd smelled that same scent in Cristin's room.

Her stomach churned. Carolyn's face and body seemed to undulate like highway heat waves under a burning sun. Lysi's voice seemed to come from underwater. "It's the tea. You put something in the tea."

"Amazing, you're so much more perceptive than Cristin. She didn't even notice the bitter taste and the bad smell of the toxic oleander; but then she had already drowned herself in another poison—alcohol."

Lysi felt the color drain from her face. *She poisoned Cristin and now she's going to kill me in the same way.* Lysi tried to think of what to do.

A dark feeling of isolation squeezed her chest. The cabin sat far from the main road, hidden among thick trees and shrubs. She wondered if anyone besides Hank and Carolyn knew its location or even that it existed. It seemed unreal to be alone with a murderer. Should she scream? No one would hear her. Should she try to run? What good would it do? Carolyn would catch her before she reached the road. If she tried to escape to the woods, she'd get lost a few steps from the door.

"You'll never get away with it. People saw us leave." Lysi heard desperation in her own voice. "Jade Green from the restaurant saw me get into your car."

"It doesn't matter. Hank and I are the only ones who know about this old abandoned cabin. By the time they find you, we'll be on a plane to the Bahamas. They'll never catch us."

Lysi blinked several times trying to keep her eyes from drooping shut. Carolyn took Lysi's shoulders and leaned her against the back of the couch. "You're tired. Poor thing."

She took the cup from the table, held it up and gazed at it. "You know Lysi, Cristin liked oleanders, just like me. I know because when I dripped some nectar from the blossoms right into this same cup, she drank it down. I guess you could call this the 'Cristin Cup.'" Carolyn giggled. "I took it with me when I left her room. I never thought you'd be drinking my special tea from it, too."

Now Lysi knew why the police found no evidence of poison in any of the glasses in the motel room.

Carolyn set the cup back on the table and looked at Lysi. Her voice softened. "Lysi dear, you're exhausted. You really should rest."

She lifted Lysi's legs and laid them on the couch cushion.

Lysi tried to protest, but her feet and hands felt like lead when she struggled to get up. Her whole body trembled from a deep inner cold.

Carolyn lifted Lysi's head and placed a pillow under it, gentle as a mother and smoothed Lysi's hair back from her forehead. "There, you'll be much more comfortable now." She covered her with an afghan. Carefully tucking it under her chin she cooed, "There, there now. Just close your eyes."

In a tone suddenly cold and filled with vengeance Carolyn said, "No one crosses me. I told Cristin that but she didn't want to listen. She just flung the door open and told me to get out. Well, there was really nothing more for me to do there after she'd finished her drink so I left."

She looked at Lysi tenderly. "Just like there's nothing more for me to do here now that Mother Norris's tea is working. You're about to go into a coma. You'll be dead in a few hours. It's too bad. I really liked you, Lysi. I hope you understand. I just couldn't let you interfere with Hank and me."

Lysi's gaze followed Carolyn as she cleared away the remains of the lunch with meticulous care—gathering placemats, napkins, food, and placing them in the picnic basket; washing the teapot and her cup. She left Lysi's half-filled cup on the coffee table.

When she'd finished, she sat on the edge of the couch and looked at Lysi through eyes that seemed filled with regret. "I'm sorry you felt so deeply for Hank you decided to commit suicide when you found out he loved me instead of you. Hank and I are going to start a new life together. It's a pity you have to lose yours to enable us to do that."

She stroked Lysi's cheek, leaned over and kissed her cool forehead. Lysi wanted to push her away but couldn't move. Carolyn's lips pulled away from her teeth in the semblance of a smile. "So I'll leave now. Goodbye, Lysi."

She picked up her picnic basket and strolled to the door as if she had all day to escape.

Lysi stared through heavy lids as Carolyn, her hand on the doorknob, looked over her shoulder and scanned the room one more time. Ideas plodded through Lysi's head. She'd wait for a few minutes after Carolyn left then try to make it to the door. She'd scream for help.

A sad feeling of resignation crept into her consciousness when she realized that even the effort of forming words exhausted her.

She heard the door latch click open. Strangely, it seemed that her senses sharpened. She could hear the mellow whistle of a bird in duet with the rustling leaves of the cottonwood trees. A burst of fresh air from the half open door sent a chill cascading over her. Through half-raised eyelids, she focused on some cobwebs in the corner and inanely thought they needed to be swept away, while the terrible truth struggled to surface. She was dying.

Chapter 35

James bounded into the cabin through the half-open door, nearly hurling Carolyn to the floor. He ducked as Carolyn recovered her balance, swung her picnic basket at his head and sent it flying against the wall along with her purse.

When he ducked, she sprinted past him and collided with Sam Spitz who threw his arms around her waist and clenched her against his chest.

She flailed and screeched. She hammered his arms with her fists, jabbed her elbows into his ribs and kicked him in the shins. Suddenly, with the speed of a rattler, she wrenched her head around and sank her teeth into his upper arm.

Sam yanked his arm away and as the teeth marks turned scarlet, he shouted an expletive and locked one arm tightly around Carolyn's slim white neck.

She struggled to free herself, coughing and gagging. James grabbed her right wrist and twisted it into a hammerlock behind her. He wrenched the other around and cuffed them both.

"Read this lady her rights, Sam." James thrust her out the door.

Sam, a stunned look still on his face, grabbed her and shouted, "This is no lady. I'm gonna need a rabies shot."

The contents of Carolyn's purse lay scattered on the floor—wallet, lipstick, keys, Kleenex. A large envelope next to the wallet caught Sam's attention. He scooped it up and pulled out two

Bahamas plane tickets printed with the names Carolyn Norris and Hank Jones.

He shouted at James, " I'm arresting Jones for aiding and abetting a felon. He was planning to leave the country with Norris."

James wasn't listening. He had already rushed to Lysi's side. "Lysi. Lysi. It's James. You're safe now." He joggled her shoulders.

"Lysi, was it oleander?" He joggled her again. "Was it oleander?"

Without opening her eyes, she tried to speak. James lowered his ear close to her lips. She mouthed, "Tea."

Without taking his eyes off Lysi, James grabbed his cell and punched in Dr. MacKinnon's number, clenching his jaw impatiently as the phone rang several times. He hoped the town doctor was not with a patient or out on a call. When the doctor finally answered, James relayed the Billings doctor's report to him, barely stopping to take a breath. "I found out cardiac glycoside can come from oleanders. Carolyn Norris from Nerium has an oleander garden in her office. She put some kind of poison in Lysi's tea. I'm sure it was oleander.

"Cardiac glycoside from oleanders, you say. I don't think I've ever had a case of that."

"Dr. MacKinnon, please. I need your help," James blurted out. "I had Dr. Goldfein fax you his Cause of Death report, along with antidotal information. I hope he got to it right away. I need you to—."

"James, slow down. Let me understand what you're telling me."

"I'm sorry." James took a deep breath. "I suspect that Carolyn Norris from Nerium might have poisoned Cristin Holden. I know she poisoned Lysi Weston, the woman who conducted the sexual harassment seminar.

"She picked Lysi up this morning and took her to some isolated cabin. I don't have time to explain everything right now. I need you to get an ambulance equipped to administer advanced life support equipment and antidotes required for a person who has ingested oleandrin—everything's listed on Dr. Goldfein's fax. You have to get out here before it's too late."

The line remained silent for what seemed like an eternity to James. He wondered if Dr. Mackinnon had grasped what he had told him. Then he heard the doctor take in a slow breath through his nose. "James, I have a pencil in my hand. I want you to speak very slowly when you tell me the directions to the cabin. Okay, I'm ready."

James realized the doctor had reacted with professional calm to the panicky tone of his voice. When James spoke again, his words were clear and concise. "Go about ten miles east on Highway 39. Watch for a gravel road that takes off to the left. There won't be a sign, just a reflector on a low post. Follow it for about three miles and you'll come to a dirt lane that takes off to the right. There's a cabin at the end of it." James swallowed in frustration. "I know these directions are pretty vague. The cabin's hard to find, but—."

"Not hard at all." The doctor's voice remained calm and reassuring. "Why, that's the old Smithington cabin. I know it well. I made many a house call there, first to deliver each of Dora Smithington's eight youngsters and then to keep them healthy. Hold on a minute, I'll check to see if Dr. Goldfein's fax has come through already."

James heard Dr. MacKinnon shuffle across the room and back to the phone. "It's here. I found it in the machine."

James exhaled in relief. The line was quiet for a few moments except for the sound of Dr. MacKinnon clearing his throat. James assumed he was perusing the fax and didn't interrupt.

The doctor's quiet voice almost whispered in James's ear. "How long ago did Miss Weston ingest the poisonous tea?"

James stared at Lysi. She lay limp with her eyes almost closed and lips slightly parted. He knew she wouldn't be able tell him. He would have to guess.

"I know it had to be less than two hours ago," he said recalling that Lysi and Carolyn had left the Big Sky at about 10:30.

Without further explanation, Dr. MacKinnon said, "Don't worry, I'll get the ambulance loaded and see you out there in less than forty-five minutes. Try to keep her awake."

James grabbed Lysi's shoulders and joggled her. "Lysi. Lysi. Stay with me, Lysi. The doctor's on the way. Open your eyes. Lysi!" She raised her eyelids.

*

A siren and squeal of brakes cut through Lysi's lethargy. She scrunched her eyes shut and gritted her teeth against the jarring of what felt like the entire cabin jouncing over boulders. She fought against waking, but something squeezed her arms, lifted her head, grabbed her shoulders and wouldn't stop shaking. From far away she could hear someone shouting her name. She wanted to stop the shaking, drown out the persistent calls.

A shuffling of feet and loud voices announced the ambulance crew. Dr. MacKinnon hurried through the door and pointed out the picnic basket to an EMT who understood the unspoken message and picked it up for later analysis.

Dr. MacKinnon nudged James aside and touched Lysi's cool cheek, leaving a tingling of warmth where his hand had rested. He lifted her eyelid and shone a beam from a small flashlight into her eye. Her pupil contracted.

"Keep your eyes open, Lysi," the doctor said. She tried to obey, but the urge to drift into the restful darkness overpowered her. He placed a stethoscope on her chest while the technician took her blood pressure.

A tear trickled down her cheek. Dr. MacKinnon wiped it away with the back of his hand and told her not to worry, that she would be fine.

James stood silently watching. Dr. MacKinnon turned to him. "I can't determine how long ago she ingested the oleandrin. Skin's cool. Blood pressure's low. But the heartbeat's still regular. Good sign. We'll begin antidotal treatment immediately." He shook her. "Lysi, stay awake."

Lysi struggled to stay awake as two technicians lifted her onto a stretcher and carried her to the ambulance.

*

James stood nervously outside the ambulance watching the paramedics slide Lysi into the truck as Sam Spitz walked Carolyn past the ambulance to the squad car. He turned at the sound of Hank's voice. "Carolyn, what have you done?"

"Don't pretend you don't know," Carolyn said.

"Does this mean I don't get my promotion?" Hank's voice dripped with sarcasm. Carolyn spat on him and kicked a mound of spongy soil that speckled his spotless pants with sticky leaf mold.

Sam Spitz yanked Hank's arm. "Shut up and get back in the car, Pretty Boy. You two can yell that over all the way to the Sage Deer jail." He shoved Carolyn into the backseat of the car.

"Wait a minute." Hank looked astounded. "Why am I under arrest?"

"For aiding and abetting a murderer to escape. We found your tickets to the Bahamas."

"What tickets? I don't know anything about flying to the Bahamas."

Carolyn smiled at Hank. "Why Hank honey, you know you told me to buy those tickets."

"Are you crazy, woman?" Hank started to get into the front of the squad car, but Sam grabbed his neck and slammed him into the back. "If I'm lucky, maybe you two'll kill each other off before we get back to town."

Sam secured the door from the outside and examined his swelling arm, then turned towards the ambulance. He stepped up into the back and an attendant swabbed his arm with antiseptic and covered the throbbing wound with a gauze band-aid.

"Are you okay?" James asked as Sam stepped down from the ambulance.

Sam patted his shoulder. "I'll be fine soon as I get my rabies shot. You go with Lysi. It'll be my pleasure to get the proud peacock and pit viper caged."

Chapter 36

At the Rosebud Health Care Center the next morning, Lysi awoke early. She looked around at the sterile white walls and the stainless steel service tray next to her bed, then up into the crinkly eyes of Dr. MacKinnon sitting by her side. "Well, young lady, you gave us quite a fright. You look a lot better today. How are you feeling?"

"I feel pretty good, tired but starving."

"Starving is a good sign. Stomach pumping increases the appetite. We'll get you some gourmet hospital food. Jello sound good?" He reached over and pressed the nurse call button.

Lysi wrinkled her nose.

"Fortunately, you ingested a relatively small amount of oleandrin, but when we pumped your stomach everything else came up with it. The fact that you had food in your stomach kept the oleandrin from rushing into your blood stream. And we got to you quickly, thanks to Detective Tennyson."

Lysi's face hardened. She grappled with the inconsistencies of James's attitude. Conflicting feelings of gratitude and humiliation sloshed around in her head when she thought of him. His harsh words on the phone had wounded her deeply. Yet, she remembered his worried, almost loving expression when he sat next to her in the ambulance on the way to the hospital.

She now understood that Paris Spyer had painted an ugly picture of her visit to Hank's office. But she could not understand why James so easily accepted Spyer's lies. Why he could so easily believe the worst about her. She asked herself the same question over and over—Why had he bothered to save my life if he despised me? But of course, the answer was simple. He had to do his duty.

"When can I leave?" she said.

"Probably today. Now that you're awake, we can give you a final examination and you can be on your way." The doctor rose from his chair with a little grunt. "I'll let Detective Tennyson know you're awake. He's outside waiting to see you."

"I don't want to see him." She turned her face away from the doctor and stared out the window.

"But he's been waiting all night."

She turned and looked into the doctor's brilliant blue eyes. He wore a perplexed expression.

"You don't understand. I need time to think. Please, just tell him I appreciate all he's done, but that I…I…I'm not up to seeing anyone right now." Lysi turned away again.

"Suit yourself. I'll see to checking you out." Dr. Mackinnon squeezed her shoulder then left the room.

*

James rose heavily from a functional plastic chair when Dr. MacKinnon walked into the waiting room. The dark circles under his eyes, his stubbly face and wrinkled clothes spoke of the kind of night he'd passed.

The doctor looked at him with affectionate concern. "She's going to be fine. Probably go home this afternoon. She'll need a final exam, then I'll have the nurse check her out."

Relief spread over James's tired face. "Is she able to have visitors?"

The doctor tried to choose his words carefully. "She says she isn't up to seeing anyone."

"You mean she isn't up to seeing me." James stared at the black and white floor tiles. "I know she's angry and hurt. It's my fault. I need to talk to her, to explain, to apologize."

Dr. MacKinnon peered over his spectacles and examined James as though he were one of his patients. "Not a good idea right now."

He watched James's shoulders droop under the weight of disappointment. "However," he said with a roguish gleam in his eyes, "I could err on the side of caution and keep her in the hospital a few days more—for observation, decontamination and cardiovascular monitoring. I've heard that in some cases, oleandrin is eliminated very slowly from the body, sometimes it can take up to two weeks."

James's haggard face registered fear. "You said she'd fully recovered and would check out today."

Dr. MacKinnon breathed an exasperated sigh. He grasped James's shoulders and gave him a little shake. "Jamie, my boy, how can you be so thick headed? If I checked her out today, she'd be on a plane to San Francisco before sundown. Is that what you want? I thought you wanted time to talk to her?" He released his grasp and patted him on the shoulders. "Go home, Jamie. Come back this afternoon. I guarantee she'll be here."

James started for the door, then turned back to the doctor. "Will you give her this for me?" James handed the doctor an envelope.

He had spent a lot of time writing the letter. In it, he wrote he was ashamed of his words on the phone. He should have known better. He didn't expect her to forgive him, but he did want her to know it was his deep feelings for her and the profound emptiness he felt at losing her that had clouded his judgment.

"Of course." Dr. Mackinnon took the envelope from James's shaky hand.

*

Two days later, James tried for the third time to see Lysi. This time he requested that the attending nurse, an old schoolmate, not announce his visit. He paused before entering. The hospital room was cool. Lysi lay on her side, back to the door. The restful play of shadow and light through the waltzing leaves of a giant elm framed by the window resembled an impressionist painting. She didn't turn when James approached the bed. He saw the unopened envelope lying next to the water pitcher on the stainless steel service tray and his chest tightened. He sat down on a chair next to the bed and watched her, trying to decide what to say. After a moment, she jerked around to him, as if she suddenly felt a presence. She didn't smile. He couldn't quite read her expression—not hostile, but not inviting.

"Hi," he said.

"Hi," she said.

They looked at each other for several seconds, not speaking, yet communicating over the sound of nurses' voices and footsteps passing through the hall.

He reached for her hand. She allowed him to enfold it in both of his. Then he broke the stillness with a flurry of words. "I've been such a fool. I'm sorry. I know there's no excuse for what I said. I just want you to know that I'm a clumsy oaf when it comes to women. I guess I felt...too soon...then when I thought I'd lost you, I said things I—"

She quieted him by placing her finger over his lips.

"James, I know. Neither of us was ready for what happened between us."

He started to speak again. She interrupted, leaving his comments dangling in the antiseptic air. "There are some things you need to know about the case. Carolyn confessed to me that she murdered Cristin. She did it with oleandrin, the same way she tried to kill me. She found out through her father about Cristin's marriage to Hank."

James frowned at the sound of Hank's name. Lysi didn't seem to notice.

"She went to Cristin's room to tell her she was marrying Hank and to warn her to stay away from him. When Cristin refused, she dropped oleander blossom nectar into a drink. Cristin probably didn't notice because she'd been drinking with Hank just before.

"She's denying any part in Cristin's murder," James said.

"I can prove she did it. She's wearing a diamond and ruby ring she took from Cristin the night she poisoned her. Hank had given it to Cristin. It's engraved with the letters C and H for Cristin and Hank. Ask him about it."

James nodded and squeezed her hand.

"There's more. When KiKi told me she'd seen Hank leave Cristin's room, I went to see him because I was almost certain he murdered Cristin. That's how I found out he and Cristin had been married. He was grieving for her, as I was. I took his hand to comfort him. That's what Paris Spyer saw—nothing more. She reported it to Carolyn as a sexual encounter and that's when Carolyn came after me."

"Oh my God, I'm sorry."

*

Later that day Lysi laughed as Dr. MacKinnon pushed her wheelchair down the hospital ramp to James's car. "Just how long did you plan to keep me in the hospital for *observation*?" she asked.

"Well, the medical book says I could have monitored your progress for as long as two weeks. I just kept you as long as was needed. Three days seemed to do it." The doctor winked at James as he opened the car door for her.

James shook Dr. Mackinnon's hand. "You're coming to the farewell dinner aren't you, Doc?"

"Nope, can't make it."

He turned to Lysi who stood next to the open door. "I won't say goodbye. I'll say *Beannachd leat,* a Scottish blessing to you, Lysi." He put both arms around her, gave her a bear hug and kissed her forehead.

Chapter 37

As the car glided along Highway 39 towards the Wild Flower Inn, Lysi peered through the window with new eyes. The setting sun had created an abstract painting of reds, yellows, blues, and greens, all spilling into each other. Large boulders, blue under the darkening sky, reclined on a blanket of golden grain fields, under gently swaying cottonwoods. She had heard songs praising silvery sage before, but never understood its incredible beauty until tonight. Turning to James, she whispered, "Stop the car for a few moments."

Without comment as though he could sense her feelings, James pulled onto the gravel shoulder of the road. Lysi rolled down the window and breathed in the clean scent of the sage. She listened to the soft lowing of cattle trying to keep track of each other in the gathering darkness, and the chorus of crickets celebrating the end of the day. In her mind, she was seeing Montana for the first time. She wondered how she could have missed it.

James took her hand. Neither spoke, yet they expressed with perfect clarity their shared joy in this warm Montana evening. After a few quiet moments, James let go of her hand and started the car. They both knew it was time to go.

Before he could pull onto the road, Lysi stroked his thigh and a come-hither smile spread across her lips. "Any chance of skipping the dinner and going directly to James's Place?"

James grasped her hand and removed it from his thigh. "Now stop that. There's nothing I'd like better than to keep you all to myself tonight. But your fans would draw and quarter me if you didn't show up at their farewell extravaganza."

Lysi knew he was right.

"I'll make it up to you after the party." He winked. "I promise."

"Yes you will." She winked back at him.

As they drove, James answered Lysi's questions before she asked them. "I knew how concerned you were about Denny Robbins, so I called him to my office to file a formal report about the sexual harassment."

James shook his head in dismay. "You know, the weirdest thing happened. Picture this: Robbins comes waltzing into my office with Bill Pitt right beside him, practically holding his hand. They both sit down, and Robbins looks at Pitt. Then Pitt slaps Robbins on the back and says, 'Do it boy. Just like we talked about.'"

Lysi barely controlled her urge to laugh when James imitated Bill's gravelly voice.

"The irony of the whole thing was that Robbins reported Pitt as one of his harassers, but wouldn't file charges against him. He did file against Noah Pry.

"The Pry kid admitted writing the notes when I confronted him with the packet of evidence you gave me. I've charged him with stalking Robbins, assaulting Cristin Holden and harassing you. I've requested that a psychiatrist peer into Pry's twisted brain. I expect they'll ship him off to a psychiatric institution. He'll end up in either a hospital or a county correctional center. In the meantime, I'm holding him in a cozy little cell without bail because he's proven himself to be a flight risk."

The worn-out face of Noah's hard-working mother drifted through Lysi's mind. "His mother tried everything she could to help him. Such heartbreak to raise a son and have him turn out so badly."

James nodded sympathetic agreement and continued. "Carolyn Norris called her daddy. The great Hubert Norris, himself, hopped on a plane, landed in Billings, hired a limo, drove to Sage Deer and bailed his little princess out the day after we arrested her. We did manage to get her passport. She can't leave the county until her trial is over. It's on the docket in the Sixteenth District Court. Could be a year before it comes to trial."

Lysi said, "I don't think Daddy considered Carolyn a princess. A long-time acquaintance of hers told me he set her up in a job at Nerium Montana just to get her out of his hair."

James laughed. "Now comes the best part. Right after Carolyn walked out of her cell, Sam and I watched the two of them march over to Jones's cell. We could hear big Papa and Princess yelling in duet at Jones. Carolyn used words no lady I ever knew would use. Then Papa told Jones if he ever saw his face again he'd blackball him so the only job he'd be able to get would be swabbing toilets or cleaning up after horse parades. I tell you, Sam and I almost passed out we were laughing so hard. I have no idea where Jones went. We had to release him after we corroborated his story that he didn't have a passport and couldn't have gone to the Bahamas even if he'd wanted to."

After James finished his story, he said, "Now you know everything I know. Any questions?"

"No questions," Lysi said.

But she did have questions, all stemming from the unanticipated affection she had developed for so many people during her stay in Sage Deer. How will Elizabeth Scot cope with Hank's leaving? Can Denny Robbins survive much longer in manly Montana? What about Ominotago, Namida's Festival Princess niece and Honehe, the Cheyenne boy she loves?

Lysi imagined a comical picture of big, burley Bill Pitt and his clumsy effort to disengage from KiKi and prove himself to Maggie and his son. *The sparks are going to fly when KiKi gets wind of that.*

And what about Jade Green, who had anchored Lysi during her stormy days in Sage Deer? *My friend Jade—a shoulder to cry on, an ear to listen, an encyclopedia of knowledge about the people in this town. She saved my life by telling James about Carolyn picking me up.* Jade, an intelligent woman who never had the opportunity to realize her dream of a college education. Sometimes life can be so unfair.

A warm feeling flowed through Lysi when she reflected on the wonderful life Deborah Tennyson and Namida had carved out for themselves—two pillars of the community. Lysi gazed at James. Could she ever find happiness in a place like Sage Deer, so different from the world she's always known? After all, his English mother did.

The sun had set. The world on the narrow country road had turned black except for the white path of the car headlights. Before Lysi saw it, James turned onto the gravel drive leading to the Wild Flower Inn. A rainbow of lights twinkled on the shrubs along the lane. Beyond the lights that brightened the arbor, Lysi saw a banner stretched across the porch eaves. In large blue letters she read, Celebrate Our Lysi.

"Oh no. This is too much. I never expected anything like this. Let's leave. Quick!"

When they entered the sitting room and everyone cheered, Lysi's knees nearly buckled in surprise and embarrassment. At the sight of so many eager faces, her eyes prickled with tears. Looking at all the warm expressions, she understood James's reply when she had asked him why he loved Montana—"Most of all, I like the people." Then everyone started chattering at once. They all wanted to share something with her.

Deborah Tennyson, in an elegant burgundy sheath, maneuvered her way through the crowd and put her arm around Lysi's waist. "Let's give our guest of honor a bit of breathing space, shall we?" She led Lysi to a plush chair by the rock fireplace.

Denny Robbins got to Lysi first, his cheeks rosy against a red silk mandarin-collared shirt. "Lysi, great news. They hired a finance director. The sooner I get him trained, the sooner I go home. I've asked for a transfer to Nerium San Francisco."

Lysi threw her arms around Denny and gave him a warm hug. "Great news."

Denny stepped back and glanced around the room uncomfortably. "My partner and I plan to take a month off and concentrate on restoring our Victorian. Here's my At Home card. Call me when you get back to the Bay Area. We both want to invite you to our housewarming. And thank you for making my life bearable."

"You couldn't keep me away from that housewarming. I'm so glad your transfer came through. The new guy's going to have a tough time filling your shoes."

Elizabeth Scot and Jade Green sat nose to nose on a small mauve settee a few steps from Lysi. Though deep in conversation, Jade winked at Lysi. "Hey Lysi, Elizabeth's offered me a trainee position in Information Technology at Nerium. Thanks for putting in a good word for me."

Elizabeth, in her quiet understated way, nodded affirmation.

Lysi approved of both Jade's new job and her new look. Jade had updated her hairstyle to a smooth bob with a light fringe of bangs. She had traded in her tight stretch pants and low-necked shirts for pale blue pleated pants and a cobalt silk shirt that gave her a professional look. Lysi guessed Elizabeth had had a hand in the makeover. "Good luck to both of you."

Deborah Tennyson tinkled a little bell to signal dinner. Everyone moved into the dining room to an English style dinner that included individual Beef Wellingtons, Brussels sprouts with chestnuts, carrot custard and baby lettuce salad.

When Lysi found her place card, Bill Pitt rushed over and pulled out her chair for her. When he pushed in the chair, it banged the back of her knees and she had to stifle a little "ouch".

He plopped down beside her and seemed quite satisfied with his chivalry.

She looked around for KiKi.

"KiKi's not for me. I took your advice and told Maggie again that I'm crazy about her. This time she didn't treat me like a doorman. I think she might be willing to give it a try over time. I can be patient. She's worth it."

Lysi nodded approval. *Why Bill, I think you're shedding some rough edges.*

When everyone finished the raspberry trifle dessert and Deborah had offered a choice of liqueurs, Bill hammered his water glass with his spoon. "Now listen up everybody. You know I volunteered to give a farewell talk for Lysi. So here goes."

He pulled a wrinkled scrap of paper from his pocket, tugged at his collar and cleared his throat. He looked down at Lysi. "I speak for everyone when I say you've done a lot of good things for a lot of people in this town in a pretty short time. We all want to thank you.

Well, I guess that's about it. So, thanks." He raised his glass. "To Lysi."

The crowd echoed his toast. "To Lysi."

Lysi beamed, while a quiet voice inside her whispered, "And to you, Cristin. Wherever you may be."

Lysi hugged Bill while everyone applauded. The tears in her eyes showed her gratitude.

Deborah Tennyson and Namida approached Lysi after dinner ended. Namida grasped her hand and whispered a Native American blessing, "May the Great Mystery make sunrise in your heart."

Deborah slipped a package of Montana wildflower seeds into Lysi's hand. "Remember, 'Flowers must be gathered in their prime, else they fade and die.' Just a bit of advice from one of our English boys, William Shakespeare." She put her cheek close to Lysi's and whispered in her ear. "I gathered mine and never regretted it." She put her arms around Lysi. "I hope to see you again soon."

Chapter 38

James was quiet at the Billings Airport. His last night with Lysi had strengthened his resolve to spend the rest of his life with her. He knew he had to wait for the right time and was willing to meet any compromise. When her plane's departure was announced, he held her close, and reluctantly let her leave.

Just before she turned to board the plane, she reached into her carryon bag, pulled out a lavender foil-wrapped gift and handed it to him. "Open it after I'm in the air."

Clutching the gift to his chest, he hurried to the observation deck and waved to the plane until it disappeared into the light cloud cover. Then he slowly pulled the lavender foil off a white box. The scent of her perfume wafted from the box. As soon as he spread apart the tissue paper that covered the gift, a big Montana grin spread across his face. He looked up into the empty sky where the plane had been, then threw his head back in a hearty laugh. Two people standing a few yards from him shot him a curious glance.

On top of a silky, lilac nightgown lay a card on which Lysi had written, "Keep this handy. I'll need it when I come to see you. Lysi."

About the Author

Nancy Curteman has lived most of her life on the majestic Pacific coast. After graduating from San Francisco State University she studied at the University of Nice in France.

She has a Masters in French literature and a Masters in Administration. She has taught college French and worked as a school principal. She is a member of Mystery Writers of America.

Curteman's passions are reading, travel and writing. She loves to read mystery novels so of course she loves writing them. She is currently working on her seventh novel.

Curteman sets her novels in the countries she has visited. Her novel, *Murder in a Teacup*, set in Montana, placed second in the California Writers Club Jack London novel contest. *Murder Casts a Spell*, set in South Africa, was voted 2013 Best Mystery by The Readers' Poll. *Murder on the Seine*, set in France was rated in the 2015 Top Ten Best Mysteries by The Readers' Poll. *Murder Down Under*, set in Australia, and *Lethal Lesson* were released by Solstice Publishing.

On her blog, Global Mysteries, Curteman posts writing and travel tips. Her website is Nancy Curteman.com

Acknowledgements

First, my sincere appreciation to my husband, Larry, for his loving encouragement.

Special thanks to original members of my writing group, Art Carey, Carol Hall and Jane Lester. They taught me the basics. I couldn't have written this book without their powerful suggestions.

Thank you to my two book clubs. Champagne and Chapters members: Laurel Gonzales, Sandy Grandbois, Janyce Hummel, Kim Kelly, Trudie Mathiesen, Trish Murray, Catherine Rost , AnneMarie Sylva and Carol Wilson. Book Babes members: Carrie Douglas, Wisty Olsson, Valeria Sandusky, Leslie Traber and Barbara Wong. They were my cheerleaders. They gave me the courage I needed to try.

www.ingramcontent.com/pod-product-compliance
Lightning Source LLC
Chambersburg PA
CBHW071234250626
47163CB00001B/177